THE
Sun Goes Down

THE
Sun Goes Down

A MITCH MITCHELL MYSTERY

James Lear

Published in the United States by Cleis Press, an imprint of Start Midnight, LLC, 101 Hudson Street, Thirty-Seventh Floor, Suite 3705, Jersey City, NJ 07302.

Cover design: Scott Idleman/Blink
Cover photograph: iStock
Text design: Frank Wiedemann
First Edition.
10 9 8 7 6 5 4 3 2 1

Trade paper ISBN: 978-1-62778-162-6
E-book ISBN: 978-1-62778-163-3

I

THERE WAS A SOLDIER LEANING ON THE RAILS, LOOKING BACK AT the white wake cutting through the dark Mediterranean water. His sleeves were rolled up, exposing tanned, hairy forearms; one leg was bent, allowing his ass to stretch the khaki of his pants to near breaking point. This wasn't the thick wool stuff they wear back in England, with layers of unappetizing underpants beneath; this was tropical-weight cotton, as thin as a second skin. If the crossing had been longer I'd have joined him at the rail, engaged him in conversation and used all the Mitchell charm to get him into a cabin or a cupboard. As it was, with just a few minutes to go, I watched his wake as he watched the ferry's.

He lit a cigarette and moved fore, trailing smoke behind him.

A little farther along the deck, huddled in chairs and surrounded by excessive amounts of luggage, was an English family with thin, pinched faces, gray hair and ill-fitting clothes that were quite unsuited for the weather. That is how the parents looked, at least: could have been a schoolteacher and his do-gooding wife. The son was a different matter. Nineteen, maybe twenty. Young, perfectly blond, rosy cheeked. Dressed as if he'd just come off the cricket pitch: a white wool sweater knotted around his shoulders; white shirt; cream trousers. He shaded his eyes with one hand, squinting towards the horizon where the land mass of our destination was now clearly visible, getting larger. Gozo, smaller sister of Malta, separated from the main island by three or four miles of deep-blue sea, half an hour on the ancient vessels that ply the route day in, day out, steaming past the brightly painted fishing boats that bob along the waves, nets cast, waiting.

"Look," he shouted, turning a bright, eager face to his parents. "We're nearly there!"

They glanced up from their reading matter (religious tracts?), frowned in perfect unison and looked down. The boy's face fell, his pink lips hanging open, blue eyes bright and wet, perhaps just from the stiff sea breeze. This wouldn't do. I strolled over.

"There she blows," I said, standing next to him. "Journey's end."

The boy smiled and jumped to his feet, grateful for any attention. "At last! I thought we'd never get here!"

The parents turned stony, disapproving faces towards me. If I'd been wearing a hat I'd have raised it. Instead I said in my best Beacon Hill tone, "Dr. Mitchell. Pleased to meet you." The "doctor" part always works wonders. They looked away, content to let me babysit their son.

"You travel over from England?"

"Yes. We come here every summer."

"Lucky you."

The boy sighed and looked to the island. "I suppose so." The side of his face was smooth, soft, his ears red from the sun. "It's very beautiful."

"Sure is," I said, not meaning the island. His neck was like a column of marble disappearing into the cool whiteness of his shirt. For someone who'd been traveling for so long, he was remarkably unruffled. "I've never been before. Perhaps you could show me around."

"I'd be delighted." He smiled, revealing a set of perfect white teeth. I hoped he knew how to shield them with his lips because he was going to need to before long. My dick was getting hard just looking at his mouth.

"Henry. Come here. We are about to dock."

They must have read my mind... But one look at his parents, with their thin lips and flinty eyes, was enough to cool me down. At least I had a name. "I'll see you around, Henry."

He glanced down at the deck, bashful. "I hope so," he mumbled, then scuttled back to the family nest. They loaded him with ticket and jacket and suitcase and hat, until the poor boy looked like a scarecrow. I smiled and winked, hoping at least to cheer him up; a holiday with that pair of stiffs, even on the most beautiful island in the world, would be a mixed blessing. But he didn't see me; he stared into the middle distance, a look of utter dismay on his face.

I turned to see what he was staring at and there, on the starboard side like a mirror image, a negative, was a young man entirely in black, his hair dark, brows drawn down over deep-set eyes in a gloomy scowl, just one dazzling spot of light in the whole silhouette at his neck. A dog collar. Tall and slim, he was rooted to the spot, moving only with the motion of the boat, arms by his side, fists clenched in readiness to run or fight. They faced each other, white and black, port and starboard, across the rolling deck, until suddenly the spell was broken. The boy was absorbed into the disembarking crowd, and the priest was engulfed by a swarm of nuns, habits and veils billowing and flying, concealing him from view.

I was traveling light: just one small knapsack containing food, water and the latest Agatha Christie novel. Everything else—my clothes, my books and so on—was in the hold. My fellow travelers seemed reluctant to entrust their possessions to foreigners. The English family carried enough to withstand a three-week siege; the nuns were laden with cases, not to mention the weight of their habits. Thrusting her way to the front of the boat, a tall, heavily made-up woman of a certain age commanded various members of the crew, in accents straight from the London stage, to transport her collection of hatboxes and valises to dry land. "If you imagine," she said, loud enough for the whole ferry to hear, "that I would consign Paris creations to the bowels of a rust bucket like this, you are very much mistaken." She lit a cigarette, smearing pillar-box red over the butt, and exhaled, as her black, wavy hair fell over her shoulders. I guess I must have smiled. She blew a kiss.

I was in no hurry; the promised bus was not going to leave without me. I like to take my time at the end of journeys, particularly if, as in this case, there's a handsome soldier in tight pants and a sweat-stained shirt, the only other passenger traveling without excess luggage.

"Here on leave?" I asked, as we watched the growing scrum around the gangway.

"No," he said, in a London accent. "Work. Worse luck."

"You stationed in Valetta?"

"Yeah."

I offered him a cigarette, which he took, and lit it for him.

"How long you on the island for?"

"Just one night."

"Can I buy you a drink?'

He smoked for a while, eyes narrowed, an amused look around his mouth. "American?"

"Yep." I put out my hand. "Edward Mitchell. My friends call me Mitch."

"Mitch. My name's Bill. I expect I'll see you around." He winked, shouldered his bag and swaggered off, his ass rolling in a figure eight.

"I'm staying at the Continental," I shouted, but my words were carried away on the wind.

The vehicle that collected us at the harbor was a heap of rusting metal and worn rubber that hardly seemed fit for the steep and bumpy roads. But somehow we were loaded on, six of us and our luggage, and we began the slow, wheezing climb away from the harbor. Once on the top road we could see most of the south coast of the island—a series of cliffs and inlets, green-gray foliage, warm yellow sandstone carved into weird sculptural shapes by the wind. For the first time since leaving London I felt that I was truly, properly abroad, on holiday, escaping from everything and everyone I'd left behind.

This was an escape—from loneliness, sorrow and disappointment, and most of all, from guilt. I'd screwed everything up—again—and for the last time. Vince, my lover, my companion, the man I was supposed to be building a future with, had finally tired of my infidelities and accepted a job in the Far East. We'd parted on good terms, allowing ourselves the comforting lie that this was a marvelous opportunity for him, that when he came back we could pick up where we left off, but neither of us believed it. I'd fucked too many asses, sucked too many cocks, come crawling home at two, three in the morning smelling of other bodies, full of promises that lasted until the next time. And then Vince had enough. He shipped out to Singapore leaving me in London, far from my family in America, with few friends and none at all that I neither worked with nor fucked. When I wasn't working in the hospital or screwing some fresh, young ass, I was alone.

And then, although it pained me to admit it, there was Morgan.

Harry "Boy" Morgan, my old college chum, the man I had spent more time pursuing and seducing and adoring than anyone else, my beloved friend and the best lay I have ever had, was now irreversibly married, and we were estranged. What started as a sunlit frolic in the English countryside—fucking as much for fun as for love—became something dark and destructive, hurting both of us, hurting the ones we loved even more. I knew it had to stop. He wouldn't see me anyway, but that hadn't prevented me from trying and plotting and hoping, even hanging around outside his house watching shadows on the blinds. But now...well, perhaps even I had grown up a little. Enough to know that if you keep touching fire, you get burned.

Thanks to a maiden aunt back home in Boston who had the decency to die just at the right time and leave her money to her favorite nephew Edward, the doctor of whom she was so very proud, I'd quit my job and accepted an invitation from an old pal from medical school who had wound up working for the British Army in Malta. There are worse places to be, I thought, than a beautiful Mediterranean island in the summertime, particularly one with a sizeable military presence. On his advice I'd booked accommodation on Gozo, Malta's smaller, prettier neighbor, the place where everyone (military personnel included—I checked) came to relax. With Aunt Dinah's legacy in the bank I could afford an indefinite stay at a small, comfortable hotel, while Frank Southern, now

Lieutenant Colonel Frank Southern, brigade surgeon to the garrison at Valetta, would introduce me to people and entertain me when possible. And, he said, there was a "delicate professional matter" on which he needed my advice; he would tell me more in person. It was a far more attractive proposition than summer in stuffy, dirty London, exhausting myself caring for the sick and obeying the whims of my capricious dick, with nothing to come home to but absence and regret.

And who knows? Here on Gozo, surrounded by the darkly sparkling Homeric seas, under the broiling near-tropical sun, I might find adventure. Sex, for sure, with all those soldiers and sailors. Love, even, if I was lucky, but without the oppressive need to be faithful—it could only last as long as I stayed. *And*, I thought, fingering the pages of the Agatha Christie that lay unread in my lap, *I might stumble upon a crime*. The setting was perfect: picturesque enough for novelty, surrounded by water to limit escape, a place where people of all types came together, a melting pot. It would be quite literally melting, if the sun kept beating through the dusty glass windows of the bus like that. The English parents, in their hopelessly inappropriate tweeds, looked ready to expire. They were staying at the Continental Hotel as well, it seemed, the mother, the father and their unlikely son, all freshness and coolness where his parents were crabbed and hot, the beautiful fruit of bony loins. What if he was scheming to push one or both of them off the highest cliff on the island and make it look like an accident, playing the grief-stricken son while planning how to spend his inheritance? He looked like an angel, but wasn't it always the seemingly innocent who were the guiltiest?

What of the aging glamour queen, she of the commanding manner and multiple hatboxes? Was she hiding a gruesome secret? Was she, perhaps, a notorious murderer in disguise, starting a new life in this unlikely corner of the Empire? Maybe it would be her body that we'd find bludgeoned to death on an isolated beach, or bobbing in the harbor, rough justice meted out by grieving relatives of her victims. The only other passenger on the bus was a hefty local woman with a string shopping bag digging into her plump wrists, stuffed with bottles of vinegar and olives and capers that she'd brought back from the market—but was she all she appeared to be? Was her native costume a disguise? If anyone was going to find out it was me, Mitch Mitchell, private detective, for so I styled myself after an accidental involvement in a handful of murders. Admittedly I'd detected the killers more by accident than deductive skill; I'm too easily distracted to be a second Holmes or Poirot. My chief, or perhaps my only, advantage as a detective is a willingness to blunder into the murkiest of secrets, unashamed and unabashed by anything I might find there. I've usually discovered guilt when I've been looking for cock and ass, but if that's the Mitch Mitchell method, I'm happy to claim it, with all its fringe benefits.

As for secondary characters and red herrings, I was spoiled for choice. The tall, young priest on the ferry, swallowed up by a crowd of nuns as we disembarked, whisked off to God knows what monastic cell—was he all he appeared to be? And "my" soldier Bill: what was he really doing on the island? Did his cool swagger conceal a deadly intent? Undercover army business perhaps, rooting out enemies of the Empire in the villages, or perhaps turned traitor, selling secrets to His Majesty's foes...

The heat was rising as we labored through the dust and potholes, the engine singing a high, cracked note each time it negotiated a rock. Even I, who can sail the roughest seas without the slightest *mal de mer*, was starting to feel queasy. Cigarette smoke wasn't helping; someone behind me was puffing away, and I could guess who. The English couple started coughing noisily, tutting and opening windows, which just let the dust in.

I felt a jab on my shoulder and saw a bright-red nail.

"Look at them, darling," said a husky voice, low enough to be intimate but quite loud enough to be heard, "staring at me in that oh-so-disapproving way." She took a long, theatrical drag on her cigarette. "I suppose they think a lady shouldn't smoke in public. Well between you and me, darling,"—and here she put her mouth to within two inches of my ear—"I'm not a lady. There."

I turned in my seat and managed to put some distance between us. "Perhaps they just don't like the smoke. It's kind of stuffy in here."

"Don't tell me you're the puritanical type," she said, rearranging her dark curls to flash diamond earrings at me. "You don't look it, but you never can tell with Americans."

"No, ma'am. The pilgrim fathers wouldn't think too much of me."

"I'm delighted to hear it. Perhaps, when we have freshened up from our travels, you would like a cocktail. Don't be shocked. I don't see why it should always be the man who asks. A girl could wait forever."

Forever and ever in my case, I thought, but I mustered what gallantry I could. "That would be very nice."

"Been here before?" she said, and without waiting for an answer continued: "I come whenever I can. I call it my island paradise, a perfect getaway from the hurly-burly of London. Oh! All those crowds, the parties, the endless round of society." She pronounced it *ser-SAH-ty*. "Sometimes I just want to give it all up—I can hardly be bothered to do my face in the morning. When I'm on holiday I let myself become an absolute hag. Honestly," she said, waiting for a compliment, "within a couple of days you won't recognise me."

"I'm sure I will."

"Oh, you Americans. Such flatterers! A girl will have to watch herself, I can see that." She simpered like Shirley Temple, which didn't show her to her best advantage. The English couple glanced over in disgust. Young Henry noticed nothing—he spent the whole journey staring out the window, his face impassive, his thoughts who knew where. Contemplating murder? It didn't look like it. Wondering if he could escape from his parents for long enough to sneak off to my room? I glanced down at his pants, hoping to see some tell-tale bulge, but there was nothing, just the usual folds of fabric. Oh well. We had days, weeks even, of sun and sea ahead of us, and I would surely see him naked, or as near as dammit, even if I didn't get inside him.

There was plenty to look forward to. Apart from soldiers and sailors and young blond Englishmen, there was my host Frank Southern, a great beauty when I knew him during our medical training, the sort of square-jawed Englishman upon whose broad shoulders the Empire rested. Years had passed since I saw him last, and maybe he'd run too fat, but it seemed unlikely, given his job. All soldiers, even medical officers, keep in shape, don't they? Frank Southern had the kind of looks that lasted: in his early twenties he already looked thirty, and would probably stay that way forever with his thick fair hair, big straight nose, and wide mouth. Why, if Miss Glamourpuss got a look at him, she'd be booking herself in for a checkup. In the back of my mind was the hope that Frank's invitation was more than just a holiday. Perhaps, as the years had passed, he'd realized his true nature. Perhaps that was the mysterious "professional matter" on which he needed advice. When we trained, he was devoted to his work and only took his recreation with the occasional nurse, like most of the doctors. I always wondered if his heart was really in it. He seemed more interested in sports—rugby, to be precise—than women. And so, as usual, I was quick to jump to conclusions.

That must be it. After all these years, he'd decided he wanted me. *Mitch, I've come to the conclusion that I want to suck your dick and fuck you up the ass, and to that end, have booked you into the Continental Hotel on Gozo for an indefinite stay...*

"Penny for your thoughts." She didn't give up easily, my new friend.

"I'm sorry," I said. "I was thinking of someone."

"Are you, too, running away?" She delivered the line as if it was penned by Somerset Maugham. "I wonder if we all are. If that's what life really is. Running from one disappointment to the next, to the next..." She sighed, and for the first time she sounded vaguely sincere. A long piece of ash curved down from her cigarette then dropped onto her dress. "Damn it," she said, brushing furiously, and for a moment the mask dropped: she was an ordinary middle-aged woman, worried, tired. She quickly recovered. "Smoking and swearing and inviting handsome young men for cocktails," she said, in a carrying voice. "What must you think? My name is Claire." She held out a hand weighed down with jewelry. "Claire Suther-land." She glanced up coyly from beneath lowered lashes, obviously thinking that I should recognize the name. I didn't; I'm not much of a theatergoer.

I said "Ah," in an understanding sort of way and squeezed her fingers. "Edward Mitchell."

"Mr. Mitchell. I have a feeling we're going to be *great* friends."

And that's all, sister. "I do hope so."

"And look!" She gestured out the dusty window. "We're almost there!"

The rubbly, barren landscape gave way to the green of oleanders and tamarisk, large hibiscus bushes along the roadside, even palm trees. Instead of stone huts there were elegant houses with white walls and red-tiled roofs, terraced gardens, bougainvillea spilling over walls. The road dipped steeply as we approached the shore.

"Aaaah!" said Claire, throwing her head back and twinkling those earrings for all they were worth, "I am home! My real home! A life of natural simplicity—how one yearns for it!" She ran scarlet nails through glossy, dark curls. "My lovely Xlendi!"

Xlendi—pronounced Shlendy, but, like all Maltese words, designed to baffle foreigners—was a small fishing village boasting a perfect little bay around which a cluster of new villas were being built. There were unfinished houses here and there, piles of bricks and sand, shovels and hammers, although no sign of any actual work being done. People sat on stone benches shaded by trees, smoking, gossiping, watching the bus as it trundled down the road. We stopped just short of the sea; another fifty yards and the front wheels would have been wet.

"Hotel Continental!" shouted the driver as the engine died. As the doors creaked open, the scramble began. The English family clucked and fussed over coats and bags; Claire Sutherland strutted down the aisle like a Ziegfeld girl, placing one foot directly in front of the other, her ass swaying as she made damn sure that she was first down the steps. I got the impression that Miss Sutherland was accustomed to getting what she wanted. Perhaps it was I who would have to watch myself.

I sat awhile, watching Henry shouldering his burdens, enjoying the way his shirt stuck to his damp back and revealed something of the smooth curves beneath. We could all do with a bath. The sea looked mighty inviting. I said as much as I got up.

"We do not bathe in the sea," said his father, scowling at me through tortoiseshell glasses. "It is particularly treacherous here."

I looked out at the calm blue waters, so smooth they reflected the yellow sandstone of the cliffs like a mirror. "Looks okay to me. I can't wait to jump right in."

"At your own peril," said the father. Henry tutted and sighed. I caught his eye and smiled. He blushed as he struggled with the bags his parents refused to consign to the porters.

"Let me help you with that." I picked up a suitcase. His parents squeaked in dismay, but their son had better manners.

"Thanks."

"Don't worry, folks. I'm not going to steal anything." Except your son's cherry, perhaps. "After you."

The family got down from the bus, glancing back all the while to ensure I hadn't vanished with their precious luggage. I followed.

We were standing on a cobbled promenade, tiny shops and houses on one side, the Mediterranean on the other. There was nothing remotely resembling a hotel to be seen.

"Come, come," said the driver, beckoning towards a dark, narrow alley between two ancient buildings. "Hotel. Here, hotel." Shallow steps led up into the gloom. Claire Sutherland was way ahead of me, heels ringing like gunshots on the stones.

"Isn't there an easier way?"

"God no, darling. One of the many charms of this island, to which you will soon become accustomed, is that there's no easy way to do anything. Cars and buses and suchlike can't get anywhere near the dear old Continental. A donkey can just about struggle up these steps, but that's it. One has to rely on the boys." She was carrying nothing but her purse and the portable wealth with which she adorned her fingers, neck and ears. Only a brave woman walks down dark alleys with that much ice on display, but I guess Miss Sutherland knew what she was doing. One slug from those expensive knuckle-dusters would lay anyone out.

The rest of the party tailed behind us. After a minute's climb we emerged into a dazzling square of light; once my pupils had adjusted I saw white walls surrounding a sandy courtyard, trees and shrubs in neat beds, a pillared door with a fancy tiled surround and, tinkling merrily in the middle of it all, an ornamental fountain.

"The dear old place," said Claire. "Still standing."

And out of the cool, dim interior emerged a young couple, a beautiful woman and a handsome man, smiling and stepping towards us with hands outstretched.

"Welcome to the Continental," she said. "We're so happy to have you."

II

"TILLY, DARLING." CLAIRE SUTHERLAND STEPPED FORWARD, hands outstretched, lips pursed and ready. Her black curls brushed against the other's immaculate blonde waves. "I said I'd be back, and here I am. Martin," she went on, turning to the young man in the navy blazer, "you're even younger and better looking than last year, damn you." Another kiss, this one a little more sincere.

"Claire," he said. "You look wonderful. I don't know how you do it." Martin smiled. He had dazzling white teeth, a flop of dark-blond hair and deep laugh lines around blue eyes. He looked like the leading man of a West End show, right down to his tennis shoes. I half expected him to burst into song. "And you must be Dr. Mitchell," he said, turning the beam on me. "Welcome to the Continental. I'm Martin Dear, and this is my wife Tilly."

"We hope you'll have a wonderful time, Dr. Mitchell," said Tilly. The petite, curvy blonde bombshell was, in her way, just as charming and theatrical as her husband. The perfect proprietors of a nice little hotel. "We're all friends here, aren't we, Claire?"

"Oh yes, dear, we are. Now if someone could just…" She gestured around as if conjuring spirits.

Tilly clapped her hands, and an elderly man in an ill-fitting white jacket emerged from the darkness. "Ralph, take Miss Sutherland's things to her usual room."

"Darling, you remembered. I need peace."

"Of course I remembered. I hope you'll find things exactly as you like them."

"I hope so too," said Claire. Was there a note of warning in her voice?

Trunks and bags were being carried up the stairs by a small army of children, black haired and bare limbed, the offspring of the fishermen who acted as the village's unofficial fetch-and-carry service. Martin pressed some coin into the oldest one's hand. Claire strode through the door as if she owned the place, and I followed.

"We've put you at the very top, Dr. Mitchell," said Tilly, who was wearing a white dress with a bold design of red roses, tightly fitted over her narrow waist and big bosom. "The stairs are rather killing, but you look as if you'll manage. And the view! Well, I'll let you discover that for yourself. Ralph will bring your things."

"Are you sure he'll make it? He's kind of old."

"Oh, they all look ancient here. It's the sun. They will go out without hats. And the salt water—terribly ageing. I won't go near it. He's probably only forty or something." She handed me a key hanging from a chunk of driftwood. "Quaint, I know, but people just kept losing them. Take the stairs and when you can't go any farther you'll find a door. Will you join us for dinner? I think Stella is making something rather special. One of her wonderful fish things. Drinks at seven, shall we say?"

And she was off, greeting the English family, cooing over how much "darling Henry" had grown in a year, what a handsome young man he was becoming...I climbed the stairs until I was out of earshot.

The staircase curved around, an architectural eccentricity that appeared to have been cut into the rock of the cliff. The walls were cold and rough, and soon I was in darkness. A few more steps and the light returned, a bright beam shooting through a small aperture in the wall, enough for me to see a heavy wooden door at the top, shot through with black nails. It looked more like the entrance to a dungeon than a hotel room, and I wondered if I might have to ask Frank Southern for alternative accommodation.

A little jiggling with the key and the door opened.

The room was large and round—octagonal, in fact, with four of the eight sides given entirely to windows that looked out to sea, the view unimpeded, save for the uppermost branches of trees on the promenade below. The light was intense yet the room was cool, shaded from the fiercest heat by a solid ceiling, and clearly designed to catch only the weak but picturesque setting sun. There it was, turning from dusty yellow to orange as it sank towards a headland on the other side of the bay, leaving a glittering trail of gold on the water beneath.

I gasped and went straight to the windows. They opened inwards, giving access to a small balcony, big enough for a couple of canvas-backed chairs and a little folding table. The floor was paved with large, square marble tiles. There was a double bed with a hideous brass bedstead; a table with, of all things, an aspidistra on it; a wardrobe and little else. A small door led to the bathroom.

Claire Sutherland was right. Even I, who had never set foot on the island before, felt as if I had come home.

A sudden stab around my heart. Home—the place I left behind in London—was home no longer. Vince had gone, and there was nothing for me except regret, the hollow echo of all the apologies I'd made, each worth less than the last. And then, when sorry meant nothing anymore, Vince decided that his future lay elsewhere. Not in London, waiting for me to come home at night, wondering where I was, who I was with, if I was safe. Somewhere far away, where he could build a new life and forget me. Oh, we'd told each other all the comforting lies—we'd take a break, we'd concentrate on our own careers, we'd come back together when the time was right. Maybe I believed it at the time, but I don't think Vince did. I betrayed him too many times, and love—even Vince's love, the truest and purest I've ever found—can't survive that. I was free now, which I suppose is what I wanted. I didn't need to miss another opportunity because of guilt or scruples. I could fuck every ass that came my way, and nobody would care. Nobody would care. Nobody. That was it.

Not even Morgan, the man I'd spent years chasing and seducing, loving and fucking and, in the process, almost destroying his marriage and family. What kind of friend had I been to him? A false friend. In the quiet hours of a sleepless night I can tell myself that Morgan's true nature is being denied; that it's me he loves, not his wife; that it's society and the law and Morgan's innate cowardice that has torn us apart. Now, in the brilliant light of an island sunset, those illusions vanish. Morgan is what he is, a normal married man who has enjoyed a few adventures and settled down. The fact that my dick felt so good up his ass, so right, doesn't mean that's where it belongs. Time to let it go. And maybe here, far from the mess of my life, freed from the immediate responsibility of earning a living by receiving an unexpected inheritance, I could make a fresh start. Tabula rasa. No regrets, no memories. A new Mitch Mitchell. Others can do it. Why not me?

Start with washing off the dirt of a long and tiring journey. Through the door was a claw-foot tub with curving brass taps, a toilet and a basin. Thank God that modern plumbing had reached this little outpost of the Empire. I proposed to spend as much of my time in the sea as possible, but I'm still American enough to insist on hot water and flush toilets.

I ran a bath—the water gushed out, satisfyingly steamy and smelling slightly of salt—and stripped. You probably know me well enough to realize that I was already thinking about how to get laid, and taking my clothes off made things more urgent. For all my sorrows and regrets, which I believe were sincere, there was a concurrent train of thought: how could I get into that English boy's pants? Where was the sexy soldier from the ferry—or even the tall, young priest? What about Martin, my genial host? Just how hospitable would he be? My dick was rising at the thought of all these options when there was a knock at my door.

Someone's read my mind, I thought, adjusting a towel around my waist. Soldier, son, priest, host? Or a surprise…

I opened the door.

"Your luggage, sir."

The ancient porter, having lugged my trunk up the twisting stone stairs, was wheezing as if he was about to die at my feet. I didn't want to start my holiday by delivering the kiss of life. "Jesus, you didn't have to do that."

"Quite all right, sir." His accent was thick, rattling out of congested lungs. He looked as if he smoked eighty cigarettes a day. "Where shall I put it?"

"Just there." I gestured to the foot of the bed and rummaged for change in my pants pockets. "Here. What's your name?"

"Ralph, sir."

I gave him a handful of coins, and he looked pleased. It's always a good idea to make friends with the help, especially if you're relying on their discretion.

"Is there anything else, sir?" he asked, glancing at the front of my towel.

"No thanks. That's all."

"Perhaps you would like to go to a cafe later, sir."

"A cafe?"

"My sister, she runs a very nice cafe in the town. Very clean, nice girls."

It took me a few seconds to figure out what was on the menu. "Thanks, Ralph. I'll bear it in mind. At the moment I just need a bath."

"Very good, sir. If you would like some company, I know many ladies."

"That's great. I'll be fine, thanks."

He seemed reluctant to leave, perhaps hoping to see me get into the bath. Perhaps the whole hotel was riddled with spyholes. I've stayed in places like that before.

"Goodbye, Ralph." I pointed at the door, and off he went.

While the tub filled, I looked out from the balcony. The sun was almost down now, the sky a fantastic mixture of pink and gold, the sea already turning black. Lights were coming on along the promenade. Looking down from my eyrie I could figure out something of the layout of the hotel. Beneath me were two identical balconies, one on either side; the house tapered towards the top. Further down there were three more balconies. Six rooms at the front, then, and perhaps others at the back, looking onto the cliffs. I wondered who was where. Miss Sutherland, with her repeated plea for peace, was perhaps at the back, where she could allow herself to fall to pieces (no makeup, no jewelry, no wig—*was* it a wig?) unobserved. And what of the English family? Were they all camped out in one room, or had they given the son—an adult, for all his boyish looks—the privacy he deserved? At the moment all the doors were closed, the balconies unoccupied, but from my vantage point I could see everything, as well as keep an eye on the comings and goings around the harbor, the bars and cafes, the fishermen's huts and the promenade. At its left-hand extremity the promenade turned ninety degrees to the right, following the edge of bay and providing a paved pathway over the undulating rocks that led out of the village. On the right, it terminated in a sheer rock face full of small caves—dug either by time and the elements or the hand of man—where the locals kept nets and floats. Steps were cut into the rock leading up a steep path that disappeared to the west; the cliffs there climbed towards the bulky, square headland behind which the sun had now dropped.

There was much to explore, both inside and out. But first, that bath.

The ancient Ralph and his unwelcomed offers had effectively quelled my excitement, but the hot, salty water soon did its work and by the time I was clean in body I was once again very dirty in my thoughts. Trusting the twilight and railings to conceal the details, I stood naked on the balcony and looked down.

Below me one set of windows was open. A towel, identical to the one I'd discarded on the bathroom floor, was draped over the rail. I leaned a little farther and there it all was—a blond head; a long, pale neck; bare arms and shoulders, just the straps of a fresh white singlet across each. He was sitting watching the sunset, and he appeared to be alone. I watched him long enough that my cock started to rise and then, making sure it wasn't visible, called down a salutation.

"Hi! Henry! Lovely evening!"

He jumped and looked up into the shadows. "Who's there?"

"It's me. Mitch."

"Oh, Dr. Mitchell." He sounded pleased. "I can't quite make you out. I've been staring at the sunset. Isn't it beautiful?"

"Lovely," I said. "You going for a swim?"

"I don't know. I'd very much like to."

And then, like sinister figures on a Swiss clock, his parents popped out onto the adjacent balcony. "Henry! Come inside!" shrilled his mother.

"Who are you talking to?" barked the father. I withdrew into the shade of my room; it wouldn't do young Henry any good for his parents to see a naked man hovering above him.

"Just the gentleman in the room upstairs," said Henry, who was obviously the honest sort. "Dr. Mitchell. He was asking me if I'd like to go for a swim."

"Have you finished your unpacking?"

"No, but..."

"I told you to put all your things away," said the mother. Some holiday they were going to have. "Perhaps tomorrow you may bathe."

I dressed quickly and went down to the lobby. Martin Dear was leaning on the front desk, greeting the guests as they came and went.

"Drinks at seven, Dr. Mitchell," he said, flashing a smile. Were it not for his glamorous blonde wife I'd be putting my host right at the top of my hit list. "Do hope you'll join us."

"Sure. Just thought I'd take a little stroll first. Get the lay of the land. Which way would you recommend?"

"Follow the prom round to the left," he said. "Skirts the bay and climbs up to the salt pans, which are worth a look. Lots of good places to swim as well."

"Where do you go?"

"There's an inlet about four, five hundred yards along that way, if you can climb down the rocks. Some of the local kids jump straight in. The water's deep, and there's a lot of fish. Jellyfish too, sometimes, so you need to look before you leap."

"I'll bear that in mind. Don't want to get stung."

"If you're a strong swimmer you can go right across the bay to the caves and rocks on the other side. Not many people go. It's very private."

"You go over there?"

"Sometimes."

"With your wife?"

"God, no. She won't go anywhere near the water. Terrified of it, if you want the truth. I mean, she says it's bad for the skin and the hair and so on, but really she's frightened. Won't even paddle in the bay with the children. Just one of those things."

"Seems strange that she works in a hotel by the sea, then."

Martin laughed, throwing back his head; he had one of those thick, strong necks that I always want to bite. "That's what I say to the old girl! You must be the only seaside landlady who's terrified of water!"

"You're not, though."

"Not me." He made a few breast stroke moves. "I like a dip. Keeps me in shape."

"So I see. Perhaps you'll show me those caves some time."

"How long are you with us, Dr. Mitchell?"

"Three weeks for starters. Maybe longer. And please—call me Mitch."

"Mitch." We shook hands. "Martin."

"Okay, Martin. Drinks in half an hour."

I trotted down the stone steps from the Continental courtyard to the promenade. The light was fading, but the path was busy with tourists and locals taking the evening air—the delightful Mediterranean tradition of *passeggiata*,[1] that little break between work and dinner for seeing and being seen. A trio of handsome black-haired youths were sitting on the wall that ran alongside the promenade, smoking and picking their teeth and watching the girls go by. This could be a happy hunting ground for me, with a hard dick and a wallet full of Aunt Dinah's dollars.

"Ah, Dr. Mitchell!" It was Claire Sutherland of course, in a blue evening dress, wearing diamonds around her neck. "I wonder if you would be so kind?" Without waiting for a reply she put her arm through mine. "I'm not old-fashioned—far from it—but really, an

---

1   http://www.fodors.com/news/story_4117.html

unaccompanied woman simply isn't safe here! The way they look at me!" She glanced back at the three young men, who were staring with great interest at a blonde teenage girl. "Positively carnivorous! And I'm sure I understand enough Maltese to get the gist of what they were saying. Quite unrepeatable!" She leaned into me, squeezing my arm. "So what brings you here, if I may ask?"

"Just a holiday. An old colleague works over in..."

"I come every year, or as often as my career allows." Miss Sutherland was obviously not one of life's listeners. "It's absolutely marvelous. It was, anyway. We shall see what the new people make of it. Haven't managed to muck it up too much, by the look of things, but time will tell."

"How long have they been here?"

"This is only their second summer. They were very wet behind the ears last year, and one made allowances of course, but I do hope things go smoothly this summer. One simply wants to relax and just *be*, don't you think? To allow oneself to *live*."

"Who ran the Continental before Martin and Tilly Dear?"

"Oh, the most wonderful couple, the Andersons. Couldn't have been more devoted to me. They had seen me on the stage many years...a few years ago, and were most insistent that I should come as their guest, you see. Their way of saying thank you, I suppose. The tributes of audiences, really." She put one hand to her breast. "So humbling. And I repaid their loyalty by coming back again and again. As I've said, it's quite a second home to me. Perhaps when I retire I shall make the move permanently." She sighed. "Not that that's going to happen for years and years yet. As long as audiences want me, I shall continue to give."

"Of course."

"But not the Andersons. They simply threw in the towel." She sounded bitter. "Just like that. Out of the blue. Sold up. Took the money and ran. I suppose it's up to them, but really, one did feel just a little disappointed."

"Perhaps they had personal reasons."

"None that I knew of," said Claire, as if somehow their decision should have been run by her first. "But of course these people have lives of their own about which we know nothing. I know all too well what it is to have one's private life scrutinized. The price one pays for success, they tell me, all that press and gossip, but really…" She sighed. "I don't see the need. One is simply an actress. A devotee of the craft."

"You don't get that in my profession, fortunately."

"Well, no, of course not. Let us give the new proprietors the benefit of the doubt," she said, switching subjects abruptly. "There's no denying they've made some wonderful improvements. The new plumbing is a joy—all that lovely hot water, and so clean! My goodness, they've spent a pretty penny on the old place. One rather misses the old ways, but I say progress! Youth at the helm! The Continental is a good deal smarter than it was. And the clientele too. Not the ragtag bohemians we used to be—now it's doctors and professional types. I hope it doesn't become too smart, though. Wealthy people are so dull. Are you wealthy, Dr. Mitchell?"

"Not terribly."

Her grip slackened a little. "Well of course in the old days we got all sorts here. I mean, the Andersons were broad minded. Very tolerant. That's why they loved artists. There were many painters in the old days, bearded types, you know, and their models, shall we call them. Writers too. Somewhat irregular lives, but the Andersons never minded. Liberty Hall, as long as one was discreet. Oh, I've seen them all coming and going. Clergymen, bluestockings, really some of the most unlikely combinations, but love knows no laws."

"Indeed."

"I remember last summer—no, it must have been the summer before last, the Andersons were still here—there was one young woman here who was just the most mousy little thing you can imagine. Stringy brown hair; awful, shabby clothes and, my dear, she was as flat as a pancake, no sex appeal at all that I could see. But there she was, carrying on with a gorgeous young man—a priest, would you believe! A dog collar and everything, quite blatant. There was talk of course, but the Andersons didn't mind one bit. Treated them the same as the rest of us, not that she ever was one of us. Nasty, stuck-up little piece she was."

I sniffed the jealousy of the older woman, whose *amours* were, perhaps, more mercenary. Claire adjusted her smile and continued. "Never any scandal though. Discretion above all. I do so hope that the Dears will keep up the tradition."

We walked in silence both, I suspect, looking out for likely male companions. I saw a couple of men in uniform, which was encouraging. Perhaps the soldier from the ferry was nearby...

"Oh, but really, these people." Claire jerked to a halt and whispered in my ear. "My heart sank like a stone when I saw them on the ferry. Just the type we don't want."

The English parents descended the Continental steps; their son was nowhere to be seen. Perhaps he'd slipped the leash.

"I mean, what are they? Missionaries or something? They come back year after year, and I swear they never even speak to me. Absolutely cut me dead. That poor boy of theirs."

"You know them?"

"Only by name. A Mr. and Mrs. Jessop. The son is Henry."

"What are they doing here? They look very out of place."

"I know, darling. They belong in Margate rather than Malta. Perhaps they're international jewel thieves in cunning disguise. They send the boy climbing over the rooftops and then sell their ill-gotten gains to some shady lascar over in Valetta! For all I know he could be rifling through my things as we speak! Oh, my imagination! That's the thing about the artistic temperament, you see. One has these marvelous flights. Well, well." Her attention was wandering towards an unattached gentleman in a navy-blue blazer with a carnation in its buttonhole. He had passed us a couple of times and now bowed slightly in greeting. Claire smiled back and withdrew her arm from mine. "Perhaps I shall see you at dinner, Dr. Mitchell," she said, and moved off without a backward glance.

It was too dark now to explore the eastern path that led, according to Martin, up to the salt pans, and I had no intention of starting my holiday with a broken leg, so instead I turned to the bright lights of the waterfront cafes and bars. One of them, at the farthest corner where the fishing boats were tethered for the night, seemed popular with the locals, and it was here that I decided to slake my thirst with a beer. It had the advantage of commanding a good view of the whole promenade, in case Henry or other prey appeared.

I took a seat and waited to be served.

"Yes sir, what would you like?"

A gray-haired, weather-beaten old man—although, like Ralph, he could have been in his forties—was wiping his hands on an apron. The great advantage of Malta, I reflected, is that everyone speaks English.

"A beer, please."

"American?"

"Me, or the beer?"

He laughed as if this was the funniest thing he'd ever heard. "You, sir—our beer is Maltese! Best beer in the world." Then he shouted over to the three handsome young men I'd noticed earlier, sitting on the harbor wall watching the girls go by. "Hey! Joseph! Come! We are busy!" As he turned back to me, he shrugged as he said, "My son. Lazy, lazy fellow. He is supposed to be working tonight but he thinks he is too good for work."

The shirker in question loped across to the bar, chewing on a toothpick. His shirt was unbuttoned to his chest, his sleeves rolled up to his elbows. He was confident in his good looks, and he treated his father with a sort of affectionate disdain.

"Papa."

A tirade of incomprehensible Maltese followed, but Joseph simply smiled, flicked his toothpick into the water and ambled off towards the bar.

"No wonder my hair is gray. That I should have such a lazy, good-for-nothing...I'm sorry, sir. These are not your troubles."

"Mitchell," I said, extending a hand. "Nice to meet you."

"Thank you, sir, thank you." He wiped his hands again. "Anthony Vella at your service. Joseph!" he roared. "Where is the beer!"

He bustled off in search of his errant son, and I looked around me. Vella's place was little more than a cave hollowed out of the rock, a few tables and chairs and a wooden bar with, I hoped, some way of keeping the beer cold. I may have lived in Britain for a long time, but I've never accustomed myself to warm beer.

My fellow customers were a mixed lot—certainly not the smart clientele that would soon be gathering for aperitifs at the Continental. A few fishermen, deeply tanned, bearded after days and nights at sea. Some of the village elders, stooped and white haired, bent ruminatively over drinks and pints. All locals, by the look of it, but for me and a stout, red-faced gent in a dusty old jacket, a cravat around his neck and a cap of somewhat nautical style perched on his white hair. He sat and watched, sketching in a pad—one of the artistic community of which La Sutherland had spoken, perhaps.

"Beer, sir."

The son returned with a reassuringly dewy bottle on a tray with a glass. He laid them in front of me and seemed in no hurry to depart. That suited me fine: he was tall and handsome, and for all his laziness he appeared to be strong. I was glad of the beer, but there was something I needed more—and maybe he could provide it.

A plan popped into my head. "I need a guide," I said. "Someone to show me the sights."

"What you want to see?" His voice was rough and guttural, more thickly accented than his father's.

"The local beauty spots. I'll pay you for your time."

He shrugged, looking down into my eyes, trying to figure out what I wanted. "Okay. Tomorrow?"

"Now. Show me the clifftops. There must be some great views of the harbor."

Joseph nodded towards the back of the bar. "There's a path there, takes you way up. If you can climb."

"I can climb."

"Then come."

I took the bottle and followed him to a narrow alley cut into the rocks, which seemed to serve as a combined drain and trash dump; it was wet and smelly. A few yards up, however, a path led through the rocks and scrub; Joseph sprang up it like a goat.

"Watch your feet."

"I can't. It's pitch black."

"Then hold on." He reached back, grabbed my hand and pulled. I half climbed, half scrambled up the steep path, spilling beer as I went. There was a house at the top, and a broad, flat path that was visible even in only the very last of the evening light. I was panting by the time I reached it; Joseph seemed to have barely noticed the climb.

"There," he said, pointing down to the harbor, "the village. It is very pretty."

"Yep, sure is." Crickets were singing up here, seabirds making strange mewing calls above our heads. I swigged my beer, then offered it to Joseph. He took it and drank. "What's up that way?" I pointed up a bit, in the direction of the sunset.

"Cliffs. Caves. Other villages."

"Show me."

"You pay?"

"Sure." I patted my pocket where my wallet was. "American dollars."

"This way." He put an arm around my shoulder and led me along the high path. It was not quite the affirmative gesture I was hoping for—many of the young men of the southern Mediterranean walk hand in hand with none of the implications it would have in America or England—but still, it was good to feel the weight of that strong, dark limb at the back of my neck. "Be careful," he said, leading me away from the cliff edge. "It is dangerous up here. There have been accidents."

It was cooler on the clifftops, a stiff breeze ruffling our hair as we crunched over the stony path. I shivered, and was glad of the heat from Joseph's body. We passed the bottle of beer to and fro.

"You're cold," he said, pulling me closer with his hairy arm.

"I'm fine."

"You want my shirt?"

"What?"

He was already undoing the last few buttons; even in the failing light I could see that his stomach was flat, brown and hairy. "Here." He put it around my shoulders. "Better?"

The material was still warm from Joseph's body and smelled faintly of sweat.

"What about you? Don't want you catching a cold."

He put his arm around me again; now I could feel a good deal more skin. "Up here there is a hunter's place. You see?" He pointed ahead. I could vaguely trace the gray outlines of a hut. Empty now. I come up here sometimes. Sleep, drink..."

"I see."

"Bring girls." He pulled me closer. I put my arm around his waist, feeling the firmness of his flanks. He didn't pull away. "Do you kiss?"

This was unexpected; most men of Joseph's type pretend nothing's happening even when you're swallowing their cocks. "Of course I do."

He looked into my eyes, smiling. "Good. Some don't. I do."

"You do this with many men?"

He shrugged. "A few. Here." We were at the hunter's hut, and he was fiddling with the lock. I wanted to ask if this was a financial arrangement, or simply for the sake of pleasure, hoping it was the latter but confident in the power of the dollar.

There was just enough room to stand up inside. It was dark, a few cracks in the wood allowing dim rays of light to penetrate. I wanted to see Joseph—and I wanted him to see what we would be doing—but that would have to wait. He took me in his arms and kissed me, large flat hands pressing against my shoulder blades. There in the dark, with the warmth of his hairy body against mine, the salt tang of sweat, it felt like it meant something—as if someone wanted me for myself, someone cared about me, loved me even. I was tired from the journey, and I guess my emotions were near the surface. I was missing Vince and marking time over Morgan, and for a moment I allowed myself to believe that here in this ancient hut perched above the Mediterranean I had found something of meaning...

"I want your cock."

Well, that was meaning enough, I guess. His hips were grinding into me, his tongue plunging into my mouth, and when I reached down to slide my hand to the front of his pants I could feel something long and thick and very hard down there. Love and regret are all well and good, but I'm shallow enough to forget them for a fistful of penis.

We pawed at the front of each other's pants for a while, our breath loud in the confines of the hut, the heat from our bodies rising. One of us was going to have to take the initiative, and for all Joseph's claims that he had sex with "a few" men, I'm pretty sure I was the more experienced party. I unbuckled my belt, unbuttoned my fly and hauled the goods out. I was well over half erect, in some ways my favorite state: the surge of arousal, the anticipation, the intoxicating sense of possibility. It's probably all explained by the drain of blood from the brain.

"Suck it."

I didn't have to ask twice. In the gloom of the hut Joseph dropped to his knees, drank the last of the beer, put the empty bottle carefully on the floor and took my cock in his mouth. I'd been on the island for barely a couple hours and already some handsome, hairy native was sucking my dick. I can't fault Mediterranean hospitality.

My eyes were adjusting, and I could see Joseph looking up at me, dark-brown eyes gleaming, brow furrowed. What kind of life did he lead? Was he playing a part, the typical arrogant, young islander with his easy good looks and lazy disposition, all the while hiding his true nature, waiting for men like me to come along? Or did they see things differently in the south? Were things less black and white? I've fucked enough men to know that it's not always a simple choice between queer and "normal"; plenty of us have a foot in both camps. Perhaps that was more acceptable in Malta and its islands. From the efficient way Joseph was sucking my dick—which was now fully hard and plunging into his throat—they got plenty of chance to practice.

I wondered how much further he'd go. I like a challenge, and the idea of bending Joseph over and fucking him in that rickety little hut was very appealing. Would that be a step too far? There are plenty of guys who will let you do anything with their mouths but are nervous as hell about their asses.

"Stand up."

He did as he was told, holding onto my cock with his hand; now that he'd gotten it, he was in no hurry to let go. I pinched a tit and pulled him in, slipped a hand around to the back of his pants and squeezed a buttock.

"Get naked."

He gasped, kicked his shoes off and undid his pants. He was wearing nothing underneath, which is either a Maltese custom or a sign that Joseph liked to be ready for action. From what I could feel he was good and hairy on his legs and ass. When he stood up again, his dick stuck straight out from his body; I grabbed it and pressed it against mine. Joseph's knees buckled.

"You like that?"

"Yes."

"You want my cock?"

"Yes."

"You really want it?"

He said something in Maltese, which could have been an insult or a witty retort, but I chose to interpret it as "I want you to fuck me hard up the ass, but I'm too much of a 'man' to tell you directly."

"Turn around."

Obedient again—really, I don't know what his father was complaining about. To me, Joseph seemed to be a diligent and enthusiastic worker. I pressed my hard cock between his cheeks and rubbed it up and down, enjoying the softness of the fur against my head and shaft. Joseph pressed back against me and spread his legs. If he came up here for regular fucks, I'm surprised the old hut was still standing.

I spat into my hand and slicked up the head of my cock—there was nothing else available, unless Joseph had a stash of Vaseline up here. I lined up with the target and pressed. He didn't complain; I guess he was used to rough fucks. That suited me fine. He wouldn't suffer for long; after the journey by land and sea from London to Xlendi my balls were full to bursting and needed relief. I was leaking clear, sticky juice in great quantities, a sure sign that I've got a big load to shoot. It was enough; I got the head in, and after letting him relax and breathe for a few moments it only took a little extra pressure for my whole cock to slip inside him. His insides were as smooth as silk, as juicy as a peach. Soon my pubic hair was mingling with his ass fur, and we were in business.

I like my men to enjoy being fucked, so I reached around to check that Joseph was still hard. He was, his dick pressing up against his stomach. That told me all I needed to know. If he was half as ready as I was, we'd be back down the cliff path in time for cocktails at the Continental.

But Jesus, I didn't want it to be over. It wasn't just his ass that felt good—it was his broad, muscular back and his hard, hairy thighs. It was the smell of beer and hair oil and sweat, the sound of his grunting and my own heavy breathing, the squelches and clicks as I plunged into his hole; it was the eerie cries of the seabirds around us in the cooling evening air, the distant hiss and roar of the sea. I felt my mind emptying of thought, filling up with pure sensation; I could even taste his lips on mine from that long, deep kiss. No more regrets about what I'd left behind, no more fear of a friendless future, just here and now in this ancient hut with a naked man and my cock inside him.

I heard myself groan before I realized that I was coming, emptying a huge load inside Joseph's wet ass. His fist pumped as he bent over, shooting his own sperm onto the sand-worn timbers at our feet.

He was quiet when we'd finished, not making a sound even when I withdrew. I wiped my dick on a handkerchief and put it away; Joseph was still naked, and facing away from me.

I put a hand on his shoulder, damp with sweat. "You all right?"

He said nothing. The mask was slipping back into place. What now? Threats? Anger?

"Give me five dollars."

Ah, that was it. He pretended to be a whore in order to hide his real desires. Not the first to do so, and not the last.

"Or what?"

"I tell the police."

"What will you tell them exactly, Joseph? How you brought me up here? How you kissed me and sucked my cock? How much you shot when I fucked you up the ass?"

"I know the police here." He still wouldn't turn around and look at me. "My father knows them."

"And what else does he know?" Silence. "Shall I tell him?"

He turned around now, still naked, his cock still half hard, swaying as he moved. "Please, no."

"It's okay, Joseph. Get dressed. Listen, to show there's no hard feelings, I'll give you five bucks. Not because you asked for it, and not because you threatened me, but because I said I'd pay you to be my guide. Besides, I might need someone with a bit of local knowledge while I'm here." I was thinking ahead; every detective has a slightly more stupid sidekick, and mine have to be readily fuckable as well. "If you want my cock again, just ask. But no more blackmail. We don't have to do that to each other."

He said something like "Oh" or "Ah" and started kissing me again.

The job was his.

III

I WOKE THE NEXT MORNING WITH A SORE HEAD—TOO MANY OF
Martin Dear's martinis—and a stiff cock, thinking about Joseph
Vella's silky, hairy arse. It had been a short evening: drinks with
the other guests, a plate of delicious, freshly caught fish straight
from the pan, a little stilted conversation with my fellow guests, and
early to bed. There was no scent of mystery. Tilly and Martin Dear
were the perfect hosts, friendly but not overly familiar. They asked
politely about my plans; I told them I was meeting an old friend,
and they nodded and smiled. Claire Sutherland was as horny as
I was, albeit twenty or thirty years older; she dined with her new
friend from the promenade and, presumably, took him to bed. The
Jessops remained as dull and unbending as they had been on the
ferry, ostentatiously refusing alcoholic drinks, nibbling their fish as if
they feared poisoning, exchanging looks of distaste every time I tried
to speak to them. The other guests—a mixture of Italian families
and elderly Brits—kept to their own established groups. As a young,
single American, I was the odd man out. I kept my ears open for any
hint of scandal or hostility—I wanted, like Poirot or Miss Marple—
to sense a crime before it happened, but there was nothing. I would
have to look farther afield than the lounge of the Continental Hotel.

To that end, I rose and dressed early for my breakfast appointment with Frank Southern, who was due on the nine o'clock ferry. The sea was sparkling as I stood on my balcony, the sky a pristine pale blue. Out in the bay I saw a sleek wet head and strong white shoulders gliding through the water; Henry Jessop, I was fairly sure, was getting an early-morning swim before his parents started bossing him around. I made a mental note to follow him one day; for now I was sufficiently excited by the idea of seeing Frank again. Was he still as good-looking as he used to be? And what was the secret business he wanted to discuss? Would he like to come to my room and show me?

I took the rattling, smelly old bus across the island, passing herds of goats, ancient footsore crones, wild children playing in the dust—sights unchanged on the island for centuries. We reached the harbor just as the ferry docked.

My first glimpse of Frank Southern answered one question. In his short-sleeved white shirt and regulation pants, his cap pushed back on his head, he was just as beautiful as before. More so, perhaps: the sun had darkened his skin to golden brown and bleached the hair on his head and arms to the color of wheat. He stood at the top of the gangplank surveying the quay, and I had time to take in his flat stomach, his strong jaw and sturdy legs, before he spotted me.

"Mitch!" He sprang down the steps like a mountain lion and grabbed me with both arms. "It's good to see you." Southern was Scottish; we trained together for a while in Edinburgh. I'd forgotten what an effect those rolled Rs and shortened vowels had on me. Add to that his strong arms around me, his hard body pressed against mine, and you can figure out for yourself how I responded.

Frank stepped away before this became compromising, and held me at arm's length.

"You look well, Mitch."

I didn't feel it; those martinis were getting their revenge, and the rigors of the journey were catching up with me. Compared to Frank Southern I felt haggard and exhausted—by life, by sorrow, by drink. However, the company of a handsome man always works wonders, and something of his glowing good health was reflecting on to me.

"Ready for breakfast? I'm starving." He patted his stomach, which sounded as tight as a drum. "I've got an hour and a half before my clinic. Another morning looking at old ladies' feet and old men's arses. Oh well. The burden of the Empire."

"I thought you just looked after the garrison at Valetta."

"We have to show a bit of goodwill to the natives as well. It's all politics, Mitch. If I can cut a few corns and reduce a few hemorrhoids among the civilian population, everyone's happy."

"Small price to pay for all those soldiers and sailors," I said, checking Frank's eyes for any hint of reaction. All he did was laugh.

"Same old Mitch," he said, slapping me on the shoulder. Frank knew all about me and accepted my preferences as he accepted my hair color. "You haven't changed."

"Not me. Have you?"

"Sorry, still normal."

The word rankled a bit. I've never considered myself to be abnormal, and I've fucked enough "normal" men to know that the world isn't quite as simple as Frank Southern implied. But I didn't complain. At least Frank accepted our differences.

"So what's the big mystery you wanted to discuss?"

"All in good time. Here." He steered me into a waterfront cafe, a cluster of white metal tables and chairs under a green striped awning. "The best breakfast on the island." A motherly woman in a black dress emerged from the darkness, arms extended. "Doctor Frank!" She squeezed him in an embrace and kissed both his smooth-shaven cheeks, the lucky girl. "My favorite man in the world! Look at me!" She stepped back, turning this way and that. "Would you believe it?" She was addressing me now. "Last year I could hardly walk my legs were so bad. Now I am dancing the Black Bottom!" She shimmied her ample black-clad posterior in support of her claim. "All thanks to my wonderful Doctor Frank!"

"Ulceration as a result of varicose veins," said Frank in an undertone. "I gave her some support stockings. She thinks I'm a miracle worker." Then aloud he said, "Ah, Mama Melissa! I'm so proud of you! You look ten—no, twenty years younger!"

Melissa simpered like a teenage girl and ushered us to a table.

"Now, gentlemen, what can I get you?"

"Two of your delicious fry-ups, please. Tea for me, you know how I like it. And coffee for my friend. You still drink coffee?"

"Of course."

"Wait till you try Mama's coffee. It's so strong it should only be available with a prescription."

"Just what I need. Long journey yesterday."

"Good, good," she said, bustling off to the kitchen.

"And a skinful of cocktails at the hotel last night."

"They're looking after you, then? The Dears?"

"Very well, thank you. I'm grateful for the recommendation."

"How long will you stay, Mitch?"

"Three weeks for starters. Maybe more. There's no reason for me to rush back."

"Oh." He was about to ask something but thought better of it. He knew Vince, and he knew enough about my habits to assume the worst. I was in no mood to discuss it—or to admit to my failings. "Well, if you decide to hang about, we might find you an apartment somewhere. There are always locals who are happy to rent to visitors."

As I discovered with Joseph in that clifftop hut, I thought. "I'll bear it in mind."

"It's good to see you, Mitch," said Frank, looking directly into my eyes. I thought for a moment he was about to make a declaration, but instead he said, "To be honest, I need your help."

"What's the matter? Not getting laid enough?"

He blushed—it was visible even through his tan—and frowned for a moment, two deep lines between his thick eyebrows, several shades darker than his blond hair. "Don't you worry about me, Dr. Mitchell. I'm married to my job."

"What a waste."

Melissa returned with drinks, much to Frank's relief. He was right about the coffee; it looked like molasses and tasted like heaven. Frank sipped his tea and stared out at the boats in the harbor.

"Back home," he said at last, "you were involved in a couple of—I don't know. Strange situations."

"Crimes," I said. "Murders, to be precise."

"Exactly." He turned back to face me. "And I believe you were in some way responsible for bringing the guilty parties to justice."

"I helped," I said, not yet ready to assume the arrogance of my idol, Hercule Poirot. "I just happened to be in the right place at the right time."

"And you asked the right questions," said Frank.

"That's what we learned in medical school."

"Exactly. You ask the right questions based on your expert knowledge, and you are not afraid of what you might find."

He was frowning again, obviously wanting to say something but unsure how to start.

"Go on. Don't be shy."

"I'm going to ask you to do something for me. You can say yes, or you can say no, I won't mind. Just promise me one thing."

"Anything."

"You won't be offended by my asking."

"We're old friends, Frank. Nothing you can say will offend me." I tried to sound carefree, but my heart was pounding—and not just because of Mama Melissa's lethal dose of caffeine.

"Right. Here goes." Frank looked around to make sure we weren't overheard. "A couple of years ago, a young soldier stationed at Valetta committed suicide on Gozo."

"Ah." There was a queer element to the case, obviously. That's why he was asking me. Young soldiers don't kill themselves unless they have something to hide. "Go on."

"At the time, everyone accepted it at face value. There was a suicide note, and it appeared that the soldier was being blackmailed."

"What about?"

Frank scratched his chin. "Not sure," he said, "but these things tend to get hushed up. He was known to be...like you."

"I see."

"Some of the boys are. Some of the officers too, for that matter. Doesn't bother me, but it's against the law and they're playing a dangerous game." He shrugged. "Sometimes they lose."

"But you're not satisfied."

"I don't know, Mitch. I was. It's sad, of course, but these things happen all over the world."

"They shouldn't."

"I'm not saying they should. I'm saying they do, and it's going to be a long time before that changes."

Our breakfast arrived, huge oval plates full of bacon, eggs, sausages, tomatoes and mushrooms, with a rack of toast and a plate of butter. Frank made the appropriate remarks to Melissa, who left us in peace.

"So what's changed, Frank? Why are you telling me all this?"

"Last year another soldier came to me suffering from insomnia, loss of appetite, fits of uncontrollable weeping, all the usual symptoms of neurosis."

"And the connection?"

"He was a friend of the dead man."

"More than a friend, I assume."

"Well..."

"Come on, Frank. If I'm going to help you, you're going to have to be forthright. Talk to me as a doctor, not as a friend, if that helps."

"Lance Corporal Edward Porter. That was the boy who died. I say 'boy,' but he was twenty-two years old. Not that much younger than us, but they seem like children, some of them who come out here. Full of life and hope and illusions. Innocent. Naïve."

I didn't ask Frank what had made him so disillusioned, but I stored it up for further investigation. "And his *friend*?"

"What would you prefer me to say?"

"Friend is fine."

"Alfred Lutterall. Private. He's twenty-two now; he was twenty when Ned Porter died. It seems to have broken him. He hasn't told me as much, but they were clearly..." He hesitated for a moment, then said "lovers."

"Does he think he'd get into trouble if he told you that?"

"He would put himself in a very vulnerable position. It would compromise me as well, if I failed to report him. So we're going round and round the houses, avoiding the subject."

"And that's where I come in."

"Officially, I'm bringing you in for a second opinion. I hope you don't mind, but I've represented you to my superior officers as a nerve specialist from London. I had a hell of a job persuading Major Telford to give me permission. He's very keen to hush the whole thing up and send Alf Lutterall home as a mental case."

"But if I examine him, he can tell me all the juicy details, and I'm under no obligation to report them to anyone."

"That's the general idea. Also—well, forgive me, Mitch, but I wouldn't know the right questions to ask in a case like this. About their involvement."

"Honestly, Frank, we're not so different from the rest of humanity. We fall in love, we fuck, we fall out of love, we cheat. We have the same joys and sorrows as the rest of you. As for the mechanics of it—well, you're a doctor. You know what goes where, and what it does when it gets there."

"You're right. I'll be honest with you, Mitch. I'm embarrassed. Every time Alf Lutterall comes to see me, we sit there stammering like a couple of idiots. I'm a bloody awful doctor. I blame my Scottish upbringing. Presbyterian. We don't talk about these things."

"We'll have to work on that, Dr. Southern. In the meantime, you want me to see your patient?"

"As soon as possible. I'm seriously worried about him. He's developing what looks very much like a persecution mania."

"What are the symptoms?"

"He's convinced himself that Ned Porter was murdered."

Murdered! The word I'd been waiting, hoping to hear ever since I stepped off the ferry. Here it was at last, my very own Mediterranean murder mystery! I realized I was smiling, and Frank Southern was giving me a very strange look. I composed my features and tried to look appropriately concerned. "Do you think there's any substance to his suspicions?"

"I don't know. He seems otherwise sane."

"Apart from his sexual inversion."

"Don't put words in my mouth, Mitch. I am not one of those doctors who believes that your kind of affections are a form of mental illness."

"I'm delighted to hear it."

"As far as I can see, Alf Lutterall is suffering from shock and depression. He may be having some kind of breakdown, and people in that condition make up all sorts of stories to explain what's happening to them. This whole murder obsession may be a fantasy, in which case he is ill enough to be sent home and possibly discharged on grounds of unfitness. But there may be another explanation."

"You mean Ned Porter might really have been murdered?"

"I can't discount the possibility."

"So you need someone with experience in solving murders who's not too embarrassed to ask questions about irregular sexual activities, is that it?"

"That's it," said Frank. "And who else could I possibly call on?"

"Mitch Mitchell at your service," I said as I tucked into a large, juicy sausage. All trace of a hangover had disappeared, perhaps due to food and coffee but also the excitement of a new case. Because that was how I was already treating the death of Ned Porter, and the suspicions of poor Alf Lutterall—a murder case that only Mitch Mitchell dare solve. I had my method: no stone unturned, no cock unsucked in the quest for truth. I even had my local sidekick lined up in the pleasing shape of Joseph Vella. All I needed now was information.

"Tell me about Ned Porter's death."

"He jumped off a cliff, just across the bay from your hotel. Straight down to the rocks below. He's not the first person to do it, and I don't suppose he'll be the last."

"Aside from what Alf Lutterall thinks, is there any suspicion of foul play?"

"None. He left a note."

"Did you see it?"

"Not personally, but the inquest was satisfied."

"What did it say?"

"I have no idea. Goodbye cruel world, I suppose."

"Do you think it still exists?"

"The military police would have it. It was addressed to his commanding officer."

"And you said the dead man was being blackmailed."

"Apparently."

"Did he tell you?"

"No. I barely knew him. I did his medical when he arrived. I used to see him around the place. That was it."

"Who told you he was being blackmailed, then?"

Southern scratched his chin again; it made a crackling noise that went straight to my balls. "Do you know, I can't remember."

"Alf Lutterall?"

"No. He knew nothing about it."

"Well?"

"It must have come up at the inquest. I mean, everyone seemed to know that it was happening, but now that you ask, I can't remember where that information originated."

"Perhaps evidence was found in Porter's room?"

"It's possible, but it seems unlikely. The younger men are impulsive, reckless even, but they're not stupid."

"And if it exists, the police would have it."

"Yes." Our eyes met; we were both thinking the same thing. *How trustworthy are the military police?*

"Tell me, Frank. Did Ned Porter strike you as the suicidal type?"

"No. He was a cheerful enough bloke. A bit of a joker. But of course you never know."

"Was there any change in his behavior before his death?"

"I didn't notice anything, but as I said, I didn't know him that well. Nobody else mentioned anything."

"What does Alf say?"

"He is adamant that Ned was as happy as a lark. He had no reason to kill himself. He's suggested that he had a lot to live for, without going so far as to tell me exactly what."

"They were in love."

Frank shrugged. "I suppose so."

"And do you doubt Alf's word? He seems to be the only person so far who actually knew Ned Porter."

"I have no reason to doubt him."

"You just think as a general rule that queers are liars and lunatics who may kill themselves at any moment."

40

"I think nothing of the sort."

"Very well. In that case, I prefer to believe Alf Lutterall. Happy young men don't just kill themselves, especially when they're in love."

"You think he was murdered?"

"It seems as good a theory as any."

"But who on earth would want to kill Ned Porter? He didn't have an enemy in the world."

"By your own account, Frank, you hardly knew him. And in my experience of murder, it always looks implausible at first glance." I thought back over the bodies I'd encountered—a mysterious house guest falling out of a cupboard, a passenger in a train compartment, a man in a locked bathroom. All of them seemed the least likely people in the world to be murdered. Popular, normal, inoffensive, a threat to nobody. Nice, regular guys, just like Ned Porter. And yet in each and every case there was a hidden story, a tangled thread leading inexorably to murder.

"I bow to your superior knowledge. And here." He reached into his case and presented me with a white envelope. "A letter of *bona fides*. You'll have to show this to Lutterall's CO to prove you are the well-known nerve specialist from London."

"You're taking a risk, aren't you?"

"I am. Because, you see, I rather think that Alf Lutterall may be right. I think something has been covered up. Something that I am in no position to uncover."

"Thank you." I pocketed the letter. "And when will I see my patient?"

"Tomorrow, if all goes well. I've got to get Major Telford to sign off on it. I'll slip it in among a lot of other routine business and just hope the old bastard doesn't notice. Fingers crossed, I'll send someone to collect you."

And with that, he finished his breakfast, gave me a reassuring hug and went on to address the corns and hemorrhoids that fell within the scope of his official business.

By the time I got back to the Continental they were laying up for lunch in the dining room. Ralph, the ancient, lecherous porter, doubled as a waiter; Martin Dear supervised the bar; Stella, the sturdy cook and housekeeper, provided food with just a couple of village girls to assist. This left Tilly as hostess, a role to which she was born. Attractive, effusive and with an obvious love of gossip, she was the perfect person with whom to commence my investigations. If there was anything to know on the island, she'd know it.

"Dr. Mitchell!"

"Mitch, please. I'm on holiday."

"Very well then, Mitch. Did you have a pleasant morning? I hear you went over to Mgarr." There, you see—she knew everything.

"I had breakfast with my old friend."

"Doctor Frank?"

"How on earth could you know that?"

"Stella's sister-in-law runs the cafe where you had breakfast. Her son delivers some of our fruit and veg. It's better than a local newspaper."

"You know Frank Southern?"

"Who doesn't? All the women on the island think he's a dreamboat. And he's so tantalizingly unmarried." She gave me a searching look, hoping perhaps for some explanation of Frank's mysterious celibacy.

"I'll tell him that next time we meet."

"Oh, don't." She put her hands to her cheeks; it was hard to tell, under all that paint, whether she was really blushing. "I'm sure he has girlfriends all over the place. Now, will you be joining us for lunch?"

After Melissa's mighty breakfast I had no desire to eat ever again; in fact, I was ready for a siesta. But I wanted company and conversation. "Something very light, if that's possible, in an hour or so."

"An omelette and a salad?"

I'd already eaten two eggs and feared constipation, but I assented. "I had a very nice walk last night," I said, unwilling to let her get away. "Up on the cliff path. It's beautiful."

"Oh, yes. So they tell me. Personally, I'm terrified of the cliffs. I can't bear heights. I go quite swimmy. What's it called?"

"Vertigo. And you don't like the sea either."

"Madness, isn't it? I suppose you doctors would have a special name for it, and might lock me up in the booby hatch."

I was about to say I wasn't that sort of doctor but remembered just in time that Frank was representing me as a nerve specialist. "Don't worry, Tilly. You seem sane enough to me. And I can't blame you for being frightened of the cliffs. They're dangerous."

"Terribly dangerous. They ought to fence them off or something. It's quite criminal how they let people wander up there." She shook her head.

"Have there been accidents?"

Tilly lowered her voice. "I don't know about accidents exactly. But one poor chap fell to his death. Before our time, thank God. The very thought of it makes me shudder." She matched the action to the words. "Suicide, they said."

"How awful."

"Isn't it? A soldier from the garrison at Valetta. Can you imagine?" She sighed and wiped her eyes. "Sorry. I always get upset when I think about it. How can anyone feel so desperate? So alone?" She blew her nose on a tiny handkerchief. "Forgive me. I'm just glad it didn't happen when we were here. Things like that make me go to pieces."

"Death?"

"Yes. I'm not very good at the serious side of life."

"Perfectly natural. It's only doctors like me who are hardened to it."

"Poor Doctor Frank had to deal with it, of course. I expect he mentioned it to you."

"He mentioned it, yes."

"I wonder—do the authorities have any idea what happened? I mean, there was a lot of talk, but nobody ever got to the bottom of it. That poor boy." She dabbed her eyes again.

"I have no idea, I'm afraid. What have you heard, Tilly?"

"Oh, there was some nasty gossip around the village. I just can't stand those narrow-minded old crones—it's none of their business! Live and let live, that's my motto. It's always been the philosophy of the Continental Hotel, and it's something we're proud to continue."

"You haven't been here long, have you?"

"Frankly, no. It's only our second season. I'm well aware that we're still on probation. There are plenty of people who would love to see us fail. It's always like that when someone new comes along, isn't it? People can be very uncharitable. But we'll show them. Martin and I can run a hotel just as well as anyone else, I suppose."

"Was it something you did back home?"

"Good Lord, no. But we always used to dream about it. I suppose we thought it was something we'd do when we retired. We'd find a nice little nook somewhere and open up a guest house. Then we came into some money, and we thought—well, why not?"

Just like me—suddenly, unexpectedly, rich. I kept that fact to myself. "And why here on Gozo? Was it somewhere you knew?"

"Never set foot on the place. It was a leap in the dark. But the people who owned it before, the Andersons, were friends of my parents. Sort of like an aunt and uncle to me, although we weren't related at all. In fact, I hardly saw them after they moved out here, years and years ago. Then suddenly they announced they were selling, and they were desperate for a buyer. We just thought, why not? Quite the most terrifying thing I've ever done. But we had the money, and there was no particular reason for us to stay put in cold, gray England. It was the best decision I ever made." She corrected herself. "*We* ever made. Martin and I. We're a good team, I think, don't you?" She nodded towards her handsome husband, mixing more of his dangerous cocktails at the bar. "He's as happy as a little boy on a playground. Look at him, the darling."

I was more than happy to look. Martin Dear, with his matinee idol looks and floppy hair, was easy on the eye.

"Oh, and here comes the dear Captain." I recognized the red-faced, white-haired old boy from the harborside bar last night. "He's an absolute poppet. Lives up there on the cliff."

"The house at the top of the path?"

"That's it."

"I saw it last night."

"He drops in here now and then for a drink and a bit of company. And really, he's absolutely harmless. You know, of course, they say that he *had* to leave England, but I don't like that kind of talk. What he chooses to do in his private life is nobody's business but his own, and as far as I'm concerned if he's not hurting anyone he's just as good as the rest of us. I hope he understands that his type will always be welcome at the Continental, just as before."

Was she trying to tell me something? She knew everything about my morning's movements already; perhaps she'd learned what I was up to with Joseph the previous evening. Joseph told his friend, who told his sister, who worked in the kitchen with Stella, who mentioned to Tilly... Nothing would surprise me.

"Not everyone shares my view, though," said Tilly. "There's an awful old woman in Victoria who likes to stick her nose into everyone's business. One of those church types. Always wearing a black shawl, like a horrid crow. She writes letters—you know the sort of thing. Mend your ways or you will burn in hell. I won't let her into the place, of course. Some of the locals think she's a witch; you see them warding off the Evil Eye." She made a horns sign with her index and little finger. "Superstitious nonsense, but I can't say I blame them. She gives me the horrors. She's even sent us a letter, can you imagine? No doubt telling us that the hotel is worse than Sodom and Gomorrah, calling me the Whore of Babylon and so on and so forth. Martin threw it on the fire before I could read it, bless him."

"Now now, darling," said Martin, sauntering over from the bar with a drink in his hand. "Mitch isn't interested in ancient history."

"Is that for me? Goody." She took the cocktail, the glass dewy, the contents crystal clear, and had a large sip. "Oh, nectar. Or is it ambrosia? Whatever it is, it's fit for the Gods. You know Odysseus stopped off here, don't you, Mitch? For his little liaison with Calypso. If you're interested, you can go and see her cave."

"Romantic twaddle," said Martin. "People on this island will believe anything. It's best to take it all with a very large pinch of salt."

"Martin thinks I pay too much attention to local gossip," said Tilly. "But I say it's part of my job. What do you think, Mitch? Aren't you just as fascinated as I am?"

"If you've got any sense, you'll ignore it like I do," said Martin. "That letter went straight in the fire, and if we get any more they'll go exactly the same way. I don't know why you let these things upset you so much, Tilly. They're nice enough in their way, these islanders, but they're like children, and should be treated as such when they misbehave."

There spoke the true son of the British Empire. Martin Dear could have been running some African or Indian colony instead of shaking martinis in this little backwater. Perhaps his heroic consumption of his own drinks—I saw him knock back at least four cocktails last night with no obvious effect—had something to do with it.

"Did you tell the police about the letters?"

"Good God no," said Martin. "Think I'm going to dignify that old bag's insane rants by getting the police involved? That's exactly what she wants. No, I shall continue to put her trash on the fire, and she can die in a madhouse and do us all a favor."

"Oh, Martin! Really! You shouldn't say things like that." Tilly put a finger to her husband's lips. "I know you're joking, but other people might not."

"Don't worry," I said. "Unless I find her body at the foot of the cliff, I won't think anything at all."

Martin barked with loud, rather artificial laughter. "Look, darling," he said, "guests are coming down. Excuse us, Mitch. Duty calls." And off they bustled around their business, smiling and kissing and showing people to their tables. Mr. and Mrs. Jessop appeared, dressed for a formal parish luncheon, sailing past the bar with eyes averted, as if the very sight of alcohol could endanger their immortal souls. Young Henry was nowhere to be seen—perhaps he was alone in his room. With this in mind, I slipped out of the lobby and up the stairs.

From my balcony, I surveyed the scene. The morning mist had burned off, leaving the colors vivid and harsh: the gray of the rock, the yellow of the sandstone, the dark-blue of the sea with its millions upon millions of diamonds. Here and there were patches of green or the acidic colors of the flowers; the browns and burnt pinks of flesh. I scanned the scene for anything worthy of my attention but it was all families now. I turned back indoors, almost ready for a siesta. And then, as I glanced down, I noticed a flash of white—a towel thrown over the railings of the balcony below. And behind it, concealed from all eyes except those above, was Henry Jessop.

And he was naked.

IV

Henry appeared to be asleep. He was lying on his back, stretched along the full length of the balcony, one arm thrown over his eyes, one leg bent, one hand resting lightly over his groin. He was not moving. It seemed he was simply taking advantage of the fresh sea air and his parents' absence for a little *al fresco* nap. This suited me fine; ever since I caught sight of him on the ferry, I'd been wanting to see him naked. Now I had time and a good vantage point from which to study him. An uninterrupted view from the top of his blond head down his sculpted neck, across the smooth, taut skin of his chest, his flat stomach with a little fuzz of golden hair extending above his hand to his navel, then down his shapely legs to his feet. Needless to say I wanted to lick every inch of it before turning him over and eating his ass—my aesthetic appreciation has its limits and always gives way to baser desires—but for now I had to restrict myself to using my eyes.

So I gazed my fill for a while, dick painfully hard in my pants and pushing through the balcony railings. It would have been so easy to whip it out and, with a few strokes, wake Henry Jessop up with a hot shower. That, however, would have had the entire village down on me, and I had no desire to end my holiday in a Maltese prison cell. I considered going downstairs to tap on his door. *Hi, excuse me, I wonder if you have a spare toothbrush that I might borrow? Oh, look, you appear to be naked. I'll just close the door behind me, shall I?* I was almost ready to put this plan into action when Henry stirred. To be precise, his right hand stirred—the hand that covered his cock. It wasn't a big movement, just a slight pressing of the heel of the palm down into the groin, but it was enough. Henry wasn't asleep—at least, not all of him was. He moved enough for me to see the base of his dick stretching down, the skin taut from the pressure of his hand, pale white against the gold of his body. He was still—perhaps it was just the movement of a dream—and then his lips parted, showing ivory between two bands of coral.

Was he awake? Could he know that I was there?

His hips raised a fraction of an inch from the floor, and his hand pressed down farther. He turned his head slightly beneath his arm, the tendons in his neck standing out, and I could see his jawline curving up to the base of his ear—just the place where I wanted to kiss him. Looking down again, I saw his hand moving rhythmically now, pressure and release, pressure and release, just as I do sometimes on waking, lazily enjoying myself before the real business of the day begins. His fingers were curled over, containing his cock and balls and concealing them from my hungry eyes, but soon he would let go and expose himself. He was a young man after all, no matter how crazy his parents.

His chest rose and fell, rose and fell. His stomach hollowed with each breath, his hips shifting against the tiles, his head rolling gently from side to side. If he glanced up now from beneath the sheltering arm he would see me looking directly down at him.

Come on, boy. Move. Show me. See me.

And there, the hand was gone and the cock, released from its cage, moved rapidly upwards like the hand of a clock, six o'clock, eight o'clock, ten o'clock, high noon as it finished its trajectory. For a moment he let it lie there pulsating, stretching his legs away and tensing the muscles in his stomach, and then, at last, he grabbed it. One hand starting stroking and tugging, and the other hand moved to the back of his skull, lifting his head slightly. Henry Jessop's eyes met mine. They widened for a moment, glanced from side to side to make sure there were no witnesses and then, when he knew that I was his only audience, he stared straight at me and wanked.

To anyone watching from the cliffs or the beach, I was just a guest enjoying a view of the bay from his well-appointed balcony. The more observant might have wondered why I was looking directly down; perhaps I was lost in thought, contemplating the mystery of life. In fact, I was looking into the blue eyes of a slim blond youth as he stroked himself, lips parted, tongue occasionally appearing to moisten them, panting as he moved rapidly towards his climax. It didn't take long. White jets arced from his cock and fanned out over his stomach, glistening and running down his sides. He never took his eyes from mine. We stayed like that, gazes locked, as his breathing slowed and his cock began to soften. And then, quick as a rabbit, he grabbed the towel that had shielded him from all other eyes and scuttled into the darkness of his room.

I will fuck you, boy, I said to myself, pressing my cock against the bars. I will ride you again and again until you can feel me inside you all the time, until you don't feel complete unless my dick is up your ass.

And with that pleasant thought in mind, I realized that I was hungry again, and I headed down for lunch.

I enjoyed my omelette and salad along with a glass of cold white wine—but not half as much as I enjoyed watching Henry Jessop, now demurely dressed in navy shorts and a white shirt, making polite conversation with his parents just two tables away from mine.

Time for a walk and to reflect on the case—as I already considered it. There was a queer mystery on the island, and the military authorities had closed ranks to conceal it. Officially, nothing of the sort ever happened in His Majesty's Armed Forces. Of course there was as much fucking and sucking as there would be in any predominantly male environment; soldiers and sailors, in my extensive experience, aren't overly worried by the civilian preoccupation with correct sexual behavior. Let us take it as a given that Ned Porter and Alf Lutterall were lovers, that either or both of them were active with other partners, that someone had found out—perhaps the self-appointed Fury who had also been persecuting Martin and Tilly Dear with her poison-pen letters. Ned's death may have been suicide, of course, but there was another possibility—that someone wanted him and his compromising affairs to disappear. There were other motives: jealousy is always likely, or money. I struggled to see how a young lance corporal in the British Army could have enough money to make him worth killing, but it was not to be dismissed without investigation.

The sexual motive seemed the most persuasive, and certainly the most interesting; with that in view I needed more information about the secret life of the islands. Joseph would be a good starting point. Joseph, with his smooth, tight ass and his hard, brown dick, all of it available for a price. He would know all about the networks, the rumors, the anxieties of men in Malta. But Joseph was nowhere to be seen, not in the bar or anywhere around the bay. I strolled out along the promenade, heading towards the inlets and salt pans where, Martin said, the bathing was so good; I had my trunks and a towel, ready for a postprandial dip.

And there, perched on a rocky promontory that commanded fine views of the eastern coastline, I saw the top of an easel, a familiar blue blazer and the back of a head bent forward in concentration as the right hand dabbed away with a brush. The Captain, of course, the other notable queer on the island and, it appeared, something of an amateur artist.

I've spent enough time in studios around London to know that artists fall into two camps: those who can't bear to show or discuss their work until it is complete, and those who prefer talking to doing. The Captain, it soon appeared, was of the latter persuasion. I hovered over his shoulder for a while, admiring his pretty, conventional watercolor of the Gozo coastline, rocks in the foreground, the shimmering horizon a white band across the center. Then I coughed discreetly.

He wheeled round, his face red and sweaty.

"Sorry. I didn't mean to startle you."

"Good God!" He mopped his brow with a clean white handkerchief. "What do you mean, creeping up on people like that?"

"I apologize. I was struck by your wonderful painting. I had to stop and admire it. I will leave you in peace." Moving closer, I saw two young men bathing in the inlet —islanders, sixteen, maybe seventeen years of age. Their bodies moved like blades through the water, black hair slick as seal fur. Was that why the Captain was so jumpy?

"Lovely day," I said.

"Nature at her finest." He waved his brush around. "The sweep of the coast, the play of light on water, the wonderful palette of these islands, the greens, the yellows...I never tire of it."

"Me neither," I said, watching the young men climbing onto the rocks, water showering off their brown bodies like diamonds. "You've certainly found the best view on the island."

The Captain frowned for a moment and gazed out to the horizon. "Perhaps."

"Do you exhibit your work? It's very good. I take it you are a professional." Few artists are immune to flattery.

"Some visitors have been kind enough to buy my little daubs. But of course I don't do it for pecuniary return. Simply for the love of beauty."

"Indeed."

"Some of the paintings I work up more fully in the studio, in oils. Heroic scenes." He sighed. "These islands are steeped in mythology. Odysseus. Homer. All the wonders of the Greek world." He glanced at the swimmers as they dove and ducked in the water, flashing their hairy tails, their tight balls. "The human figure, of course, I place in the landscape later, just as the old masters did."

"Do you use models?"

That furtive glance again. "Occasionally, but they are expensive. I always carry my sketchbook and, of course, my trusty camera." He patted the brown leather case that hung around his neck on a worn strap. "Invaluable for recording those fleeting moments of physical perfection."

"Such as this," I said, nodding at our frolicking water nymphs.

"Quite so, quite so. A perfect Leander breasting the Hellespont, or the young Achilles, blissfully unaware of his tragic destiny..."

I'm no classical scholar, but even I know that Leander was the plaything of Poseidon, and that Achilles was fonder of Patroclus than he should have been.

"And where do you show these paintings? I can't imagine they're for the tourist trade."

"There are one or two periodicals in London and New York who think them worth reproducing," he said with a simper. "Although the shipping costs are ruinous. But people appreciate my work, which makes it all worthwhile. Letters reach me, even in this little corner of the world. Commissions, even. I struggle to keep up with demand."

"I would love to see your work."

"Indeed?"

"And perhaps some of the photographs."

"They are strictly for artistic reference, you understand."

"Absolutely."

The old man was warming to his theme and looked at me with friendlier eyes. In time, I thought, I could win him over completely.

"I gather the water is good for bathing just here."

"As you see. Very popular with the young men. Less so with families, on account of the rocks."

"Do you think I might manage?" I unbuttoned my shirt.

"You certainly appear to be strong."

"I am. Solid New England stock." My shirt was open now, revealing my hairy chest and stomach.

"Ah," said the Captain as I stripped off, "one would paint you as a satyr, perhaps. The spirit of nature. Pan himself."

"Half goat."

"And the upper half, the human form divine."

I unbuttoned my pants and took a few steps down the rocks, concealed now from all eyes but those of the Captain above and swimmers below. "Look away now, if you're of a nervous disposition."

"Dear boy, I was in the Navy for thirty years. Very little shocks me."

"Fine." I dropped my pants and took my time folding them

neatly. The Captain devoured me with his eyes. "Forgive me," I said. "I haven't introduced myself. Edward Mitchell. My friends call me Mitch."

"A doctor, I gather. News travels fast on this island, my boy. And I am George Hathaway, retired Captain of the Royal Navy, at your service." He saluted and picked up his camera. "Perhaps, if I might be so bold?"

"I'd be honoured."

I stood with my hands behind me, knees slightly bent, hips thrust forward. I was still aroused from Henry Jessop's balcony show, and the experience of being naked in front of the smartly dressed Captain was adding fuel to the fire.

"Splendid, splendid." He fired off a few exposures. "My goodness, yes. Excellent." I was almost fully erect now. "Perhaps you had better jump in, my lad, before you get us both into trouble."

"Sorry. It's the sunshine. Always has that effect on me." I clambered down the rocks and, for the first time since I arrived, immersed myself in the sea. The cold salt water was enough to tame my cock, and for a moment my brain was clear of all thought but the wonderful buoyancy, the taste and smell of minerals, the utter blueness beneath me. The water was deep in the inlet, and when my eyes adjusted I could see fish shimmering and flickering around me. I remembered what Martin Dear said about jellyfish and had a moment of panic—but if the local boys were swimming here, it must be safe. I let myself float, gazing at the sky, toes, knees and dick breaking the surface. The other swimmers were now perched just above me, sharing the contents of a bottle, brown thighs touching, toes gripping the sharp igneous rock. The Captain had a point; stripped of twentieth-century trappings, they could be the shepherds of legend, and I the satyr, ready to prey on them.

They saw me watching, pointed, exchanged a few words in Maltese, laughed and punched each other. The Captain was busily sketching with a stub of pencil, too nervous to photograph them. For a few moments, this strange triangular game of watching and showing seemed about to be played out as something quite different. My cock was stirring again, and if either of the boys had given me the slightest encouragement—hell, even if the Captain had made a move—I was more than ready to give someone the big load I'd built up watching Henry Jessop's slim, young body writhing around on the balcony. But at the crucial moment a small motorboat puttered around the headland, bringing a party of trippers to the village, and in a split second we adjusted our behavior to look perfectly innocent. I submerged my hips, the Captain turned the page of his sketchbook and stared at the horizon and the boys grinned and waved at the passengers, taking good care to keep themselves decently covered. That told me a lot about life on Gozo: there was opportunity, but there was also danger and the need for concealment.

And in that climate, the death of Ned Porter took on a new dimension of interest. Frank Southern was right to call on me. There were things here that only an initiate could discover. Secrets that were cunningly concealed, and a whole range of people—locals, visitors, even the British Army—extremely practiced at dissembling.

The sun was getting unpleasantly hot and the Captain was packing up, taking a last lingering look at the view before returning to his house, I imagined, for siesta. I wasn't ready to let him go without a few questions, so I scrambled up the rocks and took my time drying, allowing him a flash and a peek before I got dressed. It worked; he put his easel down and perched on his canvas stool.

I made a few remarks about the landscape, the village and so on, before getting to the point. "And I heard that there was a tragedy a couple of years ago, up there on the cliffs." I gestured across the bay to the highest point. "A soldier, was it?"

"Yes," said the Captain, betraying nothing more than conventional regret. "A sad business."

"They say it was suicide."

"Apparently so."

"Did you know him?"

Obviously the question was too direct. The Captain fiddled with his paint box and pretended not to have heard.

"I wondered if you knew the dead man. Edward Porter, I believe?"

"Yes, that was his name."

"Sad that he was taken so young. By all accounts he was a fine person."

"Yes."

"And a very happy person, I've heard. Not the type to take his own life."

The Captain was about to say something, but a couple was walking past us on the path, and he clammed up again.

"I said…"

"I really must be going," the Captain said, shouldering his traps. "Do enjoy your stay."

This would not do. "I would love to come and see some of your paintings."

"Hmmph."

"Perhaps I could model for you."

He'd seen enough, surely, to know what was on offer. "Perhaps."

"I've always taken care of my body."

"So I see."

"I'm not inhibited."

"Indeed not."

"Sketches… Photography, even, if that would help."

"Yes, that would be…" But he didn't complete the sentence. His mouth hung open and his cheeks, usually florid, became pale. I looked over my shoulder and there, like a living shadow, was an old woman swathed in a black shawl, covering her from head to foot, her skull face and gnarled hands the only things visible. She stood above us on the rocky path, swaying slightly as if she might at any moment dissolve into smoke. A low, sinister hissing came from between her thin lips.

The Captain fled, moving faster along the path than I would have believed possible. This, I guessed, was the local Fury, the writer of letters, the scourge of all that was not strict and pious and joyless. She stared at me with red-rimmed eyes and apparently expected me to gibber and quake in her presence. Instead I smiled and, in my most ingratiating Boston accent, said "Good afternoon, madam. What a beautiful day." I was still shirtless.

She glared.

"Going for a swim, baby? The water's lovely."

Her jaws worked as if she was chewing a wad of tobacco, and her claws reached towards me in malediction.

"Hey, hitch up that skirt, grandma. It's 1932." And I sauntered back to the village, whistling a merry tune. If looks could kill I'd have dropped like a stone into the water.

The heat was overpowering now, the beach emptying as people retreated to the shade of rooms for a siesta. I don't much care for afternoon naps; if I'm going to bed in the daytime, I prefer to have company. I looked around the bay for any sign of Joseph. I needed to ask him a lot of questions about life on the island and enlist his help in unravelling the mystery of the suicidal soldier, but he was nowhere to be seen. His father was snoozing in a chair in the shade of the bar; there were no customers. The Jessops' balconies were empty. I climbed the steps to the Continental and entered the cool lobby. Perhaps Martin Dear would like to come up to my room to discuss the finer points of Maltese plumbing. After breakfast with Frank, watching Henry Jessop come over his belly and swimming naked for the Captain, I was ready to fuck anything.

I don't often resort to masturbation. Why waste what you could give to another? I'm generous like that. But things were getting pretty desperate, and if I closed my eyes I could still see Henry's slim torso writhing and rippling as he milked himself for me... It would take a minute, no more, and I'd shoot.

I closed the door of my room, kicked off my shoes and lay on my bed, ready to take matters—quite literally—in hand.

An hour and a half later I woke up with a dry mouth and a headache. I must have fallen asleep in seconds. Sometimes I wake up with a raging hard-on that demands attention, but on this occasion my brain was the more stimulated organ. I had a lot of thinking to do, and in the cool light of my room, with the sounds of children playing on the beach below, I had a chance to do it.

Poirot, Marple and Holmes get their facts in order and look for shapes and patterns in what appear to be messy, random phenomena. I would do likewise, mentally tabulating what I knew, what I suspected and what I needed to find out.

First, the death of Ned Porter. He was found at the base of the cliffs, smashed to bits on the rocks—but I had no way of knowing whether he was alive or dead when he fell. For all I knew he had been murdered elsewhere, the body dragged to the clifftop for disposal, the trappings of suicide (the note, the allegations of blackmail) added to disguise the crime. But by whom? The military authorities, desperate to hush up a queer scandal? A jealous lover—Alf Lutterall or a person unknown? Perhaps Porter had been involved in some crime of his own; one heard a lot about the Maltese habits of smuggling, gun-running, you name it. Porter might have tried to make some money, gotten in over his head, and been killed by gang bosses. Anything was possible.

Two facts persuaded me that this was not suicide: firstly, Frank Southern said Porter was a cheerful, easygoing kind of guy, not the type to fling himself off a clifftop. Secondly, Alf Lutterall insisted he had everything to live for. Call me romantic, but I find it hard to believe someone like that—especially if he was in love—would kill himself. Perhaps if his love was unrequited, as so often it is—God knows I've experienced enough of that with my lingering infatuation with Boy Morgan—but in this case it seemed that Ned loved Alf, and Alf loved Ned in return. Much depended on my forthcoming interview with Alf Lutterall himself: tomorrow, if Frank Southern was as good as his word.

I'm cynical (or experienced) enough to know that all you have to do with a mysterious death is blow the smoke of a queer scandal around it and people are none too eager to investigate. In the minds of most people we deserve to die; it's sad, but hey ho, that's the way it goes, men like me just can't live in the world, and perhaps it's for the best if we leave it. But I was damned if I was going to let Ned Porter's death be written off as just another lamentable suicide, ignored and hushed up. If he was really driven to killing himself, I intended to find out by whom—and punish them. If it was murder, I would bring the perpetrator to justice, however little justice may wish to know.

I knew so little about Ned Porter, his history and his activities since arriving on Malta. If I took things at face value, and believed in the suicide/blackmail theory, there was one obvious suspect: the Black Crow, as I had named that vile old woman who, according to Tilly and Martin Dear, was hell-bent on blackmailing every sinner in town. Had she found out about Ned's sex life and threatened to expose him to the military authorities? It was possible, but surely not something to kill yourself over. Surely Ned, a happy-go-lucky young soldier, would just tell the old crone to fuck off. I couldn't think of anyone else who would even think of blackmail.

And then I had a cold, sick feeling in the pit of my stomach.

Give me five dollars. I tell the police. I know the police here. My father knows them.

At the time I'd written it off as post-coital panic, the sort of tough-guy act that a lot of young men put on after they've taken a big, hard cock up the ass and loved it so much that, like Joseph Vella, they shoot a huge fucking load. And then, as the dick softens and the ass feels sore, the conscience kicks in. I didn't want to do it, he made me do it, I'll show him, I'm a real man...Joseph backed down when I called his bluff, but maybe others weren't as confident as me. Hey, I could leave Gozo anytime I liked. But what if I had to live there? What if I was really frightened of the police? Or—and here another dimension was added to the picture—I needed to hide my sexual indiscretions from the person who loved me? What if Ned Porter had been lured by Joseph Vella to that selfsame hut for a quick fuck, and then found himself facing exposure not only to the army but also to Alf, his lover?

I didn't want Joseph to be a bad guy. I wanted him to be just as he appeared: a young man with a taste for cock who didn't want the world to know about it. I wanted to help him almost as much as I wanted to fuck him again. But if he was the blackmailer, then what? If things had gone wrong, Joseph was big and strong enough to overpower another man—and he knew the island well enough to know exactly the right place to dispose of a body.

I would have to treat Joseph Vella with great care. I wanted him to be my Watson, my Hastings, and if he was the real villain of the piece I would need to lull him into a false sense of security before exposing him. He could turn vicious. I'm strong enough, but

I wouldn't place any bets on the winner of that fight. And if he was making an income from blackmail, that would explain his reluctance to work behind his father's bar.

And how much did Vella Senior know? Was he in on the act? Had he set me up with his son, sending us off for an evening stroll, intending me to become another mark?

So much for the victim and his persecutors. What else had I picked up in my twenty-four hours on the island? No fact is irrelevant, even the most trivial, the most tangential. I knew this from my own stumbling efforts in the field of investigation: it was the little detail that often held the key, the loose end, the fact the did not fit.

I went over my list of characters.

Tilly and Martin Dear, the picture-perfect proprietors of the Hotel Continental, so beautiful and gracious they were almost too good to be true. They took over the management of the hotel with no experience in the field, almost on a whim, it seemed, when the former owners—friends of Tilly's parents, she said—retired suddenly. Why would they do such a thing? The Andersons were popular and successful according to Claire Sutherland, a regular guest, and had never mentioned retiring. Was there a hidden reason for their decision? If so, were the Dears—who benefited most directly from the sudden vacancy—somehow responsible? And what of the inheritance that enabled Tilly and Martin to buy the business? It must have been a pretty substantial sum, even bigger than my own windfall from Aunt Dinah. It could be perfectly legitimate, of course, but in the mist of suspicion around the death of Ned Porter everything needed to be questioned. Had the money come by honest means? What other secrets lurked behind the immaculate facade of Martin and Tilly Dear? I'd seen the way Martin looked at me, heard his comments about swimming across the bay to private coves. Was their marriage a sham?

As for my fellow guests, they seemed like a pretty innocuous lot, but who could tell? The Jessops could be white slavers for all I knew, disguising themselves as tight-lipped English missionaries. Their "son," the beautiful Henry, could be an abducted heir, drugged and brainwashed before being sold to some perverted foreign millionaire. Or he could be the bait in a trap, luring men like me into a web of crime. He was certainly the sort that people would commit folly over. And what of Claire Sutherland? On the surface she was a very recognizable type, the second-rate actress who plays at being a star, using her charm and glamour to attract young lovers—gigolos, most of them—hiding her loneliness behind lipstick and diamonds. But what if that was all an act? Would she pull off her wig in the closing chapter of this little mystery and announce, in a Cockney accent, that "yew bleedin' interferin' Yank 'ave ruined everyfink" when I revealed her dark secret? What secret? Well, everyone has one. Could she be connected to Ned Porter? It seemed a long shot, but by her own admission she'd been here for many years. God knows what kind of entanglements she'd gotten herself into.

More transparent was the Captain, a type I was familiar with. Getting old, unable to let go of the lust that has driven him all his life, and cost him, in all probability, his family and home. Trying to conceal his true desires behind the mask of art, all that phoney-baloney about "reference photographs" and modeling for oil paintings on mythical subjects. Once he got a naked man in his sights, his interests were far from artistic. I understood the Captain—and sympathized with him. In forty years that would be me: still chasing cock, but no longer desirable enough to get it on my own terms.

One thing was certain: the Captain was scared. Jumping at shadows, watching his back, terrified of being found out. When he saw the Black Crow approaching, he went as white as a sheet; perhaps he was one of her victims, hounded by her poisonous letters. Tilly Dear said that he'd been forced out of the UK—had trouble followed him all the way here? Or was there something else, some secret that connected the Captain with Ned Porter? Did he know something about his death? Perhaps he'd even caused it. He took photographs up at the house—had he used them as a way of obtaining money after the event? Did he threaten Porter with exposure?

I was happily cooking up half a dozen perfectly plausible theories about the death of Ned Porter, each of them incriminating one or more of the guests and locals, until I realized that not a single one of them was based on a shred of evidence. I was simply writing fiction in my mind, regardless of facts. I didn't even know for certain that Ned Porter was queer. Frank Southern told me that Alf Lutterall was disturbed, grieving, possibly unhinged; the supposition that he and Porter were lovers could be based on nothing more than Lutterall's wishful thinking. Porter could have been as normal as they come; he could have committed suicide or been murdered for reasons unknown.

Everything depended, I realized, on what I could learn from Alf Lutterall, and how trustworthy a witness he was.

I got up, splashed water on my face and went down to the lobby.

"Ah, Mitch!" Martin Dear was behind the desk, as handsome as ever. Damn you, Dear, where were you a couple of hours ago when I needed you? "There's a message for you." He rummaged in the pigeonholes. "Here. Came this afternoon."

A slip of paper.

> Be ready to depart hotel 0600 tomorrow. I'm on the island now and will transport you to appointment with Dr. Southern / Capt Haymon / Major Telford. Yours, W Conrad (Sgt Mjr).

And so my investigation began. Frank had obviously managed to get Major Telford's permission for Dr. Mitchell, the noted nerve specialist from London, to examine his patient. So far, so good. But first I had an evening ahead of me, and no company.

"Any idea where Sergeant Major Conrad is staying? I need to speak to him." Not true, of course, but I have a weakness for NCOs.

"He didn't say," said Martin, "but there's a barracks block up in Victoria, right by the bus station. Couple of offices on the ground floor." He scribbled an address on a piece of paper; the street name was something indecipherable in Maltese, lots of Xs and Ks. "Try there. Bus leaves in ten minutes. Excuse me a second."

There was a commotion in the doorway, a raised voice, instantly recognizable.

"I said in any decent hotel there would have been someone to open the door for me! Now go in there and order one of their poisonous cocktails. I suppose you can manage that?"

It was Claire Sutherland, obviously the worse for drink, with her companion in tow—the man for whom she'd deserted me last night. His evening wear had seen better days—shiny at the knees, seat and elbows, showing the signs of frequent cleaning—but from a distance, and perhaps through Claire's somewhat blurred vision, he looked elegant enough. He glided through the lobby and was waylaid by Martin, who engaged him in conversation about drinks.

La Sutherland stood and swayed. Tilly came bustling out of the office, a picture of fresh, neat efficiency, as usual. "Ah, Claire, Mitch, I'm glad I caught you. Will you be dining with us this evening?"

I was about to reply, but Claire got there first. "Dining? Goodness me, aren't we grand. In the old days we called it supper, or simply 'eating.' Honestly, Dr. Mitchell, I don't know where she gets these high and mighty ideas from."

Tilly wisely ignored her and turned a smile and raised eyebrow to me.

"I'm going out, thank you," I said. "I have business in Victoria."

Claire was not so easily deterred. "You may play the part of the great lady, my dear, but remember that some of us see through you. There was none of this nonsense when the Andersons were here. They understood the artistic temperament." And she was off on one of her soliloquies. Her companion, tense and thin-lipped, offered her an arm, and with a little encouragement from Martin steered her into the lounge.

"Dear Claire," said Tilly, crossing her arms over firm, ample bosoms. "She's a lovely lady, but really, sometimes..."

"You handled it beautifully," I said, privately wondering what, if anything, Claire thought she knew about Tilly Dear. I added it to my checklist of questions, just a tiny query about the origins of our hostess.

Those questions rotated in my mind as I made my way to the bus station, hoping against hope that I would get laid before bedtime.

V

Victoria, also known as Rabat, is the capital of Gozo. It lies roughly at the center of the island on a hill from which, on a clear day, you can look out at the sea in all directions. The buildings are largely sandstone, and by the time I reached the town that evening, the walls were giving back the heat they'd absorbed during the day, making it warm enough to walk the cobbled streets without a jacket.

The barrack wasn't hard to find, an ugly concrete building with square windows, devoid of decoration. The entrance was a white-painted wooden door, cracked and peeling, with a small hand-written sign, the ink much faded, proclaiming OFFICIAL BUSINESS ONLY.

Well, my business was official, and I had Frank Southern's letter of introduction in my pocket should anyone question me. They needn't know that I'd come here looking for company for the night.

A fat man in a sweat-stained shirt sat in the gloomy, airless hall. Behind his desk were three doors leading to offices. He looked over the top of greasy spectacles and said, in a weary English accent, "Yes?"

"Is Sergeant Major Conrad here?"

He consulted a list. "Yes."

"I wish to see him." He continued to look at me, boredom and contempt on his face.

"What is your name, soldier?"

"I..."

"Your name. Now."

He spluttered out something, I forget what.

"I shall make a point of mentioning you to Major Telford when I see him in the morning." Thank God I have a retentive memory; the name worked wonders. Fatso sat up straight, adjusted his glasses and said "May I take your name, sir?"

"Mitchell."

"Well, Mr. Mitchell..."

"Dr. Mitchell." The title can be useful sometimes, especially with rank-conscious military personnel.

"Sergeant Major Conrad is here, sir. Would you like me to get him for you?"

A voice from behind me. "Who wants me?" London accent, deep, good humored. I turned. Taller than me, black hair, thick black eyebrows above heavy-lidded eyes. Heavy beard growth that obviously hadn't been shaved since early this morning. He was wearing a lightweight khaki tunic, the top buttons undone.

My soldier from the ferry. Bill.

"Conrad? Mitch Mitchell." As we shook hands, I noted his hand was large and strong. "Good to see you again." He smiled, deep lines around his eyes. He was in his thirties, I guessed, a little worn and weather-beaten.

"I was going to get you in the morning, sir." His accent took me back to the cabbies and market traders of London. "Did you get my note?"

"I did. But as I was coming into town this evening, I thought I'd track you down."

"Doc Southern tell you to keep an eye on me?"

"No. Do you need it?"

"Not me." He smiled. "I know how to look after myself."

"If you don't have plans, I'll take you for dinner."

"I'm not exactly dressed for it." He gestured down at his dusty pants and army boots.

"Let's go somewhere local, then. Any ideas?"

"Yeah. Let me get my kitbag."

He disappeared whence he had come, up a dark staircase at the end of the hall, leaving the desk sergeant scribbling away, trying to ignore me. Conrad was back in thirty seconds.

"Don't trust the thieving bastards here," he said, shouldering his bag. "Not that there's anything worth nicking. A toothbrush and some clean knickers. Right, let's go. See you, Porky." We stepped out into the warm streets. "You like the local grub?"

"I don't know yet."

"You're not one of them that'll only eat English stuff?"

"I'm not English."

"Yeah, I had noticed." Conrad had dispensed with most of the Hs and Ts in the language. *I 'ad no'iced*. "Yank, right?"

"Boston. Ever been?"

"Farthest west I've been is Hammersmith." We stopped at a bakery, rows of pastries and breads in the window. The smell from inside was delicious. Conrad exchanged a few words in Maltese with the woman at the counter, who started stuffing things into paper bags.

"Here we go. A meal fit for a king. Let's go to the park." On the other side of the main square, a row of palm trees made way for elaborate iron gates; beyond them were slightly unkempt formal gardens, the gift of the British Empire to even the most inappropriate climates. Roses struggled in dry, dusty soil, while uninvited native plants climbed, crept and flowered where the gardeners could not prevent them from doing so. An ornamental fountain depicting Neptune and dolphins appeared to have broken down. A few couples and families were strolling along the paths; Conrad led me to a stone bench at the far side.

"Right," he said, spreading the contents of his bag between us. "Pastizzi, the best food in the world." Small pastry parcels, golden and warm. "And this is the local cheese. Bit of an acquired taste, makes you stink, but I love it." White balls wrapped in paper, studded with what looked like whole peppercorns. "And for afters, if you've got room, this." He produced a large pastry ring, covered with diagonal slashes through which sticky black treacle oozed. "And somewhere in here…" He rummaged in his kitbag and produced a large bottle of beer. "Dig in."

If I stayed too long in Malta I was going to end up the size of a house. Sergeant Major Conrad looked lean enough, but he probably spent every day doing vigorous physical activity. My only regular exercise is fucking, and I'd need a lot more of that if I was going to feed myself like this.

Bill stuffed his face, washing it down with swigs of beer, wiping his mouth on the back of his hairy hand. I followed suit. He was right: the food was great.

"What brings you over to Gozo, Bill? Work, you said, I think."

"Picking you up, mate. That, and a bit of bloody silly paperwork that needed sorting out up the road. They couldn't organize a piss-up in a brewery, that lot."

"I bet you could."

"Yeah." He passed me the bottle, still wet from his lips. "My drinking days are over, though. Army life knocked all that out of me. Used to run around the pubs back home, getting pissed every night, getting into trouble. Too much of that. It was either join up and sort myself out or end up in prison. Or dead."

"And here you are, very much alive."

"Yep. No regrets." He rubbed his head. "Not many, anyway. It's not a bad life."

"Sunshine. Good food."

"Yeah, all that. Not many birds though."

"Local girls not too friendly?"

"They're friendly enough, as long as you don't mind their fathers coming after you with a shotgun. They like their daughters to be virgins. Catholics." *Cafflicks*. He tutted.

"Plenty of girls in Valetta, though." Like most ports, Valetta was famous for whores.

"Not my cup of tea, mate. I've never paid for it, and I don't intend to start."

I thought of the five bucks I'd handed to Joseph Vella. "I should think not. Besides, you don't want to catch anything, do you?"

"That's what Doc Southern's always on about. He spends half his time dealing with the clap. I had it once, when I was seventeen, and that was enough of that, thanks very much."

"So now you just take care of yourself?"

"You calling me a wanker?"

"I guess I am."

He punched me lightly on the shoulder. "Get away." And that, it seemed, was the end of that, as Conrad addressed himself to the more serious business of filling his belly, laughing as he did so. The setting sun was still warm, and when he'd finished eating he leaned back on his elbows and stretched his legs in front of him. "Lovely. And no work to do till I take you back tomorrow."

"How are we getting there?"

"I'll take one of the motorboats. They've got half a dozen of them around the place. One of them's down your neck of the woods."

"Xlendi?"

"Yeah. We use them instead of that fucking rust bucket they call a ferry. They were all out yesterday, but tomorrow I get to bring one back with you in it."

"That's convenient," I said. You can already see where my mind was leading me, I'm sure. "Are you billeted here for the night?"

"Yeah. In the fleapit."

"Why not stay at the Continental with me? It'll save a journey in the morning."

His eyebrows went up an inch. "Go on, then. Sure they won't mind a scruffy bastard like me dossing down there?"

"Of course not. You're a member of His Majesty's Armed Forces. And besides, you'll be my guest."

"All right, Mitch. I don't mind if I do. Make a change from lumpy mattresses and filthy bathrooms."

"The bed's big and very comfortable. So's the bath."

"Big enough for two?"

"The bed, or the bath?"

Bill laughed. "We'll find out. Come on, Mitch. Let's get the bus."

* * *

The Continental lobby was empty when we arrived. Most of the guests were in the dining room; Martin was fixing (and consuming) drinks; Tilly was nowhere to be seen. I dreaded the sudden apparition of Claire Sutherland, who would doubtless make a big deal of me bringing a soldier into the hotel, but the coast was clear.

Bill looked around with an appreciative glance. "They've fixed it up very nicely. I'll have to be on my best behavior."

"Wait until you see the view from upstairs. Come on."

I took the stairs quickly; Bill was right behind me. The setting sun flooded my room with golden light. I opened up the windows.

"Fuck me," he said, leaning out, his ass stretching his cotton pants. "This is the life."

"Like it?"

"It's lovely. Right. Run that bath. I want to get these boots off."

He sat down on the bed and started fiddling with his laces. We were obviously not going to waste time with preliminaries. I turned on the faucet, and hot water gushed noisily into the tub. With a little care, we could both fit in there.

Conrad's feet were bare when I got back to the bedroom, thick veins running under pale skin. "That's better. Worst thing about hot climates, wearing them boots all fucking day." He wiggled his toes. "Mind if I undress?"

"Go right ahead. I'm a doctor, remember."

"Yeah, course. Used to seeing it all."

He unbuttoned his pants and pushed them down over thick, hairy thighs.

"You joining me?" he asked.

"Would you like me to?"

Bill pulled his shirt over his head. "We haven't come here to play dominoes all night, have we? Come on." He stood up wearing only his underpants. "Last one in's a sissy."

His body was firm and strong—not the lithe, lean lines of Joseph Vella or Henry Jessop, but a man's body, a little thick around the waist, deep chested, the arms long and heavy. He was tattooed on one arm, just below the shoulder: a dark blue script, blurred to illegibility.

I wasted no time in stripping off and within about ten seconds I was naked. I wasn't erect, but I was on the way. Bill glanced down, nodded his head to one side in an appreciative manner, and pulled his army shorts off.

"That bath ready yet?"

"Nearly. Give it a few minutes."

"You better come here then." He leaned back on the bed and beckoned me over. I lay down beside him, and his arms were around me. Our hairy chests touched, warm and slightly sweaty. I could smell cigarettes and beer on his breath as I went in for the first kiss. He threw one leg across mine, turning me to face him, our cocks touching, both now hard. His hands were on my shoulders and back, pulling me closer. We kissed for a long time, our eyes sometimes closed, sometimes open and locked together.

"Fuck," he said at last, wiping his mouth just as he had after drinking his beer, "I'm glad I didn't make a mistake this time."

"What do you mean?"

"Some blokes," he said, his thick, dark eyebrows lowering, "get cold feet."

"Not me," I said, pressing my toes against his. "See? My feet are warm."

"Yeah, well you're a civilian. And a foreigner. Not that we aren't all foreigners here. But you know what I mean."

"I know what you mean," I said, grabbing his hard cock and squeezing. "Looks like you need some relief, soldier."

"Too fucking right I do. I'm getting sick of my own right hand."

"What do you want to do?"

"That's a silly bloody question. We've got all night, haven't we?"

"Yeah."

"Then I want to do everything—but first, I want that bath. Come on."

It wasn't easy getting two grown men into a Continental Hotel bathtub without flooding the place, but with a little strategic planning we managed it. Bill got in first, his hairy arms resting on the rim of the tub, his legs open, cock sticking straight up out of the water. I climbed in over and around him, interlocking my legs with his, scooting forward to avoid braining myself on the faucet. We ended up with our balls touching. Bill took both our cocks in one large hand and pressed them together.

"There you go, Mitch. That's a nice sight."

"Sure is."

His other hand disappeared under the water and started pushing and digging around my thighs. I let him through, and his fingers quickly found their goal, pressing between my buttocks, caressing my hole. I moved forward, not wanting him to think for one moment that I'm one of those guys whose ass is strictly off-limits. As you know, I'm more of a fucker than a fuckee, but in some cases—for instance, with an older, weather-beaten, tattooed military man—I'm happy to open up those pearly gates. And this seemed to be exactly what Sergeant Major Conrad had in mind. It made sense. A man who's run away from trouble back home, living and working with other men, the only women either whores or closely guarded virgins—of course he prefers to fuck men. Who in his right mind wouldn't? There must be plenty of soldiers coming through the garrison at Valetta who were happy to oblige. And it occurred to me, as Bill's finger slipped inside me, that he would be the perfect person to give me some inside information about dead Ned Porter and grieving Alf Lutterall. Perhaps he'd fucked one or both of them. Perhaps, as Sergeant Major, he had his pick of the lower ranks.

The thought turned me on even more, and I groaned.

"Want me to fuck you, then?"

I like a direct question, especially when delivered in a rough Cockney accent by a man whose dick is squashed against mine. It deserved a direct answer.

"Yes."

Bill half closed his eyes. "Good. Because I ain't come for about a week, and I need a nice tight hole to stick it in." From the way his finger was probing inside me, he knew his way around the rectal canal. "Got any Vaseline?"

"I can do better than that." One of the perks of working in a hospital is that I get my hands on top-quality surgical lubricants that give a much smoother ride than the traditional Vaseline and Brylcreem. If I was about to be spit roasted by Bill Conrad's long, crucially thick cock, I was going to need all the help I could get.

"Better get on with it, then, because if we carry on in here I'm going to come."

We washed quickly and stepped out of the bath, not bothering with towels; even in the evening, the air was warm enough to dry any moisture within moments. I handed Bill the little metal tube of K-Y Jelly.

"What's this, then?"

"Try it."

He slapped me hard on the ass and said "Get your foot up on the bath." I heard the slop and click of lubricant as he juiced up his dick. "I'm coming in."

Bill put one arm around my waist from behind and drew me towards him. His cock was perfectly aligned with my hole—and very slippery. I gasped as he pushed into me; it had been a long time since anything had been up there apart from fingers, and I was going to have to take it slowly. I guess Bill was used to breaking inexperienced steers, and he slowed his pace.

"You all right?"

"Sure. Just take it easy."

"I'll try. But I need to get in pretty soon. I don't know how long I can last."

My cock had shrunk a little at the first pain of his entry, but now Bill was stroking it again, coaxing me back to hardness. For a man with such big, work-calloused hands, he was gentle when he needed to be. My ass relaxed; his cock sensed it and glided slowly in. Soon he was balls-deep.

"Good lad," he said, still stroking my dick. "How does it feel?"

"Fucking fantastic," I said. The conversation didn't get much further than that. Bill picked up the speed of his fucking, and within a minute or two we were both getting close. I let him take complete control of me, using my ass, milking my cock, his strong arms holding me. I had one foot on the rim of the tub, the other on the floor, but he was carrying most of my weight. I had a curious sensation of floating, all my being centered on the agonizing pleasure of his cock in my hole. My prick was spewing sticky fluid which Bill scooped up and spread over me, occasionally tasting his own fingers. I wasn't sure when I started to come—it simply built and built and there I was, mouth open, eyes closed, Bill hammering away as I spat white jets over the marble tiles. He came inside me, the cadence never slowing, curling his hairy chest and stomach over my back, pulling me in, squeezing me and kissing me as he delivered those last bruising thrusts up my quivering hole.

Then, slowly, he pulled out. We cleaned up and went to bed.

It didn't take long before we were at it again. Both of us were conscious of the fact that you don't often get the combination of a comfortable bed, a willing partner and the time in which to enjoy them. Bill turned out to be every bit as versatile as me: he sucked my cock, fucked my mouth and then, when we were both ready for a second round, he straddled me and steered my cock into his ass. "This stuff is fucking brilliant," he said, applying liberal amounts of jelly. "I'll get Doc Southern to order some."

He rode me well, bucking up and down on strong thighs, and shot over my chest and up into my face as I emptied myself in his guts.

After that, we slept.

I woke at first light with Bill's arms around me, his breath on my neck, a scratch of stubble on my shoulder, and a hard cock pressing against my ass. Like the comfortable bed and the privacy of the hotel room, it seemed a shame to waste it. And so, without much to-do, I slicked him up with lube and, lying on my side, steered him into me. He was still sleepy, his eyes heavy and barely open, but he knew what to do. He fucked me good and hard, jerking me off as he did so, and when I emptied my balls all over the sheets he just kept going. He pulled out just in time, jumped up and squirted his load in my face.

Was this love?

* * *

We washed and dressed and went down to breakfast at eight; Tilly and Martin were as good as their word and didn't bat an eyelid when I brought a friend. The fact that Bill was in uniform, and I was known to be there on official military business of some kind, may have mitigated the more obvious reason for his overnight stay; at least, nobody was making the sign of the horns or snatching up their children in terror as we passed. In fact, everyone seemed preoccupied, and it was only after asking Ralph several times that we managed to get served at all. Martin passed through the lobby at one point, looking somewhat disheveled, had a hushed conversation with Tilly at the desk (which, judging by the expressions on their faces, was not a whispering of sweet nothings) then disappeared into the office. Tilly's heels clicked rapidly over the tiled floor and out of the building; she almost collided with Claire Sutherland, coming down to breakfast in a red kimono, dark hair loose around her shoulders—not quite the "hag" she'd promised me, but certainly a more informal toilette than she'd arrived with. I hoped her diamonds were in the hotel safe.

"Dear me," she said to the dining room in general, "someone appears to have got out of bed on the wrong side this morning." She raised her arms; her sleeves slipped back. "And such a beautiful morning! The sky, the sea, the sun… Ah!" She stood in rapture for a while, a faraway look in her eyes, and I wondered which play this scene was from. Then she rejoined us on the mortal plane. "Good morning Jessops," she said, waving to the silent trio in the corner. They nodded politely back; Henry smiled, blushed and looked down at his eggs. "Good morning Mitch and…" She paused, hand outstretched, waiting for her introduction.

"This is Sergeant Major Conrad," I said. "He's taking me over to Valetta this morning."

"And you're giving him a hearty breakfast before you set off. What a good idea. I can't bear crossing on an empty stomach either."

Did she wink?

She sashayed over to the window, arranged herself decoratively in her chair and signaled for service. Ralph moved as fast as his old legs could carry him. Miss Sutherland certainly commanded respect.

Tilly returned as we were leaving. She beckoned to me from behind the desk.

"Dr. Mitchell."

"Yes?"

"Could I have a quick word?"

"Of course. I'm just about to leave for…"

"There have been some complaints."

"I beg your pardon?"

"About noise."

"What sort of noise?"

"Coming from your room."

"I see. And who has made these complaints?"

"That, of course, I am not at liberty to reveal."

Without her usual smile, Tilly Dear had a thin, mean-looking face. Perhaps this was why Martin drank so much; why he took occasional trips across the bay. Was that where he'd been last night? Was that the reason for her sour mood? I'll say one thing for being a doctor—you're frightened of nobody, unless they're actually in a position to kill you.

"If there are any further complaints, please ask the concerned parties to address me directly. I won't bite."

She was not deterred. "And there is the matter of…overnight guests."

"Yes?"

"I believe this…person stayed in your room."

"Yes. Sergeant Major Conrad slept here." I offered no explanation.

"That is really not allowed."

"Says who?"

She looked slightly flummoxed. "You understand, Dr. Mitchell, that we can't give a bed to every Tom, Dick and Harry."

I raised my voice, so that everyone in the dining room could hear. "Mrs. Dear, if I'd thought for one moment that this was the sort of hotel where I have to apply to the landlady for permission to entertain friends and colleagues, I would never have made a reservation. I'm sure there are plenty of other places on the island that know how to treat their guests properly."

"I didn't mean..."

"But of course you're very new to the hotel business, aren't you? Perhaps you'll learn. If, that is, anyone comes back."

For a second she looked at me with undisguised hatred, and then the smiles were back. "Forgive me, Dr. Mitchell. Mitch."

I said nothing. Bill, leaning against the wall, laughed quietly to himself, lighting a cigarette.

"I'm afraid I have a lot on my mind."

"Uh-huh."

"I had no right to..." She stared down at her hands; the nail polish, usually immaculate, was chipped and in need of repair.

"I'll be back this evening, Mrs. Dear. If you'd like to make up my bill, I'll check out in the morning."

"Oh, I don't think..."

Claire Sutherland, who could no more resist drama than she could resist a handsome man, swished into the lobby to join us. "You're not going anywhere, Mitch." She put a hand on my arm. "What is this nonsense about overnight guests? I had a man in my room last night as well. In fact, he's still there. Would you like to evict me as well?"

"Claire, please..."

"This kind of thing would never have happened with the Andersons. They understood that their guests had a right to privacy and respect, and that their job was to serve them, not to try to run them. If you go on like this, my girl, you won't have anyone left to boss around." She turned quickly, her kimono billowing around her, and delivered her exit line in a splendidly carrying voice. "Including your husband."

Tilly Dear pulled a handkerchief from her sleeve and retreated to the office.

"C'mon, Mitch," said Bill, puffing away, "let's get out of this madhouse."

"One moment."

I followed Claire into the dining room, where she was ready to receive my thanks. The Jessops, and the handful of other guests, were deeply engrossed in their breakfast, determined not to become part of a scene.

"Thank you," I said, kissing the proffered hand. "That was kind of you."

"My dear," she bellowed, "think nothing of it! I'm simply grieved by the fact that such things should ever be heard at the dear old Continental. I mean, the comings and goings at this old place—you never knew who you'd see at breakfast. That was part of the fun. All sorts! Soldiers, sailors, even clergymen. I well remember a handsome young priest, sitting just where you were now—he couldn't take his eyes off me! He was like a film star, really, quite a Valentino. And some of the women—I mean really, the dowdiest little things, blue-stockings from England who come out here and my God! Suddenly they're not so prim. One of them, a skinny thing, all teeth and glasses like a governess—the men she had up and down those stairs! Hats off to her, I say. We should all be free! Free and in love!"

And right on cue, her companion materialized at the doorway. "Massimo darling!" She waved, blew a kiss. "Here we are!" I was quite forgotten, and returned to Bill's side to leave the hotel.

"Fucking hell," said Bill, flicking his cigarette butt into the courtyard, "what's her fucking problem? Stuck-up bitch. Shouldn't be running a hotel."

"Don't worry about her, Bill. She's got problems of her own." Money was short, I knew, and there were those blackmail letters...

"And who the fuck complained about the noise?"

"The people downstairs, I suspect. Very prim and proper."

"Those stiffs at breakfast? Jesus. I wish we'd made more noise."

"The son's cute, though."

"Yeah? Didn't notice. You're enough for now."

My ass was still agreeably sore, and I wondered how and where we'd manage to do it again. Bill Conrad was a great fuck and, best of all, he made no complications. Do what you want, enjoy it, do it again, no discussion, no analysis. Just what I needed. And when I left the islands, a fond farewell.

I put my arm around his shoulders in the locally approved manner, and we walked down to the harbor. A motor launch was moored alongside the fishing boats that put up beside Vella's bar. The bar itself was closed, the boards up.

Conrad stowed his kitbag and fiddled with the controls. "You married, Mitch?"

"Me? No. You?"

"Yeah. Officially speaking."

"What happened?"

"Haven't seen her for fifteen years. Got married when we were both seventeen. Got her in trouble, didn't I?"

"Shotgun wedding?"

"Might as well have been. We did it proper, in a church, white dress and all that, and we tried to make a go of it. But with her mum and my mum sticking their noses in, well..." He shrugged.

"And the child?"

"Little girl. Margaret. She's the only thing I miss."

Margaret. Where had I seen or heard that name recently?

"She's sixteen now. Nearly the age I was when I had her. Poor kid. Hope she hasn't turned out like the other women in the family."

Of course! Margaret, and a date, the letters and numbers tattooed on his right deltoid, the ink blurred now by time.

"I'm sorry," I said.

"Don't be. I was a rotten dad. Never at home, always in trouble. They're better off without me. At least from here I can send money home."

"Do you ever see your daughter?"

"God, no. They've brought her up to forget me. Best for all of us, probably. Anyway, I'm free to do what I like, aren't I? Got a good career out here. Good money, interesting work, plenty of responsibility, and sometimes I make a friend like you."

"Sure."

He looked me in the eye. "I hope we can..."

"Hey!" A voice from the other side of the harbor. "Hey! Mitch!" Martin Dear came pelting down the promenade, feet slapping hard on the stones. "Wait!"

My first thought was that he'd come to apologize for his wife's behavior. Bill muttered "Jesus" under his breath, and started the engine.

"Are you going over to Valetta?" Martin shouted above the roar.

"Yes."

"Any chance of a lift?"

"Tell him to take the fucking ferry," said Bill under his breath. "This is for army business only."

"Come on," I said. "We might learn something interesting."

"About what? His bitch of a wife?"

"Something weird is going on in that hotel," I said, and by now Martin was well within earshot. "Come aboard!"

"Thanks." He stepped onto the boat, a little unsteady on his feet. Could have been the motion of the water, could have been the fact that he was still semi-drunk from whatever binge he'd been on the night before. His hair was unbrushed, his chin unshaven, and his clothes looked slept in. "I've got to go to the bank." He patted his jacket pocket. "If I wait for the ferry I'll be in trouble with the manager." He pulled a face. "You know what they're like. Bloody pen pushers."

Bill unhitched the painter and reversed the boat into the harbor. He was silent, his mouth set in a grim line. He obviously didn't like Martin Dear—or didn't want his company. Perhaps he wanted me to himself.

"And what about you, Mitch?" asked Martin as we moved off to deeper water. "What takes you to the city?"

"I'm being brought in as a consultant. A nerve case."

"That sounds interesting. You're obviously an important man in your field."

Well, the letter in my pocket said I was, so I might as well go along with the deception. "Dr. Southern was kind enough to ask for a second opinion. He thought it might be worthwhile."

"The work that you mental doctors do is so fascinating," said Martin, fixing me with his blue eyes. They were a little bloodshot this morning. "I have great respect for the mind. Probably because I'm as thick as two short planks."

"It's really just a case of asking the right questions. In this particular instance, the patient is suffering trauma after the death of a comrade."

"Oh dear. What's trauma?"

"Shock, I suppose you'd call it."

"Oh, like the poor chaps after the war. We saw them at home." He shook his head. "I suppose this fellow saw one of his pals killed in action, did he?"

"Nothing like that. It was suicide," I said, and immediately realized, from Bill's stern look, that I had said too much. This was confidential business, and there I was blabbing like a school kid.

"Ah, yes. Terrible business," said Martin, his eyes watering. I assumed it was from the fresh sea breeze blowing in our faces, rather than pity for the dead. "Well, I hope you get it all sorted out. As you say, just a matter of asking the right questions."

Martin looked at me in a quizzical way; I still had half an idea that he was interested in a little extramarital action. I changed the subject, conscious of Bill's furious silence. "Wow! Look at that view!" Sea and sky, basically, but any subject would do. "You don't get this in London, I can tell you." And from that point we passed on to platitudes about how different life in the city is from life on a small Mediterranean island. This sustained us for the rest of the journey.

We made it to Valetta without further incident. Martin Dear slipped away with barely a thank-you—preoccupied, I suppose, by his forthcoming interview with the bank manager, which could only be painful. Bill was quiet as he tied up.

"Penny for your thoughts?"

"I suppose I won't see you again now, will I?" He looked mighty crestfallen.

"Why on earth not?"

"Because now I'm just a soldier again, and you're the big important doctor, and once you've had your holiday you'll be going back to London."

"Come on. We can still have fun."

"How? You going to sneak into the barracks?"

"You can get a pass, can't you?"

"I just had one."

"We'll figure something out."

"Yeah. All right." He shook my hand. "Thanks for last night, anyway."

There were other military personnel around, and I could see that Bill was turning back into his workaday self. The passionate lover of last night was fading away like the early-morning sea mist.

"Dr. Mitchell?" I was addressed by a smart young officer, fresh from home; his uniform was pristine, pressed.

"Yes?"

"I'll take you to Major Telford's office. Follow me, sir."

I turned to say goodbye to Bill, but he was already slouching off in the other direction.

VI

A BUSY PORT HAS OBVIOUS ATTRACTIONS FOR A MAN LIKE ME, and if it's a garrison town so much the better. Dockers, stevedores, sailors both merchant and military, soldiers of all ranks and ages, local men hanging around the Grand Harbour looking for work or trouble; if I hadn't just spent the night fucking, I'd have been like a kid in a candy store. The climate was good, housing was cheap, and from what I could gather it wouldn't be too difficult for me to get a job. Perhaps if I cleared up Ned Porter's death to the satisfaction of all parties, I might have a foot in the door. As for companionship— well, there would be no shortage of that. There were good-looking men everywhere. Locals, like Joseph Vella. Soldiers and sailors suffering from a shortage of women. And for something more long term—Bill Conrad? Was it too soon to be building castles in the air? Forgive me. The sun was shining, the sky was blue and I was experiencing the euphoria that only a good night can give you.

After the complexities of my life in London, a future in Valetta seemed attractive indeed. For the first time in months I felt optimistic.

My appointment was at Major Telford's office, a few streets back from the Grand Harbour in one of the imposing government buildings that dominate that part of town. Frank Southern was waiting for me in the lobby, pacing nervously up and down, his face pale.

"Mitch! Thank God you're here."

"I'm not late, am I?" The appointment was for 9:30; it was barely quarter past.

"They nearly cancelled twice already. They've decided that Alf Lutterall should just be sent home as a mental case. It's all I can do to keep them in the building. Come on."

We ran up the stairs. "Who's they?"

"The old man himself, Major Telford, and an officer in Lutterall's regiment, Captain Haymon. He's a nasty piece of work."

"Gee, thanks."

"Whatever you do, don't mention anything queer. He's rather sensitive on that subject."

"You mean he hates us?"

"Not to put too fine a point on it, yes."

"I know the type. Don't worry, Frank. I can behave."

We reached the landing, and Frank gave a sharp rap on the door.

"Enter."

The interior was gloomy, all dark wood and leather-bound books, the windows small enough to keep out nearly all the brilliant sunshine. Major Telford—large, bald, tired looking—sat behind a desk signing papers. The man I assumed was the dreaded Captain Haymon strode up and down the worn maroon carpet, hands clasped behind his back.

"Southern," he said. "This your man?"

"Dr. Edward Mitchell, sir. Fellow of the Royal College of..."

"I don't need all that. You may go. Mitchell. Sit." He pointed to a wooden chair, the sort of thing I imagine prisoners are tied to for torture purposes. When I didn't obey immediately, he simply raised his voice to a bark. "Sit!"

"I would remind you, sir, that I am a civilian."

Major Telford looked up from his papers. "Oh for God's sake, Haymon, stop acting the bloody martinet. Dr. Mitchell, I apologize." He stood. "I am Major Telford." We shook hands. "This is Captain Haymon, who is extremely anxious to get this business cleared up."

"Cleared up?" said Haymon, through clenched teeth. "It is cleared up. The man would be on a boat home by now if Southern hadn't stuck his nose in."

"Lieutenant Colonel Southern has reason to believe that his patient requires specialist treatment," I said. Men like Haymon don't frighten me. If anything, they simply encourage me.

"Nonsense," said Haymon. "I had enough of that in the War. These people simply can't cope with discipline. He should be sent home and..."

"Sit down and shut up, Haymon," said the Major. "Now, doctor, er..." He rummaged on his desk.

"Mitchell, sir. As Lieutenant Colonel Southern may have explained, I am a psychiatrist."

"Whatever that may be," said Haymon, brooding sulkily in his chair.

"A doctor of the mind. From the Greek *psyche*, meaning soul, and *iatros*, meaning doctor."

"I know what it means, man. Now say your piece and let's..."

The Major held up his hand, and Haymon was silent. "Dr. Mitchell. Please."

"I understand that the patient is suffering from a form of neuraesthenia."

"Hysteria, more like."

"We do not use that word, Captain Haymon. I believe that Private Lutterall exhibits symptoms of depression and persecution complex."

"Quite so," said Telford.

"In other words," added Haymon, "he's as mad as a hatter."

"In cases such as these," I said, warming to my theme, "there is always an underlying cause. Patients do not develop these symptoms out of nowhere. With careful analysis, I am sure I can bring him back to full health."

Haymon was about to open his big mouth again, but I didn't give him the chance.

"Untreated, he is likely to commit suicide. Then, of course, there would be a full inquest, and the reasons behind Lutterall's state of mind and consequent death would be examined in forensic detail."

"Of course, there's no need for that," said Telford.

"Oh, but there would be. My professional ethics would make that absolutely necessary."

"Lutterall is simply a weak, morbid little man," said Haymon.

"In that case, I will have no hesitation in recommending a discharge on grounds of ill health. But I must insist on making that diagnosis myself."

"I don't think you are in a position to insist on anything, Dr. Mitchell. This is a military jurisdiction."

"Quite so, Captain. I will, however, leave no stone unturned in getting to the bottom of whatever ails this man. Because it begins to sound very much as if you are trying to hide something."

My words fell into a cold, fearful silence. Had I overplayed my hand? Would I be booted out of Telford's office, off the island, sent home as a threat to imperial security?

I noticed a glance between the two officers. Telford nodded, and said "Of course, Dr. Mitchell, our facilities are entirely at your disposal. We simply want the man to get better. See what you can do."

Haymon remained silent, lips tight, jaws clenched.

"Thank you," I said. "I am sure that I will find nothing more sinister than a man who is finding it very hard to accept the loss of a friend. That type is often overly sensitive, prone to exaggerated emotions." It would do no harm to let them think that I shared their obnoxious, antiquated views. "That is why suicide is so common in such cases. I completely understand the predicament you are in, gentlemen. We do not want a scandal. But you must let me ensure that the patient is treated appropriately. I've done extensive work with shellshock patients back in England," I lied, hoping they wouldn't bother to check, "and I can assure you that the top brass takes a dim view of any attempt to sweep these problems under the carpet. If, as you say, Private Lutterall is simply a weak, morbid personality, we will say no more. But the opinion of my colleague Dr. Southern suggests otherwise. I don't think he is prone to exaggeration or fantasy, do you?"

"No," said Haymon, grudgingly.

"Very well."

"You will report to us tomorrow at oh-nine-hundred..." began Haymon, but I interrupted.

"I will do no such thing. I will work at my own pace, with official cooperation and no attempt to obstruct me. Good morning, gentlemen. I will be in touch when I am ready. And now I assume someone will take me to see my patient."

The bluff worked. Major Telford was all charm. "Thank you so much for taking the time to come in. I am sure we are in very good hands. Good morning to you."

I left Major Telford's office with two facts very clear in my mind. Firstly, there was, as Frank had suggested, an extreme antipathy in the upper ranks to anything that smacked of homosexuality. Secondly, something was being hidden or hushed up. The death of Ned Porter was compromising in some way, and the mere suggestion that I would try to uncover the truth was enough to scare Major Telford into compliance. It could be the fact that nobody wanted to dredge up a tale of sodomy and blackmail that could only bring the British military presence on Malta into disrepute. But it could be more than that. A crime may have been committed—condoned or commissioned, even, by the authorities. Had Ned Porter taken his own life? Or was he killed? By whom, and to what end? By criminal elements on the island—or by the Army itself, desperate to rid itself of an embarrassment?

Telford was trying to blow smoke in my eyes, but I could blow it right back. Pretend to be on their side, use words like "morbid" and "weak" when we all knew that I really meant "queer," and let them think I would tell them what they wanted to hear.

I had to work fast. If they had silenced Ned Porter, how long before they did the same to Alf Lutterall? Another body at the foot of the cliffs, another suicide note that mysteriously disappeared, a few grieving relatives back home, but what was that compared to the dignity of the British Army?

Frank Southern was waiting for me downstairs.

"Well?"

"Take me to my patient, Lieutenant Colonel."

"You convinced them? I was absolutely sure they were going to throw you out."

"Me? A renowned psychiatrist who has been treating shellshock patients back in London? Whose work has attracted favorable notice at the very highest military levels? I don't think so."

Frank looked so shocked I thought I was going to have to start treating him as well.

"Well, that's what you asked for. Don't tell me off for lying now."

We walked out into the sunshine. As soon as we were clear of the building, Frank laughed. "Christ, Mitch, I always knew you were a cocky bastard but I had no idea you were quite so shameless."

There was at least one soldier on the island who could testify to that, I thought, but refrained from giving Frank a blow-by-blow account of my night with Sergeant Major Conrad. Nobody could accuse him of being weak and morbid. He took what he wanted and enjoyed himself. So, he said, did plenty of the men on the island. What of Ned Porter and Alf Lutterall? Surely they were just doing the same. What was so different in their case? What had led to death for one of them and madness for the other? Had they committed the ultimate crime—the thing that really threatens the likes of Captain Haymon—and fallen in love? I would soon find out.

Frank's offices were in the military hospital a few blocks back from the main administrative center, a ramshackle collection of wards and offices around four or five irregular courtyards. God help anyone who got lost in there—it was like a maze. Frank negotiated with thoughtless ease; I was thinking of dropping a trail of crumbs to find my way out.

"Send Lutterall up," he said to the smart young lieutenant who seemed to serve as secretary and nurse. "This is Dr. Mitchell. I've brought him in for a second opinion." The solider saluted. "I have surgery in a few minutes, so I'm going to leave you and Alf Lutterall together." He looked me sternly in the eye. "It goes without saying that I expect the highest professional standards."

"You mean you don't want me to fuck him."

He sighed. "If you must put it like that, yes."

"Don't worry, Frank. We renowned nerve specialists don't actually touch our patients. We just get them up on the couch…"

"Careful, Mitch."

"And let them talk. What could be more innocent than that?"

He looked suddenly serious. "Don't let me down. I've moved mountains to get this far, because I actually care about Alf Lutterall. Please don't play into the hands of Captain Haymon."

"Understood. I'll behave."

Southern's office, where I'd been left to await my patient, was a little less plush and ornate than Major Telford's, but nonetheless it was spacious, clean and bright. Books lined one wall, filing cabinets another. There was a desk and a table and a couple of old leather armchairs. Harsh morning sunshine blazed through the windows; I pulled down the blinds to create a more relaxed and, I hoped, confidential atmosphere.

There was a sharp rat-a-tat-tat on the door, and Southern's pet lieutenant appeared, all strong jawline and bright-blue eyes. I hadn't made any promises about him…

"Private Lutterall to see you, sir."

"Show him in."

I was expecting a poor specimen, an effeminate, hysterical creature—just goes to show how far I'd been tainted by the opinions of those around me. In fact, Alf Lutterall was tall and upright, his shoulders broad, his waist slim. His dark hair was neatly barbered, parted on the left. He was very young—a few adolescent spots on his face, even, and barely shaving. But around his eyes, with their downward-sloping eyebrows and shadowed orbits, there was a look of deep sadness. At his age he should be having the time of his life, but he was already consumed by grief.

"Come in, Alf. Sit down."

He looked taken aback by the use of first names. "Sir."

"I'm a civilian, Alf. You don't need to call me sir. You can call me Dr. Mitchell if you like, or you can call me Mitch, which is what everyone else does. Now, please." I indicated the chair. "Make yourself comfortable."

He sat but didn't relax. He was bolt upright, glancing around as if for spies.

I sat opposite him. "First of all, let me assure you that anything you say in this room is strictly confidential. I will not disclose it to anyone. Do you understand?"

"Sir."

"No."

"Sorry. Mitch."

"That's better. Secondly, as a doctor, I have encountered most variations on the human condition. And in my private life, I am as understanding as the next man."

Alf shifted uneasily and looked down at his nails, gnawed to the quick.

"More so, perhaps. So let's try to talk without concealment and pretense, shall we?"

He glanced up, a glimmer of hope in those sad brown eyes.

"Shall I ask you some questions, Alf?"

He nodded and looked down again.

"I understand you have trouble sleeping."

He nodded.

"And you're prone to fits of crying."

He hung his head.

"Any idea why that might be?"

He shrugged.

"How's your appetite?"

Nothing.

"Are your bowel movements regular?"

This, at least, made him look up, but he did not respond.

"Alf, if we're going to get anywhere with this consultation..."

"I loved him, you know." He looked me in the eye for a few seconds, and then down at his fingers again.

"I see." I waited in silence, remembering that I was supposed to be a psychiatrist rather than a hospital doctor treating a stomach disorder.

"Do you understand? I loved him." Now he looked straight at me, defiance all over his face.

"Yes, Alf. I understand. I have been in love too."

"And he loved me. We...loved..." And then, before he could go on, the tears began—tears that he could not control, shooting out of his eyes like raindrops. I know that psychiatrists are supposed to remain dispassionate, and I had promised Frank that I wouldn't meddle, but I only had one short consultation with Alf Lutterall, and if we were going to get anywhere I needed him to trust me. I crouched down beside his chair and put an arm around his shoulders.

"It's all right," I said. "We're going to make this better."

"You can't."

"I'll try. And if it's any help, I know how it feels to love a man."

That stopped the tears, at least.

"You do?"

I passed him a handkerchief. "I do. I'm like you."

"Oh." He blew noisily, and wiped his eyes. "Really?"

"Yes. Really."

"Do they know?"

"Dr. Southern does. Not those other jerks."

Alf's eyes widened. "You mean..."

"Captain Haymon. What an asshole."

For a moment his jaw hung open and then, at last, he laughed. "You can't say that!"

"Quite an attractive asshole, admittedly. And I wouldn't be surprised if he was one of those queers that can't stand anyone else having any fun because he's so fucking miserable himself."

"Oh my God." Alf rubbed his face, as if he couldn't quite believe he was awake. "Do you mean I can really talk to you? I mean, you... you actually..."

"Yes. Whatever you're trying to say, the answer is yes." I resumed my seat. "I'm on your side, but I don't have a great deal of time. They want me to tell them that you're a hopeless lunatic and you should be sent back home to some kind of asylum. You're not, are you?"

"No. I'm perfectly sane."

"So tell me everything you can, and I'll see what I can do."

"I was in love with Ned. And he was in love with me. Nobody believes me."

"Why not? You were both young, and by all accounts Ned was a good-looking guy."

"He was." Alf stared at the ceiling, as if searching for Ned in heaven. "Oh God, he was beautiful. And from the moment we met, we knew."

"That's how it happens sometimes."

"There was nobody else, just the two of us. I suppose everyone else could see, and they hated it. We didn't care. We were careful— you can get thrown into prison if you get caught, though if they threw all the queers in prison there would be nobody left to man the garrison."

"Are they all at it?"

"Plenty of them are. All ranks."

Another excellent reason to stick around in Valetta. "Go on."

"We were planning to leave the army together. Go back to England. Or maybe somewhere else where we could be free. Canada. America."

"America isn't quite the land of the free you might think. Not for men like us."

"Just somewhere we wouldn't be bothered. A farm in the middle of nowhere. We could both work hard. We weren't afraid of anything, as long as we had each other." He sighed and looked back at his ragged nails. "But they wouldn't allow it."

"What do you mean?"

"They had to stop us."

"They tried to separate you?"

"No." He sounded like a sulky child. "You know what I mean. They've told you. That's why they think I'm mad."

"Tell me."

"They killed him."

"I see."

"And now you think the same as the rest of them. You think I'm making it up, because I can't accept the fact that Ned committed suicide. Go on. Tell me I'm a loony."

"I don't think that at all."

"You don't?"

"But how can you be so sure?"

Alf almost shouted. "Because Ned would never kill himself! He would never do that to me!"

"You're very certain of that."

"I told you. We loved each other."

"And did you know absolutely everything about him? Are you sure there weren't any secrets?"

"I'm sure."

"We all have secrets." I thought of the mountain of lies I'd told Vince.

"Not Ned."

"Let's assume, then, that this wasn't suicide. How do you explain the note that he left?"

"I never saw it. I don't believe it exists."

"He didn't write anything to you?"

"No."

"And he didn't say anything in the days before his death that might lead you to believe he was planning to take his own life."

"Of course not."

"There's no 'of course' about it, Alf. I'm trying to get to the truth. For your sake, and for Ned's."

"He was happy. You have to believe me. He was looking forward to the future. We were in love, but that wasn't all he had to live for. He had his family, his friends. I mean, his sister had been to visit—he absolutely adored her, they were very close, and he'd even told her about me. About us. He was so happy because she understood. She was pleased for us."

"What was her name?"

"Patricia. Pat, he called her. Pat Porter."

"Do you have an address for her?"

"Yes. I've written a few times, but I've never received a reply."

"Was she married? Has she moved, changed her name?"

"I don't think so. Ned didn't mention it."

"A lot can happen in two years."

"I know." His eyes were full of tears again.

"What was she like?"

"I only met her once, very briefly. She was nice. Quiet. Not like Ned at all—he was always laughing and joking. Pat was more like me, I suppose. Shy. She didn't draw attention to herself. Dressed very plain. Glasses. I liked her."

"Older or younger than Ned?"

"Older. She was the one who stayed at home and looked after their mother when she was ill, and after she died she had to stay and look after the father. Ned felt bad about that—but what could he do? He'd joined the army when he was eighteen, and he'd been travelling all over the world."

"Did she bear a grudge?"

"I don't think so. She loved him."

"And when did this visit take place?"

"Just before Ned died."

"Was she here when it happened?"

"No. She left a day or two before. He saw her off on the boat. It's all a bit of a blur. I suppose it's all in the records somewhere."

"Was the father still alive?"

"Yes."

"And now?"

"How would I know? I've heard nothing from anyone. It's like I don't exist. I was the most important person in Ned's life, but I've just been...forgotten."

Alf was descending into self pity, and it was time to jolt him out of it. "Was Ned being blackmailed?"

"No! That is a lie!"

"How do you know?"

"He would have told me. He told me everything."

"You put a great deal of trust in your Ned."

"I told you. I loved him."

"Love can be quite blind sometimes."

"If Ned was in trouble, he would have told me, no matter what it was."

"Even if he'd done something he was ashamed of?"

"What do you mean?"

"We all make mistakes, Alf. I've made plenty myself. Who's to say that Ned hadn't done something he regretted?"

"What are you hinting at?"

"Maybe he was involved in some kind of criminal activity. Or, who knows, he met someone else." Alf half rose, but I motioned him back into his chair. "Calm down, Alf. I'm just exploring the possibilities. Was there anything that made you think that Ned was keeping secrets from you?"

"No."

"If you won't cooperate, I can't help you. I know you loved him. I accept that he was a wonderful man. But nobody is perfect. People get into trouble. They hide things."

"I didn't know about anything, and I believe that Ned would have told me if he was worried. I don't think he was being black-mailed. That was a story put around to explain his death. And I don't believe he committed suicide." He was calm now, speaking without emotion.

"There was a note," I said.

"It must have been a forgery. I never saw it. They said it was addressed to Captain Haymon. Of all the people in the world, he was the very last person Ned would write a suicide note to. He hated him. We all do."

"Very well then," I said. "If it was not suicide, what was it?"

"Murder."

The word was out at last. I couldn't help feeling excited. Wasn't this what I'd been hoping for ever since I arrived in the islands? My very own murder mystery?

"And who would want to kill Ned? Who could possibly have a motive? Did he have enemies?"

"No." He thought for a while, and added, "None that I knew of, anyway."

"But if you believe that Ned wasn't keeping secrets, and that nobody had any reason to kill him, then we are left with the only plausible explanations—suicide, or a simple accident. Is it possible that he simply fell off the cliff?"

"No. He was careful."

"Could he have been robbed? Did he carry money?"

"Money!" Alf laughed. "Soldiers don't have enough money to make them worth robbing, let alone to make them worth pushing over a cliff. If he had the price of a pint in his pocket he considered himself rich. We all do."

"How many people knew about you and Ned?"

"A few. There's a lot of gossip in the army."

"Was there any evidence, apart from gossip?"

"We were sensible. We didn't do anything in public."

"Were there photographs?"

"One or two. Look." He pulled a wallet out of his pocket—a small black-and-white image of two shirtless soldiers squinting into the sun, arms around each other's shoulders. The sort of thing that millions of men carry around, a memento of a buddy. "That's all."

"Is it possible that something was stolen? Fell into the wrong hands?"

"Not that I know of."

"Nothing suspicious? No strange letters or visitors?"

"I've been over and over this in my mind, night after night, never sleeping, wondering if there was some clue that I've overlooked. But there's nothing. One day he was there, alive, happy and smiling and looking forward to the future. The next day..."

Alf was crying again. You're probably expecting me to go and comfort him, and for those innocent caresses to turn into something more lecherous, but for once in my life I controlled myself. We have Sergeant Major Conrad to thank for that. Without his ministrations, I would have been tempted.

"Alf, listen to me. I know you're grieving, but you have to think clearly. You are in danger. If Captain Haymon and Major Telford think you are mad, you will be committed to an asylum. They would like to do that, to shut you up and make this whole thing blow over. You're an embarrassment to them. And you know that the army does not like to be embarrassed."

He blew his nose again and sat up. "Go on."

"There are three possible explanations for Ned's death. Murder, suicide or an accident. Whatever you think, it's possible that Ned took his life for reasons we don't know. Or, someone had a reason to kill him—a motive that would drive them to the most desperate of all crimes. If it wasn't money or jealousy, then perhaps Ned knew something incriminating about someone."

"He never mentioned it."

"He may not have been aware of it. He may have seen something, thought nothing of it, but in doing so he may have been a witness to something. And someone on the island was taking no chances. They killed him before he realized what he had seen."

"But what?"

"That's what we have to find out."

"There's another explanation," said Alf. "And this is the one that really frightens me."

"Go on," I said, thinking that we were getting somewhere at last.

"They don't want people like us to be happy. They couldn't stand the idea that Ned and I loved each other, and so they destroyed us."

"They?"

"The army. Captain Haymon. Major Telford. The generals who control them."

"But you've said yourself, they'd have to knock off half the garrison if that was the case."

"Ned and I were different. We were in love."

Oh, the sadness I felt when he said that. Don't we all believe, at some time in our lives, that we are different because we are in love? We are the only ones who feel that way, so pure, so righteous, so elevated above the common herd who lie and cheat and fuck their way through life. But the truth is we're all down here in the mud together. We're none of us as perfect as love leads us to believe. Ned Porter may have been beautiful, the smile in that photograph as dazzling as the sun in his eyes, and yet he was just a man. A horny young man in need of money, hoping to start a new life, surrounded by temptation, confused and without guidance.

"I know," I said, unwilling to burst Alf's bubble. It was all that was keeping him alive. "I'm going to tell Dr. Southern that you are suffering from neuraesthenia as a result of acute fatigue of the nervous system. I will tell him that you need a couple of weeks of absolute rest, and that any attempt to move you from the island would be extremely prejudicial to your recovery. I will suggest a course of further consultations with me, in which we will attempt the talking cure. Between you and me, I think the only cure you need is to find out what happened to Ned. Right?"

"Right."

"But it won't do you any harm to have a friendly chat with an understanding doctor, will it?"

"No. I'd like that." He blushed.

"Has there been anyone since Ned?"

"Of course not."

"Then unofficially, I would suggest you get yourself laid as soon as possible. You're young, Alf, and you're very beautiful. You can't spend the rest of your life walled up like a nun. It's time to move on. That's what Ned would have told you, isn't it?"

"Yes. But Ned's not here."

"And you can't bring him back. Now come on. Dry your eyes, blow your nose and at least try to look better. We don't want them to think that Dr. Mitchell is some kind of fraud, do we?"

He smiled—the sweetest, saddest smile—and stood up. "I really do feel better. I know you're right. I just miss him so much." He closed his eyes, remembering who knows what—the touch of Ned's hands, perhaps, the taste of his lips.

"Good man. Now, are you ready to face the world?"

"Almost."

"Come here." He stepped into my arms, and I hugged him close. It seemed like the best medicine I could give.

I made my official report to Frank Southern, who was delighted and relieved, and I promised to return for further sessions with my patient over the coming weeks. To be honest there was only one kind of session with Alf Lutterall I had in mind, an unorthodox but extremely effective treatment for the blues that involved inserting my penis in his anus, but that would have to wait.

My transport back to Gozo wouldn't be ready for another hour, and after a quick coffee I set off to explore the Grand Harbour. My interest in shipping and architecture is pretty limited, but there were other attractions not mentioned in the guide. Men were coming and going all around me, most of them attractive, many of them in uniform. They had the refreshing—if slightly unnerving—habit of looking you up and down quite shamelessly, whether out of curiosity or lust I was not quite sure. One young sailor in a blue uniform, sporting a handsome beard, walked past me once, twice, three times, taking a good look, smiling, his eyes alive with invitation. Well, I thought, it will do no harm to follow him, see where the action is, perhaps have a little fun before my boat is ready...

We played that familiar game of cat and mouse around the harbor until we reached a quieter area of piers and warehouses, where cargo was loaded and unloaded. My quarry was always a few steps ahead of me, stopping for a while, looking back, checking I was following him. And unless I was much mistaken, someone was following me: a couple of times I'd seen a young man in civilian clothes and a cap sauntering along with his hands in his pockets, trying to look nonchalant. The more the merrier, I thought, wondering where this little adventure would lead me.

I'm familiar enough with docks and harbors in Boston, London and elsewhere to know that there is usually some place, honored by time and tradition, where men go for their liaisons. They seem random, but there are always sound topographical reasons for the choice: secluded from general view, of course; easy to get in and out of in a hurry should the need arise (police raids and so on); something to lean against, bend over or lie on; and in more northern climates, some shelter from the rain. The latter was unnecessary in Malta, but in other respects the disused yard between warehouses into which my bearded friend disappeared was well appointed. Wooden fences separated us from passersby. The other end of the yard opened to an area of waste ground, and there were piles of crates and pallets around that made very good makeshift beds. There was even a freestanding faucet in one corner of the yard. *What luxury*, I thought, *to be able to wash!*

Beardy was leaning against the wall, one leg crooked, lighting a cigarette, the perfect pose that so often precedes a quick, passionate fuck. He smiled as I approached, looking up at me through the curling smoke from his cigarette. I took a step towards him, faintly aware of the scuff of a footfall behind me, then there was a sharp, sudden crack and I felt a shooting pain in the back of my head, stars bursting against an enveloping darkness as my knees gave way and I sank to the ground. I saw a bright flash, which I dimly recognized as a blade, I heard a shout, and that was all.

VII

I WAS OUT COLD FOR A FEW MINUTES. I WOKE WITH AN INTENSE
pain in my skull, sat up and promptly vomited on myself. Then I
remembered the blade and was almost sick again, this time from
fear. But there was no blood, no obvious sensation of stab wounds—
I've seen enough of those in London hospitals on a Friday night
after the pubs close—and it seemed that, by some miracle, I was
unharmed. There was nobody else around. Whoever had attacked
me, and whoever had saved me, had fled the scene.

I got slowly to my feet and brushed the worst of the sick off my
jacket and pants. I looked like a drunk as I staggered back to the
harbor. Fortunately, I made it to Frank's office unmolested. He put
ice on my head, cleaned me up and told me in no uncertain terms
not to take such risks around Valetta, which was notorious for foot-
pads and pickpockets.

I had not been robbed: my wallet—and Aunt Dinah's dollars—
were intact. I didn't mention this to Frank, nor did I mention the
knife. I didn't want any police involvement; they'd just want to know
what I was doing around the back of the harbor in the first place.

It was possible, as Frank concluded, that I had been attacked by
an opportunistic robber who preyed on queers cruising the docks. I
wasn't the specific target; I just wandered into the wrong place, and

my assailant knew very well that I was not going to make an official complaint. But what if I, Mitch Mitchell, was the intended victim? Had I been lured to that incriminating crime scene in order to make it look like a routine attack? Was the man with the beard the bait in the trap? Or had he been my rescuer? I was fast coming to the conclusion that my presence on the island, investigating the death of Ned Porter, was known to someone who wished to silence me.

I pondered this as I made my way back over to Gozo. My ferryman this time was not the charming Sergeant Major Conrad who, much to my disappointment, was nowhere to be seen. This time I had a taciturn young soldier who ignored all my attempts at small talk.

It was late afternoon, siesta time, but the Xlendi promenade was unusually busy. A crowd was gathered at the end of the Victoria Road, where three large black police cars were parked up against the wall. The crowd was at its thickest outside Vella's bar at the foot of the cliffs.

Tilly stood slightly apart, at the foot of the steps that led up to the Continental. She looked as fresh as ever in a clean cotton dress that emphasized her generous bosom, her makeup immaculate and hair neatly dressed—but her face betrayed concern.

I tapped her on the shoulder. "What's up?"

She jumped at the sight of me. "Mitch! You gave me quite a shock." She took a couple of deep breaths to recover her poise. "Sorry. I'm very upset. Vella's son's gone missing."

"Joseph?"

"He didn't show up for work this morning, and they've been searching for him all day. His poor father is absolutely frantic."

"He strikes me as the sort of guy who might easily wander off."

"I know what you mean. But apparently not. The poor old man is going on as if Joseph was some kind of saint."

"I'm not sure that's strictly true," I said, thinking of Joseph's silky cheeks parting as I slid my cock into him.

"Oh Christ," said Tilly, "here comes trouble."

I heard her before I saw her, a high, cracked voice like one of the seabirds that swoop around the bay at sunset. She was saying something in Maltese, jabbing her bony fingers towards Vella's bar, raising rheumy eyes towards heaven, flapping funereal shawls like tatty wings. The Black Crow herself, harbinger of grief.

"What's she saying?"

"Search me," said Tilly. "I don't speak the lingo. Ralph!" She collared the old man as he slipped past us to gawk at the spectacle. "Translate, please."

Ralph cowered as if in the presence of authority—whether Tilly's or the old woman's I wasn't sure. "She says heaven has brought vengeance to the evildoers," said Ralph. "She says that all who defy the Lord will perish."

"What on earth is the old bitch on about?" said Tilly, her mouth turned down in disgust.

"She says God has smitten the sinners again, and that he will not rest until..."

"Oh, that's enough. Go away, you silly man. Honestly," said Tilly, long before Ralph was out of earshot, "it's like dealing with savages. They actually believe this nonsense." Suddenly she put her hand to her mouth. "Oh! God, Mitch, I'm so sorry. What must you think of me? I was unforgivably rude this morning."

"Yes. You were."

"Please accept my apologies. Those awful Jessops have been on and on at me about what they like to call immorality. I'm afraid what with one thing and another, my temper just snapped. I do hope you won't leave us."

"I'm prepared to overlook it on this occasion," I said, "but let's not have any more of that nonsense."

"I promise. I've been so worried about money and everything. Well, you don't need to know my problems."

"Martin back yet?"

She looked at her watch. "Should be here soon."

"Hope his meeting went well."

Tilly frowned.

"With the bank manager, wasn't it?"

"Of course. Honestly, that awful man. You'd think we were doing him a favor letting him look after our money." Her voice was vague.

"Martin seemed very worried."

She frowned. "We're both worried, of course, but one keeps up a brave face. Goodness me, where are my manners? How was your trip?"

"Great," I said, despite the throbbing pain in my head. No need for her to know about the attack. "Very successful."

But Tilly wasn't listening, wrapped as she was in her own concerns. "Good, good. Well, I suppose I'd better get on. We've got a big party in for dinner tonight and I still don't know what we're going to give them. Tell me if you hear anything about the Vellas."

She clip-clopped through the marble hallway on her high heels, her ass swinging from side to side, and disappeared into the office.

The bump on my head was growing nicely, and I was starting to feel sick with fatigue. The quayside drama would have to take care of itself; privately I was convinced that Joseph was holed up somewhere with his legs in the air and a cock up his ass and would return, sore and satisfied, by nightfall. I labored up the stairs to my room, closed the shutters, took a couple of aspirin and lay down on the bed. The pains and pleasures of the last twenty-four hours were overwhelming me. I fell asleep quickly, like a man falling off a cliff into the dark below.

I woke with a start in gloom and silence. Something had roused me—some sense penetrating the depth of my sleep. I lay still and listened. Nothing, save voices from far below on the harbor, the hissing of the breeze through the shutters... And then—what? A creak? The scuff of a foot? The door was ajar, and from the corner of my eye I saw it move. I jumped out of bed despite the throbbing pain in my head, yanked the door open and there, cringing and ashen faced on the stone steps beyond, was Henry Jessop. I grabbed his wrist and pulled him up the steps. He stumbled and cried out as his arm got wrenched.

"What the fuck is your game, prowling around my room?"

"Nothing..."

I closed the door behind him. He looked so scared I thought he might wet his pants.

"Are you in the habit of going into other people's rooms while they're asleep?"

He hung his head. "I'm sorry. I thought you were out."

"So you just came in to see what you could find? Is that it? Cash? A watch, maybe? Is that it?"

"No."

"Then what? You'd better come up with a good explanation, boy, or I'll go straight downstairs and tell the managers." Henry was practically in tears now, wringing his hands, and I can't say I didn't enjoy the spectacle. I'd already watched him pump a load over his tight stomach; this was a pleasure of a different kind. I like vulnerability. It can be so useful.

"I was just…I wanted to…"

"What?" I stepped towards him; there was less than six inches between our faces.

"I wanted to see your room. To see where you sleep." He looked down. His eyelashes were long, his cheeks now flushed with color.

"And you thought I was out?"

"Yes."

"No you didn't. You knew I was here, didn't you?"

He said nothing, but looked up into my eyes. I could read a clear answer there, and it wasn't quite in keeping with his clean-cut, English public schoolboy image.

"You came up here hoping to find me."

"I was just going to ask you…" He paused, obviously thinking up some plausible lie. "Er, if you wanted to come for a swim across the bay later."

"I see."

"But when I got here you were asleep."

"You didn't knock."

"I didn't want to wake you up."

"You snuck into my room hoping to find me—what? In the bath? In bed? Well, you got what you wanted. How long were you watching me for?"

"A while. Then I thought I'd better go away. I'm sorry."

Neither of us moved.

"How sorry?"

"What?"

"How sorry are you, Henry? Sorry enough to make it up to me?"

"I'd better go. My parents—"

"Go on then. Run along."

Of course he stayed put. I placed a hand on his shoulder and pushed lightly down.

"On your knees, boy."

He did as he was told, eyes and lips shining in the half light. My dick was hard, straining against my pants. My head still hurt, but thanks to the aspirin it no longer felt as if it was going to explode. Henry's hands rested on his thighs, bare below his shorts.

"Come on, then. Get it out and suck the fucking thing. It's what you've wanted ever since you saw me on the ferry, isn't it? I've seen you looking at me, jerking off when I'm watching you. You want my cock inside you, don't you?"

Sometimes you have to spell it out. Henry just about managed his side of the script, which consisted of nods and the occasional "uh-huh" or "mmm" of assent. It still took him a while to translate thought into action. I put my hands on my hips, pushed forward and waited. Finally a hand fluttered up to touch the bulge in my pants, lightly at first, then pushing, testing the solidity and size. Another hand came up, this one open to cup my balls. He stared at his hands, scarcely able to believe what they were doing. Seasoned pervert as I am, I still recall the feeling of incredulity the first time I got my hands on another man's dick. What I had dreamed about for so long was finally happening. Here on his knees in my warm, dark hotel room, the sounds of the harbor and the smell of the sea just penetrating the blinds, was a beautiful blond Englishman who was about to cross his own personal Rubicon. Either that or he was a very accomplished actor.

Henry's inhibitions were melting as rapidly as ice cream in sunshine, and now he was massaging my cock and balls, licking his lips and breathing heavily. It was time to take things to the next level.

"Don't move."

I bolted the door, just in case an irate Jessop came looking for its wayward offspring, and returned to my position. I know how difficult it is for fumbling fingers to deal with buttons and buckles, and so I did what any gentleman would do under the circumstances and undid my own pants, allowing my hard cock to spring out and hit Henry on the chin.

It was a very handsome, well-molded chin with a little dimple in the middle, in which the head of my cock rested for a while. Henry looked up at me and smiled. Oh, for the camera of Captain Hathaway, to record that moment!

"It's all yours."

His eyes widened a little, taking in the fact, and then he circled my cock with his hand, tentatively moving the skin backward and forward, squeezing lightly to feel the rigidity and girth, and his tongue came out of his mouth.

"Taste it, boy."

I'll say one thing for the Jessops, however much I disliked them personally—they had raised an obedient son. Henry licked the tip of my cock, where a clear drop of juice was forming at the piss hole, flinched a little as if it gave him a mild electric shock, tasted and found that it was good—and then there was no stopping him. From licking he graduated quickly to sucking, and after a few initial gags he learned how to take at least two thirds of my dick in his mouth without choking.

I suppose I could have just let him suck me for a while, then pulled out and shot in his face while he jerked off. That might have been enough for a first-timer like Henry Jessop. But I never claimed to be a considerate lover, and it's my experience that young men like him want to be pushed to their limits. Then, when they're nursing a sore ass and a guilty conscience, they can console themselves by saying, "It was all Mitch's fault—I never thought it would go that far." If you're tutting and shaking your head at this point, that's fine, you have my respect. I save my better nature for work.

"Get up."

Removing Henry from my cock was a bit like prising a limpet off a rock, but we managed eventually.

"Strip. I want you naked."

He pulled off his shirt and shorts with the swift efficiency of a sportsman; I guessed that, back home, Henry was a star of the football field or cricket pitch. Well, he was about to learn a new game, one that he could take back and practice on his teammates, perhaps.

I was already familiar with Henry's body, but to see it up close was like walking through the museum and seeing the Greek marbles come to life. His underpants, baggy white cotton, were the last vestige of modesty and civilization left about him. He whipped them down over his knees, stepped out of them and there he was, naked and smooth and hard and about to be fucked every which way.

I shed my clothes almost as quickly as he had; I would have been faster, but Henry kept grabbing my dick as if he was afraid it was going to disappear like a feast in a fairy tale. By now I was at full stiffness, my balls swinging heavy and low. Where Henry was smooth white marble, I was dark and furry; the contrast was not lost on him, and he ran his fingers through the hair on my chest and stomach, losing them in the dense, soft bush around my dick.

"You ever been fucked, Henry?"

"No."

"Even at school? I've heard about your English schools."

"I didn't go to that sort of place."

"I'm going to be the first, then."

"Won't it hurt?"

"Of course it'll fucking hurt." I took hold of his cock, which was jumping around, sticky diamonds hanging from silken threads of juice that smeared his thighs. "But you can take it, can't you?"

"I suppose so." He sounded so meek and submissive, as if he was about to receive punishment from a superior. If his cock hadn't been quite so hard, I might have had second thoughts. However, from the way in which he was grabbing and squeezing me, and the insistent pulsing of his own prick, I had no qualms about proceeding.

"Get on the bed. On your front. And spread your legs."

That was what he needed to hear. He practically dived through the air, landing with a twang and a creak on the rumpled sheets where, just minutes before, I had been napping. His ass was round and smooth, split like a pumpkin where his thighs angled outwards. There was no hair to block my view of the pink entrance to the interior, just a slight golden down on the upper slopes of his buttocks.

I felt like the wolf descending on the fold. Kneeling on the marble floor I grabbed Henry's calves and pulled him towards me until my face made contact with his ass. He looked over his shoulder at the first contact of my scratchy stubble, and I retained eye contact as long as I could. I pulled his cheeks apart, gazed for a moment at the perfect little asterisk surrounded by rosy-pink skin, and then I devoured him. He tasted good—clean and slightly salty, presumably from a recent dip in the Mediterranean. I lapped away, pushing my tongue a little deeper every time, and from what I could hear Henry was enjoying himself, calling on God in a way that his evangelical parents might have found surprising. I reached underneath to make sure he was still stiff, and it was so wet and sticky under there I wondered if he had come already. If getting rimmed had this effect on him, he was going to be one wild fuck.

"Please, please stop," he said, his voice rather wheezy, as if he'd just run up the cliff path. "I need to...I can't..." He pushed himself up on his hands and turned over, his face bright red, chin wet with saliva. "I don't want to...you know. Not yet."

That answered that question. I'd get my dick inside him first, then see how long he could hold off.

"Okay, Henry. Take a break. And while you're resting, suck this." I sat on the bed beside him, and cradled his head in my lap while he sucked on my cock, his eyes closed, moaning gently, almost purring, as I filled his mouth. His neck was stretched and exposed, the details of the trachea and Adam's apple clear beneath the skin, the carotid artery standing out. I caressed his throat, his jawline, his lips as they ran up and down the satin skin of my shaft.

"Now I'm going to teach you a lesson," I said, pulling him up. "Partly for breaking into my room and snooping around uninvited. But mostly because from the first moment I saw you, the only thing I've been able to think about is fucking your ass."

This wasn't true, of course, as in my short time on the island I'd already fucked Joseph Vella and Bill Conrad, but Henry didn't need to know that. There was romance in the air—the sea, the shutters, the low light, the fragrance and taste of young male flesh—and I was in no hurry to dispel it.

He said, "Can I kiss you?"

I answered him with deeds rather than words, tasting my own dick in his mouth. We embraced, smooth skin against fur, my hand reaching around to find his ass and give him a little preview of what was to come. As my finger slipped past his ring, he made a "mmmf" noise inside my mouth. I put my other hand on the back of his blond head, pulling him in to the kiss. He did not resist. My tongue pushed into him, just as my finger pushed into his ass. His neck and cheeks were flushed, his cock hard and oozing.

"Now kneel."

He was swift to obey, resting on his elbows and presenting his ass to whatever awaited it. It was already wet with my spit, and my finger had relaxed him a bit; if I'd really wanted to punish him I would have pushed in without further ado. However, I wanted Henry's first experience of buggery to be a good one, and so I made a liberal application of lubricant to my cock. The cool, clear jelly felt good, and I had the feeling that my cock couldn't get any harder. Henry Jessop was about to get the equivalent of a steel bar in his guts.

"Ready?"

"Yes." His voice was quiet and shaky, but desire was conquering fear. I reached around to feel his stiff cock, then spread his ass cheeks as wide as they would go and rubbed my cock up and down the smooth groove between them. Henry let out a loud, deep sigh of relief, as if the missing piece of his life's puzzle had been found.

Once his hole was nice and slippery, I allowed the head of my dick to rest against it, and waited. This is a little game I like to play, to find out just how badly a guy wants to be fucked. In Henry's case, the answer was "in the worst possible way." He looked over his shoulder when I stopped moving, his brows contracted in disappointment, and then pushed backward against me. My cock was at just the right location and angle (I've had lots of practice) and so hard that it slipped right into him. When he realized what had happened, his blue eyes opened wide, his mouth hung open, and then he said "Ouch!"

"Hurts?"

"Yes."

"Want me to take it out?"

"No."

"Good boy. Now just stay still, wait and breathe. Trust me, Henry, I know what I'm doing. In a minute, you're going to feel better than you've ever felt in your life."

"Really? Because right now... Oh... I mean... Oh..." He shifted around, trying to get comfortable, and then I felt his ass relax and he got very comfortable indeed. He rocked gently forward and backward on his knees; all I had to do was stay still, and stay hard, and he basically fucked himself.

"Oh, Mitch. Oh, God..."

I started thrusting forward every time he pushed back, and soon I was all the way in, all the way out, and Henry was taking it. Not just taking it—he was devouring it. I was being sucked into a vacuum, the softest, slickest vacuum you can imagine. As a doctor, it's hard not to think of what you're doing in crude physiological terms, but even so, my professional understanding of the gastro-intestinal tract, anal valves, mucosa and so on was clouded by images of velvet and roses and ripe peaches.

Henry's right hand started working on his cock; this would not do, so I grabbed him and put the brakes on. "You're not going to come yet, boy, however much you want to. I'm going to fuck you and fuck you and when I say you can come, that's when you come. Understand?"

"Yes. It's just... It feels as if I'm going to... I've got to..."

He was having difficulty completing a sentence, which meant that his brain was well and truly awash with whatever chemicals we release during sexual pleasure. I never did get around to much neurology.

"Now get up."

I pulled out, although Henry's ass lips were reluctant to let me go and actually pouted at me. "Now you're going to sit on it." I stretched out on the bed, hands behind my head, and let Henry figure out the rest. It didn't take long. He straddled me, took hold of my cock and lowered away. Within seconds his buttocks were resting on my hips. I like fucking guys this way, especially if they're as beautiful as Henry Jessop; you can watch every detail of the muscles moving under the skin; you have a perfect view of the facial expression; and you can see the cock bobbing up and down as you plunge deep inside them.

Henry had stamina enough for two. His thigh muscles, firm and strong from the athletics track or the football field, rippled and bunched as he levered himself up and down. His torso and abdomen inflated and deflated with every breath, his tits sticking out and begging to be pinched. I reached up and grabbed them, pulling him up and down none too gently. He yelped. I hoped his parents were out, or deaf, because the sound of their offspring being impaled might have distressed them.

But Henry was anything but distressed. A steady stream of juice was running from the end of his cock, dripping onto my hairy stomach where it sat for a while before being absorbed. I scooped it up on my fingers and stuck them in Henry's mouth. He took them both to the third knuckle. Whatever I had to give, he'd take.

After five minutes of bouncing, Henry was reaching the point of no return—he was going to come, even without touching his dick. And much as I liked the idea of him shooting over my stomach, I wanted him to feel my full weight ploughing into him before I gave him his release.

"Get off."

"No, please…"

I sat up, threw my arms around his waist and lifted him off my cock. He buried his face in my neck and shoulder, whimpering with frustration.

"Take it easy, boy. Don't worry. We're nearly there."

I needed a piss, and Henry needed to take a break. He followed me into the bathroom like a puppy and watched in fascination as I pointed my still-hard cock at the toilet bowl.

"Want to hold it?"

"May I?"

"Jesus, are you always so polite?"

"Sorry..."

I grabbed his hand and put it on my cock just as the piss started to thunder through it. I don't know if there is a history of equestrianism in my family, but I certainly piss like a horse. Henry licked his lips. Now, if you're familiar with my story you'll know that I'm far from squeamish about urine, and the thought crossed my mind that I could dump Henry in the tub and hose him down—but perhaps I'd leave that until he was a little more experienced. Next time, for instance. For now, it was enough that he held me while I relieved myself; a man who's prepared to do that is prepared to do pretty much anything.

"Right. Are you ready?"

He was still hard, shifting from foot to foot with impatience. I grabbed him around the neck and kissed him, rubbing the wet end of my cock against his thigh, kneading and slapping his ass.

We lurched and staggered back to the bed, and I pushed him down on his back. He seemed to know what was coming. I placed a pillow underneath him, took him by the calves and pulled him into position. My cock lined up with his hole and I was in.

It didn't take long. Henry was so fucking beautiful, and the sunshine filtering through the slats of the shutters, the fragrant breeze and distant sounds of the harbor all contributed to the intensity of the moment.

"Now you can come."

Henry grabbed his dick, stroked it two or three times and started spraying great feathery jets of sperm all over his stomach and chest. I wasn't far behind him, but I delayed for as long as I could, wanting him to experience the overwhelming pleasure of being fucked right through an orgasm and beyond. Then, when he was squirming and moaning, I pushed deep inside him and let go. He pressed himself into me, our pelvises grinding together, unwilling to relinquish this moment of absolute connection, straining his head forward for a kiss. I managed to lean down, our bodies slipping and slurping from the thick coating of jizz, and joined my mouth to his. It was an awkward position, however passionate, and as my cock began to soften I slid out of his ass.

We slept for a while, and when I awoke I was alone; Henry had left the room as cautiously as he'd entered it. I hoped he wouldn't bump into his folks before he'd had a chance to clean up and come back down to earth. I've had some good fucks in my time, and that was up there in the top ten. The top five, maybe. His blue eyes, his pink flushed cheeks, the tautness of his belly as I ploughed into him... My hand went to my cock, still damp and sticky, and started to stroke.

And that's when I heard, from directly below my window, a voice raised in brute grief—a stricken bellow, breaking as it gained in volume. I flung open the shutters. There was a crowd on the harbor wall clustered around a boat that had just been tied up. At the centee of that dark throng was Anthony Vella, hands clutching his head, gray hair standing up in crazy tufts, swaying as his knees gave way, the ghastly yell of an animal in pain getting hoarser and higher. My eye followed the collective gaze to the boat, and there, only partly concealed by a bundle of nets, was the dead body of his son Joseph.

VIII

I threw my clothes on and raced down to the harbor wall. The heat and sunlight hit me hard, and for a moment all I could see was a confused jumble of backs against the hard metallic glare. A hand grabbed my arm.

"Mitch, thank God. I was just coming to get you." Martin Dear's handsome face was pale, the eyes bloodshot. "Hey! Make way!" He pushed me through the crowd. "This man is a doctor! Let him pass!" The bodies parted, and I was ushered to the water's edge. Vella Senior was on his knees, pushing away all offers of help in the fury of his grief. Vella Junior lay in the bottom of the boat, knees drawn up to his chest, elbows tucked in like a sleeping child, the upper side of his head caked with thick drying blood. There was a massive contusion on his temple, the skin so badly torn that bone was visible. There was no doubt whatsoever that he was dead.

"Who found him?"

One of the young men I'd seen hanging around with Vella when I arrived put his hand up. It shook with nerves.

"Where?"

He pointed out towards the headland. "On the rocks. Under the cliff."

"When?"

"An hour ago."

"Have the police been informed?"

His eyes sought others, glances exchanged among the bystanders. Nobody spoke.

"Martin," I said, "go and telephone the police straight away."

"But surely...an accident."

That seemed the least likely explanation—Joseph's sure-footedness, his familiarity with the clifftop paths, was remarkable. And the firmness of his beautiful brown body, his hairy ass opening up to me, the ardor of his kisses, all of them finished, destroyed, cold.

"That is for the police to decide."

People started backing away. Clearly the Maltese police don't command the same respect as the English. The locals were closing ranks, united in their distrust of the police; I would get very little out of them, I could see. But one thing was clear: Joseph Vella's death was no accident. Young men like that don't fall off cliffs—especially not in the same place as Ned Porter had died two years ago. All it would take was some suggestion of suicide and I'd know I was on to something.

And there were other parallels. Ned and Joseph were both queer, both leading secret lives, perhaps prey to blackmail or worse. Someone was targeting men like us. Whose body would be found next? Henry Jessop's? The Captain's? Mine?

A commotion among the crowd alerted me to the arrival of the authorities. Not, as I had hoped, the police, but a priest. An elderly man weighed down with robes of purple and gold, an ornate hat on his head. He was supported by a younger man in plain black clericals and a dog collar, broad shoulders, dark hair—and with a start I recognized the priest from the ferry: the nervous, handsome face; the fine body hidden by black wool, so quickly swallowed up by his attendant nuns. A priest-in-training, perhaps, posted to Gozo for the summer, and here he was by the Xlendi shore about to administer the last rites to a beautiful, dead young man.

Joseph's friends lifted the body from the boat and took him to the shade of Vella's bar, where tables had been pushed together as a makeshift bed. I accompanied them as far as I could, but there was little opportunity to examine the wound. From the depth and diameter of the trauma site, as well as its ragged edges, it looked as if he had been hit repeatedly with a large, hard object, probably a rock. There was dried blood on his face, and no other sign of injury to the rest of his body. A man jumping off a high cliff probably gets struck several times, and is likely to land on his back or his side, not directly on his temple. I would expect further damage to the clothes, the limbs, possibly the rest of the face. This had all the signs of a setup, a dead body placed to suggest an accident, forcing a conclusion to which everyone would be eager to jump. So much easier to accept than murder. And when the whispers started about Joseph's sexual activities—people must already know; it's hard to keep secrets in small communities—then nobody would be asking questions. Another dead queer. Better off without them. Church, police, army, navy, all would agree. And nobody would rejoice more than the Black Crow, whose flapping shawl and bony hands I could see approaching down the road, attracted to the smell of death as surely as her namesake. Vile old bitch, I thought, and before I said anything that might damage my relations with the locals beyond repair, I retreated to the cool of the Continental lounge.

I was shaking, and I needed a drink. It was siesta time, so the bar was empty, just Ralph wiping glasses. I ordered a beer and took a seat by the rear window. I needed time to think.

The biggest problem was the police. From the way in which they had investigated Ned Porter's death—the unsupported blackmail story, the suicide note that nobody saw—I assumed they were more interested in covering up the truth than bringing it to light. The military authorities on Malta were little better, besides which they had no interest in the death of a civilian. In my previous encounters with murder I've had to work without police help, sometimes in direct opposition to the official line of enquiry, but here, in a country whose morals, procedures and language I did not understand, I was at a disadvantage. And what business was it of mine? Yes, I'd fucked Joseph Vella, and I'm always sorry to see a piece of ass like that go to waste, but I was a transient, a tourist, not a friend, barely an acquaintance. If the cops did start asking questions things might get difficult for me, but I was pretty sure that Joseph told nobody about our clifftop liaison, and left no record. If anyone saw us climbing the cliffs that evening, I could simply tell the truth—he was showing me the local sights. He'd been seen, safe and well, for days after that. There was nothing to connect me with his death.

My intensive reading of Agatha Christie and Conan Doyle leads me to believe that if two deaths share similar features, there is bound to be a connection between them. It could be a simple one—a single killer with the same modus operandi, picking off his victims for personal gain or to conceal a secret. One death (as is often the case for Poirot and Marple) might be a deliberate distraction, establishing an apparent pattern that leads any investigator on a wild goose chase. Whenever a murder is repeated or echoed, there is a link. It is never just chance. There was one glaring connection between Ned Porter and Joseph Vella, of course—they were queer. And that was precisely why their deaths would not be examined too closely. Except by me.

But who would know about their secret lives? Perhaps the Black Crow had a network of spies, or the police had informers, but it seemed far-fetched. It's always been my experience that you set a queer to catch a queer—isn't that why Frank Southern invited me to Gozo in the first place? If anyone on the island knew the link between Ned and Joseph, it was likely to be one of us. And that brought someone to mind: Captain Hathaway. He fit the profile, and unlike Henry and me, or the soldiers stationed in Victoria, he was a permanent resident. He must know something.

Time for me to climb up that hill path and offer my services as a life model.

I finished my beer and went to the bar to pay. I opened my wallet, felt around for money—and it was empty.

I stood and stared like an imbecile, wondering if I'd emptied it when I went up to my room; my head was spinning, I could have done any stupid thing. But no, I remembered checking the money after I'd been attacked in Valetta—it was all there, every penny—and I had no reason for emptying it. I'd put it by the side of my bed, as I always do, and then I'd closed my eyes and gone to sleep.

Someone had stolen the money.

And only one person had been in my room. Henry Jessop.

Was that what drew him—burglary? Common theft? Was the rest an act to cover his tracks? If so, it was the most thorough and elaborate act I've ever witnessed. He took my cock long and hard, shot a huge load and seemed to enjoy it to the point of ecstasy. Did he think I'd be so fuck-struck that I wouldn't report him to the police, or at least the hotel management? I was intrigued by the mixture of brazenness, stupidity and lust—and I wanted to know what would happen next. A few bucks was a small price to pay for an adventure; the bulk of my money was securely stashed in the hotel safe. I certainly didn't intend to distract the police with petty theft—they had a murder on their hands, if they bothered to investigate it. For all I knew, they might already know who killed Joseph Vella, or at least have suspects in the frame. I could handle a light-fingered boy like Henry Jessop. If he was a sneak-thief, that gave me power over him—the power to reveal his guilt to the Dears and to his parents. That might give me the leverage I needed for extra fucks.

I could imagine his blue eyes wide with shock as I gave him my ultimatum. I was hard again. Pocketing my empty wallet, I left the hotel and walked slowly down the steps to the harbor, laughing to myself.

I rounded the corner just in time to see a police car pulling away up the Victoria Road. Two uniformed officers were in the front, and in the back, his flabby face putty-colored with fear, was Captain Hathaway. His eyes met mine for a moment, and he was gone.

I know enough about how cops treat queers in America and England to fear for the Captain's safety in a police cell on a small Mediterranean island where, perhaps, standards were not even as high as at home. There were two unexplained deaths, and here was a convenient patsy on whom to pin them—a man who, by his own admission, had created a mountain of evidence of sexual misconduct. I could hear him now, trying to explain to some cigar-chomping cop that his paintings and photographs of naked men were "art," that there were publications and collectors in Europe and America

118

who thought very highly of him. They wouldn't listen. Ned Porter and Joseph Vella were both known to be sexually active with other men. They were dead, and the community, under the leadership of the Black Crow and her vengeful ilk, demanded a scapegoat. One elderly Englishman more or less wasn't going to make much difference to anyone on the island, apart, perhaps, from a handful of young men who benefited from the Captain's generosity. It would be so easy to concoct a case against Captain Hathaway. Such minor details as motivation or opportunity could be overlooked. A man like him, whose very nature was an unspeakable crime, was capable of any offence. Guilty before he was even charged. If I didn't do something, the Captain would spend the rest of his life in police custody. Perhaps they'd offer him the chance to kill himself. Perhaps they'd do it for him and make it look like an accident.

The evidence against the Captain was circumstantial but damning enough. He probably knew Ned Porter—a good-looking young soldier like that would not have escaped his attention. Had Ned modeled for the Captain? And what of Joseph? Had he dipped into the Captain's wallet as he tried to dip into mine? There had been much talk of blackmail—perhaps Joseph had found out about both the Captain and Ned Porter, and had been squeezing every penny he could out of them until Ned killed himself and then, two years later, the Captain turned on his persecutor in a fit of rage, bashing his brains out and dumping him at the bottom of a cliff. That made sense—one murder that looked like a suicide, one suicide that looked like a murder, linked by the same man, the apparently innocuous English Captain, one crime covering and complicating another, a distorting mirror...

What was I doing? Using my reading of detective stories to incriminate Captain Hathaway, the man I was supposed to be helping? There are times when even Agatha Christie doesn't provide all the answers. You have to look at facts, not fiction.

I couldn't let go of the idea of blackmail. A convenient smoke-screen, especially if there were queers involved, but there was every chance that it really had been happening. It was possible that the Captain himself was the blackmailer, sniffing out the vulnerable, flattering them into modeling for him, getting embarrassing photographs and using the evidence to generate an income. How else could he afford that nice clifftop villa? By selling his paintings? I doubted it—and navy pensions aren't that generous, even for retired Captains. Ned Porter, Joseph Vella, God knows who else. There had been talk of poison-pen letters arriving at the hotel; maybe the Captain had something on the proprietors of the Continental. Was Tilly screwing island boys? Or was Martin? They told me the Black Crow was writing those letters, but it's easy to blame a crazy old woman. Maybe she was working with the Captain. Maybe, between them, they'd driven Ned and Joseph to their deaths.

But blackmail, however despicable, isn't the same as murder. You hang for murder.

Evening strollers were beginning to appear on the promenade, and the last thing I wanted was some stupid conversation with Claire Sutherland. I needed to gather information while it was hot and fresh, so I made my way to Vella's bar. It was here that the grieving father had retreated, accompanied by the priests and one or two friends. The shutters were up, but the wailing from within was perfectly audible—streams of hysterical Maltese, in which I could occasionally make out the word "Allah," and occasional bursts of English. "That old bitch," I heard, or maybe "witch," and "the evil eye" over and over again. From this I assumed that Vella in some way blamed the Black Crow for his son's death, whether for rational or superstitious reasons it was hard to say. I know that old women like the Black Crow, once they get a bad name, are blamed for everything from failed crops to miscarriages; maybe that was Vella's immediate assumption, in the senseless maelstrom of grief. But perhaps there was more to her than met the eye; perhaps her crazy shawls and swiveling eyes were part of an act, disguising criminal intent.

The bar door opened and slammed shut, and a black-clad figure issued forth. The young priest I'd seen on the ferry, his face pale and tense as he stumbled away from the house, a hand over his mouth. I guess he wasn't used to death and grief, something that barely affects me after years in the medical profession. He leaned against the wall, mopping his forehead with a handkerchief.

At times like this any source of information is useful, particularly one as attractive as the young priest, ill at ease in his heavy black suit, the tight dog collar pressing into his neck. For want of other avenues, I'd interrogate him.

"Father. Are you all right?"

He jumped when he saw me, scowling towards the shadows.

"I'm sorry. I didn't mean to frighten you." I stepped forwards, hand extended. "Dr. Mitchell. We came over on the same boat. I'm staying at the Continental." We shook; his palm was sweaty. "How's he doing in there? Must be a terrible shock."

"Yes. To lose a son..." His voice was deep and quiet, the accent English, educated. "Father Edward is praying with him now."

"If he needs any medical assistance, I can look in on him. A sedative, perhaps."

"Thank you. His friends will take care of him."

The young priest looked around, uncertain of what to do with himself. Crowds were forming on the promenade, small gossiping huddles, fingers pointing towards the cliff, the bar.

"Why don't we take a walk, father? Looks like you need to clear your head." He seemed uncertain, so I led the way. "Come on. We can get to the cliffs up here. Nice and peaceful." That did the trick, and he followed me up the steep path, taking the steps with ease. His legs were long and powerful; underneath that ghastly black suit he had an athletic build. By the time we reached the top, I was considerably more out of breath than he was.

Rather than taking him straight to Joseph Vella's little hut and fucking his holy brains out, which I might have done had it not been disrespectful to the dead, I decided to practice my other favorite vice: detection. He may have heard things in Vella's bar or from the island gossips that eluded me.

"What was poor old Vella saying about the evil eye?"

"These local superstitions. They are persistent."

"And who does he blame?"

"An unfortunate old woman who haunts the island. She is well known to the priests."

"Does he have any special reason for blaming her for his son's death?"

"None that I can see."

"Have you spoken to her?"

"Not in person. I am, at present, only a deacon." He paused, and then said, in a lighter tone of voice than I had yet heard him use, "I'm sorry. I've just realized that I haven't even had the courtesy to introduce myself. Peter Allinson. Deacon Peter Allinson."

We shook again; his hand was warmer now. "Edward Mitchell. And how does one address a deacon? Father? Brother?"

"Deacon, if you must, but I'd prefer you to call me Peter."

"In that case, I would prefer you to call me Mitch."

Up here on the cliffs, with the wind in his black hair, he seemed to walk taller and more freely. "Beautiful, isn't it?" he said, shading his eyes against the setting sun as it dipped towards the headland. "I've had no time to appreciate the wonders of the island. Down there one does little but pray and shake hands and fill in forms."

"Yes, up here you're free. You could take off that jacket, for instance. I won't tell the Bishop."

"Please don't," he said, smiling.

"It's many, many years since my last confession," I said, "and I don't intend to start bothering priests now."

"Well, here goes." The jacket came off, and after some fiddling with studs at the back of his shirt, so did the collar. "That thing must have been responsible for more failed vocations than anything else."

"Don't you have to wear a hair shirt anymore? Or one of those spiked belts underneath your pants?"

"It's no longer obligatory," he said, "although I believe some of the older priests take the mortification of the flesh very seriously indeed."

"Not you, though."

"I am painfully aware of my failings. I don't need a reminder."

That sounded promising, and I made a mental note to undermine any vows of chastity he may have taken. "That's the difference between the doctor and priest," I said. "I don't see physical things as failings. There is nothing finer in this world than the human body realizing its full potential."

"Man is created in the image of God," said Peter, then laughed at his own piety. "Oh, it's been so long since I just walked in the sun."

"Come on then. Let's run." He didn't need to be asked twice, and, even encumbered by heavy clothes, he outpaced. He reached a sandstone outcrop that afforded a good view back to the village and waited for me to catch up.

"I've spent too long indoors."

We sat on the rock. His guard was down; I could ask more questions. "Is she crazy then? The old lady? I call her the Black Crow."

"That's not very kind. She's a widow, and she lost both her sons. They went out fishing and never came back."

I stifled a laugh, and disguised it as a cough. "The manager of the hotel I'm staying at says she sends unpleasant letters to people."

"I believe so. Very unfortunate."

"Very upsetting for the people who get them."

"Of course, of course." He stared at his feet, seemingly dismayed by the mystery of evil. "But we must have compassion."

"For her, or for her victims?"

"For all, of course."

"Even if she's destroying lives?"

"Oh come now, Mitch, you don't really believe an old woman like that would drive people to suicide, do you? She's a vindictive old woman who deals with her own grief by inflicting it on others. She believes she's doing God's work, like Jonah when he was sent to Nineveh. Every parish has someone like her. The breed thrives in England, believe it or not, but they don't go flapping around in black shawls. They arrange flowers in churches and organize bazaars, and they're every bit as unpleasant as her. As a deacon one of my jobs is to keep people like that away from the priests, which means listening to their incessant, malicious chatter. It's a penance."

"You can say that again. Who needs hair shirts?"

"Beyond that, she's harmless."

"She didn't demand money, then?"

"I doubt it very much. Everyone knows her. If she was a blackmailer, she'd have been caught and stopped by now. Probably thrown from a clifftop herself." He sounded for a moment as if he rather relished the idea. "But that is not the case. She's a harmless old creature. Vella lashed out in distress, that is all."

"Then the question remains—why did Joseph Vella kill himself?"

"Who knows the secrets of the human heart?" he said, staring towards the sea and rocks below.

"If he did kill himself."

"You think otherwise?"

"I have reason to doubt it."

"Then we must leave it to the police."

I had nothing to say on that score. What else could I discover from Deacon Peter? What possible information could a young priest, fresh off the boat from England, tell me about life on Gozo that I had not already learned for myself?

"So what brings you here, Peter? Is it all part of the training?"

"Yes, partly."

"Only partly? You mean you're having a holiday as well?"

He laughed, but his eyes were sad. "Far from it, I'm afraid." He was about to say more, but changed his mind. "And you, Mitch? Work, or pleasure?"

"I was invited by a colleague, the brigade surgeon to the garrison at Valetta, to give a second opinion on a patient of his."

"I see."

"But I also came out here to forget an unhappy love affair."

Peter looked out towards the headland, shading his eyes with his hand. He said nothing.

I forged ahead. "Through my own stupidity, I betrayed the one man I have ever really loved."

No response—but at least he wasn't crossing himself and spraying me with holy water.

"And so, to get over him, I'm taking an extended break."

Nothing.

"I loved Vince very much indeed," I said. *And what about Morgan?* said a voice in my head, but there was no need to complicate matters further.

He said nothing, but I could see from the movement of his shoulders that he was breathing heavily. I waited.

"I've been got out the way," he said at last. "I'm something of an embarrassment to the diocese."

"Why?"

"There have been…inappropriate friendships."

"Ah." Another one of us on Gozo? Was this just coincidence? Henry Jessop, Ned Porter, Captain Hathaway, Sergeant Major Conrad, Joseph Vella, me… Even by my optimistic standards this seemed like a pretty high strike rate. And now I could add Deacon Peter Allinson to the list. Who else? Frank Southern? Martin Dear? Was every man on the island a cocksucker?

"You're not shocked?"

"Me? Hardly. I don't think I've ever had an appropriate friendship."

"Everyone else thinks I'm going straight to hell. The clergy here haven't even acknowledged the reason I've been sent. The nuns feed me and mother me. They're watching me like hawks. I've been given one last chance, and if I slip up again that's the end of my career."

"Would that be such a bad thing?"

"All I've ever wanted to do is serve God."

"And you think you're doing that by making yourself unhappy?"

"If that's the sacrifice that is demanded of me, then…" He ran out of steam, as unconvinced by the platitudes as I was.

"At least with me you can be honest. You mean that if you have any inappropriate friendships while you're here you'll be sacked."

"Quite."

"But Peter, half the priests in the catholic church are sleeping with their housekeepers, and the other half are chasing choirboys around the vestry. They tell people one thing, but they do the other. They're hypocrites."

He frowned, looking utterly miserable.

"So what makes you so different? Can't you serve God and yourself at the same time? We don't live in a world of absolutes. Everything is compromise."

"I fell in love."

"Love is a good thing. It's in the Bible a lot."

"Not my sort. Perverted love."

"You seem like an intelligent guy, Peter. You can't really believe that crap." He obviously wasn't used to foul-mouthed Americans, but it was time to administer a verbal slap.

"My faith dictates certain rules."

"Well those rules are wrong."

His eyes, wet with tears, met mine. I waited. At last he spoke again, so quietly I could barely hear him over the sea breeze. "Temptation is everywhere."

"I guess so."

"Not just the passing lure of the flesh. Real temptation. Real danger."

"Anyone in particular?" I asked, hoping he was going to confess that he could no longer resist me. Peter Allinson, for all his problems, was a very attractive young man. He reminded me, I realized with a pang, of Vince.

"Yes."

"I see." He didn't pounce. Not me, then. "Someone here on the island now."

"Yes."

"Someone you've spoken to?"

"Yes."

I racked my brains, and then remembered that strange passing moment on the ferry, when Henry Jessop and Peter Allinson faced each other across the deck, one blond and dressed in white, the other dark and dressed in black, a negative mirror, and the sudden shock in the young deacon's eyes before he fled the boat...

"Someone, perhaps, that you knew before?"

"I must go back to the village. They will have missed me."

"And what will they do? Send out a search party of nuns?"

He laughed, thank God. "Probably. God, how I dread those women and their kindness. They stifle me. Up here I can breathe."

An idea struck me. "Have you been to Gozo before?"

"Why do you ask?"

The truth was that I had remembered something Claire Sutherland told me about the comings and goings she'd witnessed at the Continental Hotel in the old days, before the arrival of Tilly and Martin Dear. Something about a young clergyman carrying on with a mousy bluestocking—a liaison that had aroused Claire's jealousy and spite. Was it possible that he, the errant cleric, was Peter Allinson on a previous visit? Had Claire misread the situation? "I just wondered. You seem so fond of the place."

"It's very beautiful. But no, this is my first visit and, I suspect, my last. When I am sent home I will disappear into parish life, probably somewhere in the wilds of Ireland where I won't be tempted."

"Irish boys are the worst. Believe me, I'm from Boston."

"Is there to be no peace for me?"

"Not until you find it in yourself," I said, my hand on my heart. Not a very convincing act, is it? I was as far from finding peace in my heart as anyone, and unlike Peter Allinson I'd left a trail of misery behind me. And how was I dealing with it? By fucking every hole that presented itself.

"Thank you, Mitch. I appreciate your counsel. And now," he said, standing up and brushing the grit from the seat of his pants, "I must return to reality."

For a moment we faced each other, the glow of the sunset behind Peter framing his broad shoulders, and I wondered what would happen if I closed the gap between us, stepped towards him over the rocks and grass and took him in my arms... And then he put his jacket on and fumbled for his collar studs, and we descended the path in silence.

Down in the village, in the shadow of the cliffs, it was almost dark. Candles were burning here and there, and lights shone from behind shutters, but the promenade, usually so busy even at night, was deserted. Death had extended his hand over Xlendi again, and the people huddled in their homes—out of fear or respect I could not say.

I felt sad and lonely. In the hurly-burly of Joseph Vella's death, Captain Hathaway's arrest and my subsequent attempts at investigation, I had forgotten one painfully important fact: a young man had lost his life—a young man who, only two days ago, I had been intimate with. Everything I touched seemed to turn to ashes. When I get into this maudlin mood I need company. Male company, preferably, of the simple and straightforward kind.

But Bill Conrad was back in Valetta, and the Continental Bar was deserted, the dining room empty. The Jessops, I presumed, had retreated to their rooms, and short of tapping on Henry's door and risking the wrath of his watchful parents, I wasn't going to get any joy there. Besides, the last thing I needed now was a confused young thief. I'd deal with him in the morning.

I sat down heavily in an armchair, wondering if I could help myself to a drink. I'm not one of those that habitually turns to liquor, but my hands were beginning to shake as the shock of Vella's death sank in.

I went to the bar and surveyed the bottles, and that's when I saw, sitting on the floor with his head in his hands, his clothes crumpled and stained, an obviously drunk Martin Dear.

IX

"MARTIN?"

He looked up with red, unfocused eyes. "Oh. Mitch."

"What are you doing down there?"

"Looking for my keys." He sounded confused, half dazed.

"Come on, man. Get up. You won't find anything like that." I extended a hand across the bar and pulled him to his feet. His pants were filthy, his shirt untucked, and he stank of scotch. He leaned against the bar, nearly knocking over a tray of glasses. "Better get you outside before the guests see you. Come on."

I managed to escort him unseen from the premises. It was cooling off outside, and we were no more than halfway along the harbor when the fresh air hit Martin and he doubled over and puked into the sea. The fish, I guessed, would make short work of that, and by the time holidaymakers were taking their morning swim it would all be cleared up.

Vomiting sobered him up a bit, and he was able to walk unassisted in a more-or-less straight line. We made it as far as the inlet where I'd encountered the Captain sketching the bathers in happier times, and we sat on the rocks.

"What's your problem, Martin?"

He hesitated for a while, rubbing his face vigorously with his hands, before saying, "Money. What else?"

"I thought you'd sorted all that out when you went over to Valetta?"

Martin sighed. "Fact of the matter, old man, we're broke. Flat broke."

"How come?"

"Do you have any idea how much it costs to run a business like the Continental?"

"A lot."

"You said it. It's like a bucket with a fucking great hole in the bottom. Cash runs through it like water. I can't hold onto a penny."

"You spent a lot doing the place up."

"Tilly wanted everything to be perfect. The plumbing, the decoration, even put electricity in, a telephone. We don't employ many people, but they all cost money. Not much I can say—it's the wife's money, after all. Up to her how she spends it."

"You seem to have plenty of guests, though."

"That's the trouble. We're not charging enough. Tilly refuses to put the prices up, because she doesn't want to alienate our loyal customers. Why do you think people like the Jessops and Claire Sutherland keep coming back? They pay peanuts, that's why."

"And you don't think it's worth it?"

"All I can see is an empty bank account and an ever-increasing pile of debt. I can't keep the creditors off our backs much longer. We might just about survive the season, but after that..." His stomach heaved again. "Oh God. I feel foul. I drank half a bottle of whiskey."

"As a doctor, I have to say that's not a good idea."

"It's either that, or join the queue to jump off the cliffs." He spat onto the rocks at his feet. "Sorry. That was a rotten thing to say. Poor Joseph. Poor bastard."

"Did you know him?"

"Just in the way you get to know the locals. Good morning, good evening, lovely weather and so forth. He did a bit of work around the hotel on occasion, although 'work' might not be quite the right word. Lazy sod. Oh, damn it, there I go again. But he was. Thought he was rather too good for it."

"That's exactly what his father said."

"And now the poor feller would give anything to have his lazy good-for-nothing son back again, wouldn't he? Funny old world."

"So what are you going to do?"

He flinched slightly. "About what?"

"The financial situation."

"God alone knows. Borrow more, probably. If we could just touch five hundred quid or so, we'd be out of the woods. I don't suppose you..."

"I'm afraid not, Martin."

"Sorry. Wrong of me to ask. But I don't know where else to turn."

"Perhaps Miss Sutherland could sell some of her jewelry."

"It wouldn't raise a tenner. Paste, most of it. Costume stuff. She's all show, that one. No substance."

"And the famous inheritance has run out?"

"'Fraid so, old man."

"Bad planning on your part."

"We had a few unforeseen expenses."

"You mean the building works?"

"I've made a few blunders."

"Gambling?"

"Yes. I know I'm a fool, so you don't need to tell me. I thought I was onto a dead cert, but I got fleeced. Expensive lesson. Won't do it again."

"And is that all?"

Martin was silent for a while, then said, "Do you remember what I said about certain letters that had arrived at the hotel?"

"Of course. Poisonous stuff."

"Well there was a bit more to it than that."

"Ah." I knew what he was going to say before he said it. The word that had echoed around the island ever since my arrival.

"The fact is, old chap, we're being blackmailed."

"Who by?"

"I told you. That bloody old woman."

"Seriously? Why don't you just tell the police?"

"You don't know the police around here. They're not exactly friendly to newcomers."

"Then the British garrison. They look after their own. Malta is part of the Empire, for Christ's sake."

"I don't want to get them involved. I can sort it out for myself."

"Yeah," I said, "it certainly looks that way."

"All right, all right." Martin was getting angry; he was still drunk, and I didn't particularly want to fight him. "You can be as sarcastic as you fucking well like but you don't understand a thing."

"Try me."

"The fact is," he said, his voice sounding lachrymose again, "I love my wife very, very much indeed."

I've heard this a thousand times, usually from men who are about to suck your cock. "Of course you do."

"And I would do anything to protect her."

"From what?"

"Tilly has problems."

"Is she a gambler too?"

"Good lord no. Far too sensible for that."

"Then what? A drug addict?"

"Are you trying to be funny?"

"Yes, as a matter of fact. I can see it's wasted on you, though." I got up and turned back towards the village.

"Don't go, old man. I'm sorry. I'm such a bloody rude oaf, that's what Tilly's always telling me, and she's right. I don't know how to behave. I should never have come here. I'm not up to the job."

I sat down again. "Pull yourself together, Martin. Nobody wants to see you cry, least of all me. Now be a man, and tell me what's what."

He took a deep breath. "Thank you, Mitch. You're absolutely right. Stiff upper lip and all that. Well, the truth is that Tilly isn't what she seems."

"You mean she has a double life?"

"What I'm trying to say is that when I met Tilly I thought she was the most wonderful, vivacious, sexy girl in the whole wide world. And she is. Absolutely ripping."

"Indeed."

"None of those inhibition whatsits. Up for anything. I thought

I'd landed in clover. Couldn't believe my luck. And she wanted to marry me! Me! I've never been good for much. Just one thing. And it happened to be the thing that Tilly loves more than anything."

"Fucking."

"If you must put it so crudely. I started when I was twelve with a friend of my sister's, and I've never looked back. Women like me, Mitch. I can't help it."

"I'm sure they do. And Tilly?"

"Tilly liked me very much. Couldn't get enough. Used to wear me out, to be honest. I never thought I'd say this, but sometimes it was too much of a good thing. She was never satisfied. And then..."

"You weren't enough for her any more."

"How did you guess?"

"I know people like that," I said. "They're never satisfied with one partner, no matter how much they love them."

"Tilly to a T. She can't help it, anymore than I can help drinking or gambling. We're a pretty pair."

"And someone found out."

"She was never careful. Married men, young men, some of them very young indeed. Policemen. Soldiers. She's even had a go at the priests."

"And guests?"

"Who knows? I can't watch her all the time."

"And now she's threatened with exposure."

"Exactly."

"Forgive me, Martin, but this all sounds a bit farfetched. Who would go to the trouble of blackmailing Tilly? Why?"

"For money."

"Then pay up and tell her to fuck off."

"If I do that, she will expose us."

"So what? You think anyone cares?'

"You don't understand the people out here, Mitch. They'd be coming up the steps of the hotel with pitchforks and burning torches if they knew Tilly was screwing their husbands and sons. They don't care if a man goes out and sows his wild oats, but a woman?" He shook his head. "That's a different matter."

"And what does Tilly say?"

"She's made it quite clear that if I try to stop her from doing what she wants to do, she'll leave me. But if I have to keep paying up, we go bust. Oh God, Mitch, what am I going to do?"

"Admit defeat and go home."

"There's nothing for me there."

"Then go to France, Italy. Smarten yourself up and find a nice rich widow." He laughed, which was an improvement. "Or a sugar daddy, if you can stretch to that. They tend to be wealthier. The Riviera is full of them, I believe."

"That would certainly be one solution. Thanks, Mitch. You're a tonic."

"Well why not? If Tilly can have her fun, why shouldn't you have yours? What's sauce for the goose is sauce for the gander. You're in the most beautiful place in the world, you might as well be happy."

"If we were exposed, we'd be ruined."

"Really? I can think of several people, myself included, who wouldn't give a damn. In fact, we'd be more likely to come back. As for those that disapprove," I said, thinking of the Jessops or whoever had complained about the noises from my room, "you'd be better off without them. Come on, Martin. You're a good-looking guy. You should make the most of it."

Martin slapped his thighs. "You know what, Mitch? I will. I bloody well will. Thank you." He shook my hand. "The worm has turned. Two can play at her game, can't they? Ah, she'll see. Two can play at her game."

And he headed back to the hotel, still weaving a little, but with purpose in his step.

I went to my room, but I couldn't sleep. There was too much racing through my mind, too many questions unanswered. I tried reading, but that only made things worse: every word set me off on a new train of thought. I needed a man, but there was none to be had. I took a couple of aspirin, and finally dozed off in a chair.

When I woke it was getting light outside, the thin mauve light showing the island in so different a character from the harsher, hotter light of day. I stepped onto the balcony; the air was beautifully cool, the sea still as glass, the promenade deserted but for a couple of cats sniffing at fish heads by the boats. The silence was almost complete—and then I detected a distant rumbling, the whine of a motor, the crunch of tires getting closer. There was a police car pulling to a halt at the end of the Victoria Road. A uniformed officer got out and opened the rear door, extended a helping hand, and out came Captain Hathaway. Disheveled, stooped and sick with exhaustion—but alive and, apparently, free.

The car bore the policemen back to Victoria, leaving the Captain on the promenade. He seemed disorientated. He was an old man, and judging by his florid complexion and excess weight I suspected a weak heart. I dressed quickly and ran down the steps from the hotel.

"Captain Hathaway?"

His eyes were unfocused. "Dear boy...ah, dear boy..."

"It's me. Mitch Mitchell. Are you all right?"

"Just a little weary. I must be getting home. Out all night."

"I saw."

"Ah. Ah yes." He rubbed his forehead. "I suppose everyone on the island knows by now."

"Let me help you." I took his arm, and he leaned heavily on me. Somehow, I got him up the steps behind Vella's bar to the front of his house.

"I do hope they haven't made too much of a mess," he said, producing a door key from under a terracotta pot. "They seemed quite determined to find something, although I told them they were wasting their time. Won't you come in? I'm sure I could rustle up a cup of coffee."

"You sit down, Captain." I steered him to an easy chair in the front room that overlooked the bay. It was a pleasant room, redolent of gentlemen's clubs back in England: quantities of leather-bound books, a worn Turkish rug on the floor, a couple of the Captain's competent landscapes of Gozo on the wall, a walnut bureau in the corner. Everything was tidy enough; there was no sign of a police search.

The Captain put his feet on a stool and let out a sigh. "Oh, really, that was a most unpleasant experience. I understand of course that one has to assist the police in any way one can, and I have the utmost respect for the law, but really, some of the questions they ask, I can't see what they could possibly have to do with…" He waved a hand in the general direction of the harbor, the cliffs.

"They think you know something about Joseph Vella's death."

The Captain glanced furtively at me. "But as I told them, how could I possibly know anything about that unfortunate young man? Of course one knew him to say hello to—we were almost neighbors after a fashion, and I often take a snifter in his father's little bar, but beyond that, what could we have in common?"

I could think of a couple of things, but the direct approach was not going to work. The Captain, exhausted and vulnerable as he was, was a sly old fox, practiced in deceit. "I suppose they're exploring all the avenues."

"But surely it was suicide?"

"What makes you say that, Captain?"

He shifted in his chair. "I don't know the details, of course. But the cliffs. It's happened before."

"Why would Joseph Vella commit suicide?"

"As I say, I know nothing about him."

"But you automatically assume that he was suicidal. That's a pretty big leap of the imagination."

"One heard things."

"What sort of things?"

The Captain got slowly to his feet. "If you will excuse me, Dr. Mitchell, I need to have a look around the studio. There are several valuable works in there, and I very much fear that the police have trampled all over them."

"I'll help you."

"There's no need."

I stood in the doorway. "Are you asking me to leave, Captain?"

"You've been most kind."

"What are you frightened of?"

"Frightened? Don't be ridiculous. I'm an officer of the Royal Navy."

"I saw you when the police took you away."

His shoulders sagged.

"You looked terrified."

He turned away.

"But they let you go. What did you tell them?"

"All right, Mr. Mitchell."

"Dr. Mitchell, if we're going to insist on rank."

"Dr. Mitchell, then. I told them everything I know about Joseph Vella. Some of it fact, some of it little more than hearsay."

"Let's try the facts."

"He modeled for me once or twice."

"I see."

"There's no need to sound quite so knowing, Dr. Mitchell. It was perfectly above board."

"Is that what you told the police?"

"Of course. Why would you think—"

"Because when I met Joseph Vella, he took me to a hut just up there, along the cliff, and I fucked his brains out."

The Captain's pale, red-rimmed eyes widened a little. "That's as may be," he blustered, obviously wanting to know more, "but nothing of the sort happened between him and me."

"Right, right. He modeled for you and it was completely chaste."

"Of course, sometimes a model will become...aroused. But that is not one's fault."

"Doesn't stop you from looking, though, does it? Or did you have your trusty camera with you? Is that what the police were looking for? Did Joseph pose for photographs?"

"I may have taken a couple of reference studies, I really don't recall."

"Funny, because Joseph's not the sort of man you easily forget. I thought he was extremely beautiful. That's why I'm sorry that he's dead. I wonder if anyone else is?"

"I'm dreadfully sorry," said the Captain, sitting down suddenly. "I feel a little sick."

"That's it. Now, take a few deep breaths and tell me the truth."

"How do I know I can trust you?" For the first time, he sounded as if he was speaking honestly.

"You don't. But I've got as much to lose as you have."

"Rubbish. I live here. This is my home. It's all I've got. You're a tourist."

"I understand your circumspection. But if I were you, Captain, I wouldn't sit back and watch a young man being hounded to his death—or worse—without doing something about it."

"What do you mean, or worse? What's worse than that?"

"Murder."

"Oh come now, Dr. Mitchell. You don't seriously expect me to believe that someone is killing these boys?"

"Which boys, Captain?"

"I mean, Joseph Vella."

"And who else?"

"I don't know. You confused me. I'm terribly tired."

"You see the connection, don't you?"

"I don't know what you're—"

"The police saw it as well. That's why they pulled you in. They think you've got something to do with both deaths. Have you?"

Even though the Captain had his back to me, I could hear his labored breathing. I waited.

"I suppose you're talking about that poor soldier."

"Ned Porter."

He winced at the sound of the name. "Ned. Yes. Poor Ned."

"You knew him, then?"

"Hardly. I mean, one saw him on the island and so on."

"You're not talking to the police now."

"Very well then. Yes, I knew him. A delightful chap. Saw me painting the harbor one day, much as you did. We got chatting, he seemed to know a little about art which is always a surprise, and he was more than happy to come and pose for studies."

"Did you pay him?"

"I may have given him a few shillings for his time."

"And did Ned strike you as the suicidal type?"

"On the contrary, he was a happy-go-lucky sort of fellow. Not a care in the world." He sighed again.

"Much like Joseph Vella, in fact."

"Ah, well Joseph… One knew a little more about Joseph."

"Such as?"

"One understood that he was involved in one or two unsavory rackets."

"Blackmail?"

The Captain waved a hand. "I couldn't say. He never asked me for a penny."

"Really? He asked me, in no uncertain terms. Threatened me, in fact, when I'd only just come up his ass."

"Oh, really, Mitch." No more Dr. Mitchell now, I noticed. "Must we be quite so blunt?"

"I told him to fuck off."

He turned around in his chair and glared at me, his face red.

"Don't tell me you didn't hear that kind of language when you were in the Navy, Captain."

"Very well." He got to his feet. "If it's plain speaking you want, plain speaking you will have. Yes, Joseph Vella asked me for money once or twice. He was a dishonest young man and had absolutely no moral sense whatsoever. I told him that I would never concede to any such demands and that I would have no hesitation in going to the police."

"And what did he say?"

"He laughed. But at least he didn't ask me for money again. Occasionally I may have given him a little gift, but usually he just came up to the house, posed for me, had a drink and that was that."

"How many times did he visit you?"

"I don't record such things in a diary."

"Once or twice."

"More, if you must know. Over the last year or so he's been up here quite regularly."

"As a model."

"He helped around the house a bit. I'm not getting any younger."

"And in return, you helped him out."

He looked me straight in the eyes for the first time. "I never did anything he didn't ask me to do. Begged me to do, in fact. So yes, if you must have all the details, I sometimes lent him a hand."

"That all?"

"Yes. I am past the age of doing anything more vigorous."

"Now we're getting somewhere. And then he asked you for money."

"I paid him for his time and services, but never for his silence."

"Thank you, Captain."

"I imagine that he had similar arrangements with other people on the island. Women as well as men. He never seemed to be short of a bob or two."

"A gigolo, in short."

"Oh, nothing as respectable as that." The Captain allowed himself a short laugh. "You wouldn't have seen him in the hotel bars or anything. Perhaps sneaking out of the bedrooms in the wee small hours. He was strictly rough trade." He coughed, realizing he'd given himself away by his knowledge of such terms. "Anyway," he said, serious once again, "as I told the police, I'm very sorry he's dead, I feel deeply for his poor father but I have no idea who is responsible, if not Joseph himself."

"Did they suggest foul play?"

"They were waiting for me to say I bumped him off. But as I kept repeating, relations between Joseph Vella and I were entirely cordial."

"And relations between you and Lance Corporal Edward Porter?"

"Hmmm?"

"Poor Ned."

"Well, really. I have already told you quite enough."

"You see, Captain, I'm beginning to understand the way the police are thinking. Two young men have died on this island—young men with something to hide. And the connection between them, apart from the obvious fact of their sexual preferences? You, Captain Hathaway. You, who lured them up to your studio—"

"I have never lured anyone in my life. I resent that."

"Got them into compromising positions, of which you were careful to gather evidence in the form of photographs..."

"I have never heard such bloody nonsense in my life. I would never, ever blackmail another human being. I told you, I gave them the odd financial gift. Money never, ever went the other way."

"I only have your word for that, Captain. And I don't think you're being entirely truthful."

"Think what you like. I'm past caring. And now, with your permission, Doctor, I am going to have a large whiskey and go to bed. Unless, of course, you have any further questions?"

This was intended to be sarcastic, of course, but I chose to take him literally. "I do, as a matter of fact. If you're not behind the blackmail on this island, then who is?"

"That's no concern of mine."

"It is, Captain, because I must assume that if you're not the perpetrator, you are a victim."

"How dare you!"

"Well?"

"If there was anything like that, I'd—"

"What? Go to the police? I doubt it."

"I have asked you to leave."

"What have they got on you? Letters? Photographs?"

"Dr. Mitchell, please. I am an old man. I don't want any trouble."

"You may not want it, but you've got it. Come on. I might be able to help."

"If you must know, there was a burglary here a few months ago. Several things were taken. Nothing particularly incriminating, but if they were to fall into the wrong hands, they might be open to... misinterpretation."

"Photographs?"

"Artistic studies."

"Understood. So someone knew what they were looking for, and they've been threatening you ever since."

"That's about the size of it."

"Any idea who?"

"That's just the trouble. I honestly haven't a clue."

"You're not the only victim," I said, thinking of what Martin Dear had told me. "If you could just help me, we could stamp this vile business out once and for all."

From outside, I heard a soft thud and the sound of receding footsteps.

The Captain froze, hands clenched in fear.

I ran to the door, but all I could see in the half-light was a figure running along the cliff—a young man, by the look of it. I gave chase for a couple of hundred yards, but he was too fast for me.

When I returned, the Captain was standing in the hall looking utterly dismayed, a piece of paper in his hand.

"What is it?"

"Another one."

He passed the letter to me. Carefully printed in capitals.

YOU GOT AWAY WITH IT THIS TIME OLD MAN.
NEXT TIME IT WILL COST YOU £200 OR I TELL
THE POLICE EVERYTHING.

"How many of these have there been."

"One or two."

"The truth, Captain."

"Fine, if you insist. They started shortly after the burglary last year. At first it was ten pounds here, ten pounds there."

"Or what?"

"They would give my photographs to the police."

"Are the photos that dangerous? I thought they were just art studies."

"Some of them may have been a little more than that."

"At last we're getting somewhere."

"I don't have two hundred pounds, Mitch. To raise that kind of sum I'd have to sell the house."

The thought flashed across my mind that with Aunt Dinah's money, I could afford to buy the Captain out lock, stock and barrel and make a very pleasant new life for myself in the best house on the island. This was unworthy.

"Who's doing it?"

"I don't know."

"Very well. Let me know when the house is on the market, I might be interested."

"I'm telling the truth. Oh God." He sank into a chair, face in hands. "What am I to do? I've been a fool. Such a fool."

"Then let me help you."

"I never meant things to go this far. I really did start taking photographs to use in my paintings, as reference. And then I realized that these young men who were willing to model for art were keen to model for other things as well. I never asked them to, it just happened—and then one's finger was on the button and click! The first time I pulled the film out of the camera as soon as the model had gone and destroyed it. But the next time, I thought, well, why not? Let's develop it and see how it came out. I have a little darkroom at the back of the studio; I get the chemicals and paper sent over from Malta. It's rather fun."

"And they turned out well?"

"Very well, if I do say so myself. Just a beautiful young man in the sunlight, taking pleasure in himself. What could be more natural?"

"That's not what the police think. Or the church."

"Once I'd begun, I found it hard to stop. I felt a duty to record such beauty before it slips away. Youth is such a precious thing, Mitch. You don't realize it, but it passes so quickly. And suddenly, without knowing how it happened, you're old and lonely like me. Living in exile. No friends, no family. But I was young once too, as young as you. And beautiful, in my way. Hard to believe."

"Not at all," I said, trying to find the lineaments of youth and beauty in that jowly red face.

"As a young officer, in one's uniform, the whole of life ahead of one, there were so many possibilities. And one took pleasure where one found it. No thought of the consequences. Ah, well, they were different times. The Eighties, the Nineties. Carefree. Careless, I suppose. Never thought it would come to this."

I had a sudden vision of myself at the Captain's age—forty, fifty years hence?—friendless, loveless, endlessly searching for reflections of what might have been in the young men whose companionship I paid for, exposing myself to danger and the slow poison of regret. Was that the future I was building for myself? Was I fucking my way to a miserable old age? Was it already too late? I thought of Vince, far away, and the one chance for happiness that I'd discarded like an old shoe.

"I suppose I must face the music. I have no one to blame but myself. But I wish you could have seen me then, Mitch. We didn't all have cameras in those days, more's the pity. One was drawn a couple of times. I have a charcoal sketch hidden away in the safe that was done by a Royal Academician. Picked me up in the Cafe Royal, you know. Took me up to his studio in Albany, got my togs off, sketching away like a madman. I suppose that's where I first got the idea. Worth a few bob now, I suppose. Might come in handy."

The poor old bastard looked utterly defeated.

"Come on, Captain. Is that what they taught you in the Navy? We've got to fight back."

"The battle is already lost, dear boy. It's time for a strategic withdrawal. I have an unmarried niece in Hampshire, or is it Wiltshire? I shall throw myself on her charity."

"Don't be ridiculous. We're going to find out who is doing this and beat them at their own game."

"I wish you all the luck in the world, but I fear that Gozo is no longer a friendly place for people like me. It's changing. The old order passeth. Oh, it was wonderful before—even just a few years ago. Everyone minded their own business, we all got along just fine. The dear old couple that used to run the Continental, for instance."

"The Andersons?"

"Lovely people. Great friends to me. But then they packed up in a hurry, and there was that poor boy's death, and suddenly it's all whispering and finger pointing and policemen turning up at one's house."

"What happened?"

"The same as happens everywhere. The law, the church, all those dreadful respectable people who have never lived. They catch up with us. I've always been running from them. I thought I'd found safe haven at last, but it appears not."

"Why did the Andersons sell up?"

"They'd had enough, they said. Wanted to return to England

to be looked after when they got old. I didn't believe a word of it. Never saw a healthier, happier couple in my life."

"So what do you think?"

"They were forced out, just as I'm being."

"How?"

"The Andersons were not exactly conventional. They came from somewhat Bohemian circles, you might say. It was a happy marriage, but quite unusual."

"You mean they had separate interests?"

"Quite so. They married for companionship and respectability. I should have done the same. There were plenty of understanding girls."

"But why would they just leave? They had a thriving business— everyone seems to have loved them."

"Things went on in that hotel that were against the law."

"They still do, I assure you, Captain." I thought of Bill Conrad, Henry Jessop...

"Really?" He perked up at last. "I'm delighted to hear it, dear boy. That's one in the eye for the bloody bastards."

"Who? The new owners?"

"Oh, I've nothing against them, particularly. She's a tarty little thing, and he's rather too fond of the booze, but they're doing their best." If the Captain had known what Martin told me about his wife's sexual appetites, and my own suspicions about Martin's extramarital activities, he might be better disposed towards them, but that was not my secret to reveal. "I mean whoever it is that's persecuting me."

"And you really don't know who?"

"There's that frightful old woman. She's always calling one names."

"She doesn't seem quite sane enough to achieve all this, though. Forcing the Andersons out, and now you."

"Then I don't know. I wish I did."

"But you pay someone."

"I send money to a poste restante address in Malta."

"You have the number?"

"Of course. Much good may it do you."

"Captain, I'm beginning to think that you want to be defeated. Either that, or you're still not telling me the truth."

"The truth is that I'm very old, and very tired, and I've spent the night being bullied by those bloody thugs up in Victoria, and I'm scared, and I want to go to bed. Is that enough truth for you, Mitch?"

A church bell, clearly audible in the still morning air, struck six.

It was time for everyone to get some rest, before the village woke up to another day of deepening mystery and spiraling lies.

X

I FELL ASLEEP FEELING VERY SORRY FOR MYSELF, FOR THE
Captain, for all of us poor harried souls, always hiding, always
running from the vengeful Furies of society.

A couple of hours' sleep was enough to get over that, and decided
that by the time I'd eaten a good breakfast I would be determined
to fight back. I'd find out who was responsible for the deaths of Ned
Porter and Joseph Vella; I'd clip the wings of the Gozo blackmailer,
whoever it may be; and I'd make the island a safe haven once again
for the Captain and his kind. For me, if it came to it. Gozo seemed
like Paradise. All I had to do was hunt down the Serpent.

I went downstairs for breakfast, eager to fortify myself for a
day's sleuthing.

"Aaaaaaaaaargh!"

A woman's voice was raised in an ear-splitting scream. I entered
the lobby to see Claire Sutherland in a perfect theatrical attitude of
rage and despair, her hands clutching her hair, eyes wide, mouth
open. Grouped around her were Tilly and Martin Dear, Ralph the
porter and Stella the cook, all looking extremely nervous.

"Doctor Mitchell! Thank God!" Claire threw herself into my
arms. "Save me from this gang of thieves!"

"What on earth is the matter?"

"I've been robbed! Robbed! All my jewelry! My money! Gone!" She spun around and hissed at the Dears and their staff. "I know you're all in it together, waiting until people are asleep or out of their rooms and then helping yourselves. Is that how you're keeping the place going? Did you really think nobody would notice?" Her voice was getting louder and louder, another scream building. I'm used to dealing with hysterics, so I slipped straight into my professional role.

"Sit down, Miss Sutherland. Ralph, fetch a brandy from the bar. Now, has anyone telephoned the police?"

I caught a glance between Martin and Tilly. "Not quite yet," said Tilly, as cool as a cucumber, her hair and makeup immaculate. I may have been immune to her curves, but there was no doubt that she was a capable young woman. And if she was an uncontrollable nymphomaniac—well, that was just something we had in common. "I thought we should ask a few basic questions first."

"There is nothing to ask!" shrieked Claire, obviously enjoying her role of outraged victim. "I have been robbed, and someone knows who did it! Who has access to the rooms? You do! You and your staff!" She jabbed a red-nailed finger towards Tilly. "Thieves, the lot of you!"

Tilly did not rise to the bait. "Please, Claire. Let's try to remain civil, at least. Look, here's Ralph with your brandy. Have a little sip of that..."

Claire grabbed the glass and knocked it back in one.

"... and you'll feel better. Now," continued Tilly, "please think very carefully. Is there a possibility that anyone has been in your room?" She knew full well, of course, that La Sutherland had been entertaining ever since her arrival; any one of Claire's visitors could have slipped the bijoux into his pocket.

"My friends are above suspicion."

"Of course, of course," said Tilly. "But mistakes of this kind are so easily made. Misunderstandings about gifts, and such like."

"How dare you!" said Claire, but her voice had lost its warlike tones. "I insist that you call the police."

"Very well," said Tilly, her hand reaching for the desk telephone.

"If you're sure you want to answer all their questions. I believe they are very thorough in their investigations." She picked up the receiver. "Hello? Operator? Police, please. Yes, it's an emergency."

"Just one moment." Claire raised a hand; bracelets slid down to her elbow. "Perhaps that won't be necessary."

Tilly replaced the receiver; I was far from convinced she'd even spoken to the operator.

"Let us not be rash," said Claire. "I'm sure we can sort this out by ourselves. As you say, it's quite possible that there's been a misunderstanding. Let me think." She pressed her index finger to her temple and stared at the ceiling—stage shorthand for thinking. "I have hosted a couple of little receptions in my room—dear local friends, so pleased to see one return for another summer." Local men, more like, so pleased to see the Sutherland purse opening. "Perhaps I may have tidied my things away rather too quickly. You see, one is used to having a ladies' maid and a dresser."

Like hell, I thought. "What exactly are you missing, Claire?"

"Some diamond and sapphire earrings, and a quantity of cash."

I too was missing a quantity of cash, but I didn't mention that just yet. There was a burglar in our midst. Henry Jessop, as I first suspected? Or Martin Dear, desperate for money and with access to every room?

"Perhaps you could go up and have a look for us," said Tilly, a touch patronizingly, "before I sound the general alarm."

"I will go," said Claire, mustering what dignity she could, "but not because you ask me. This would never have happened under the Andersons, let me tell you that. Never."

"Thank you, Claire," said Tilly, catching my eye and daring me to laugh. And yes, it was funny. And yet, and yet, and yet—had other people lost things? Were they, too, unwilling to be questioned by the police? Was it just Claire's love of drama that prompted her to make her accusations? I'd kept quiet; had others?

The Jessops were in the lounge reading the newspapers, giving a very good impression of being oblivious to the whole nasty business but undoubtedly listening to every word. I strolled in and joined them.

"Good morning. Lovely day."

They looked at me with distaste, nodded, and returned to their reading.

"What a lot of fuss about nothing, huh? Miss Sutherland. I bet you she's just squirreled those earrings away in her stockings or something."

Mrs. Jessop looked shocked, as if the mention of a lady's stockings was rather improper. Her husband frowned.

"Are you missing anything from your room, sir? Madam?"

"Of course not," snapped Mr. Jessop, shaking his newspaper. "We are not the sort of people who get burgled."

"What about Henry?"

They both looked up. "What about him?"

"He's not lost anything, has he?" Like his cherry, for instance.

"Certainly not. We are a respectable family."

"Bad things happen to good people," I said, wondering how they'd respond if they'd seen what dear Henry was doing in my room a few hours ago. "By the way, where is he? Taking a swim?"

Mr. Jessop cleared his throat. "Henry has been out since early this morning. Exploring the island, I suppose. He has his freedom."

That wasn't my impression. Perhaps he'd slipped the leash. "Well, that's great. Perhaps I'll catch him across the bay."

"Yes, perhaps you will, Dr. Mitchell." And they disappeared behind their papers.

Out since early this morning. How early? Early enough, I wondered, to slip up the cliff path to the Captain's house and deliver a note? Early enough to sneak into Claire's room and steal her jewelry and money? This time, the sleeper did not awake, and he didn't get caught.

Was it Henry Jessop—young, blond, blue eyed, as innocent as the angels—who was behind it all? He'd been on the island every summer for years, by his own admission. Had he driven Ned and Joseph to their deaths? Seduced them, then betrayed them into danger? I remembered the look of shock—or fear—on Deacon Peter's eyes when he faced Henry across the deck of the ferry. His hints, when we spoke on the cliffs, that there was someone here on the island, someone he had known before who posed a threat, someone *dangerous*.

And if the parents knew of Henry's activities, condoned them even, wouldn't they with their tweeds and their Bibles and their disapproving glances be the perfect cover? No one would suspect them, surrounded as they were by obvious sinners. They, surely, were above suspicion. What a perfect disguise.

I needed to find Henry Jessop, and this time I would not be distracted by the best piece of ass on the island. If necessary, I would force the truth out of him. Surely he held the key. Who else could it be?

It was time to put distractions aside and concentrate on solving the mystery before another body was washed up on the rocks. And in order to do so, I needed assistance. Another pair of legs to cover the island, another pair of eyes, and, if possible, someone with a cock, ass and mouth that I could use whenever necessary and thus prevent myself from being led astray.

"May I use the phone?" I asked Martin in the lobby. "It's just a call to the garrison at Valetta."

And with surprising ease, I persuaded Frank Southern to release Sergeant Major William Conrad from regular duties and send him over to Gozo on a special mission.

I could hardly wait for his arrival.

Those of you familiar with my biological rhythms may have noted that it was now twenty-four hours since I last had sex—well below my usual average. Put it down to the advancing years, the blow to the head I sustained in Valetta, the heat or my preoccupation with the case, but by the time Bill Conrad was due to arrive on the island I was pacing up and down with frustration, knowing too well that if I sat down in private for more than a minute I'd have to relieve myself. To prevent accidents I walked to the harbor and waited for the boat to arrive, like Cho-Cho San scanning the horizon for Pinkerton's return.

I tried to clear my mind of the case, to allow the facts as recently reviewed to form themselves into pattern and order, but I lack mental discipline. There's only one way I've ever found to stop myself from thinking, and that's by taking a big, hard cock up my ass. And so, until the Sergeant Major could oblige, thoughts whirled like a deadly kaleidoscope. *Blackmail, blackmail, blackmail—* that's what it kept coming back to. Wasn't the truth staring me in the face? An island full of secrets, and someone had the greed and cunning to exploit them. Their motive? Money, of course—we all need money, some more urgently than others. What else? Guilt for pleasures regretted, a fear of discovery? A moral crusade, punishing wrongdoers by taking judgment into your own hands? Sheer malice, perhaps: I've come across it before, the blind, unreasoning hatred that needs no justification. Too many options, too many suspects. My brain whirred. I needed to stop thinking. I needed Bill.

And there it was at last, the thread of smoke on the horizon, and soon the high whine of the engine as Bill steered the boat into Xlendi harbor, cutting the motor and gliding to the sea wall, his sleeves rolled up, dark glasses covering his eyes.

"Mitch!" He waved and shouted, as pleased to see me as I was him, then jumped out, tied up the boat and came down the promenade in a loping run. Okay, he wasn't as pretty as Henry Jessop or as handsome as Joseph Vella, but he was exactly what this doctor ordered. I couldn't take my eyes off the front of his pants, where things were swinging free.

"Sergeant Major Conrad."

He stopped, stamped to attention and saluted, showing his teeth in a carnivorous smile. "Reporting for duty, Dr. Mitchell, sir. Lieutenant Colonel Southern said it was urgent."

"It's very fucking urgent. You need to come up to my room right now."

He touched his groin. "I've been ready all the way over. Want to feel?"

The harbor was busy as the cafes opened, but I managed a swift grab of the goods; Bill's cock was solid, and if I was any judge he wasn't wearing underpants.

"Let's go."

We raced along the promenade and up the steps like schoolboys playing truant. The Continental lobby was busy, the dining room full, and for all I knew the eyes of a dozen blackmailers were watching me taking a uniformed soldier up to my room. If they cared to listen on the stairwell, they would get an earful. If Henry Jessop chose that moment to come sneaking again, we'd both fuck his brains out.

I went as fast as I could, but it wasn't fast enough for Bill. "Hurry up, Mitch. I'm fucking desperate." He was grabbing my ass as we climbed the stone stairs to my room, pulling and poking with his thick fingers. He knew what I wanted.

We almost fell through the door. As soon as it was closed he pushed me against it, grinding his crotch into mine, kissing me, pulling my shirt open. I was as hard as he was, and when he pinched my tit I felt a surge down to my cock as if I might come right away. His mouth tasted of cigarettes and coffee, and I couldn't get enough of it. When I reached down to grab his dick, the front of his pants was wet.

"Get your trousers off and get on the fucking bed, mate."

I managed to kick off my shoes and drop my pants before Bill pushed me down, face first, onto the mattress. He wasn't in the mood for preliminaries; his big, calloused hands pried my buttocks apart and he went straight in with his tongue, loosening me up and getting me wet for what was to come.

I didn't have to wait long. Bill didn't even bother to take his boots off; he unbuckled his belt, unbuttoned his pants and pushed them down his hairy thighs, then climbed up onto the bed, spat in his hand, smeared his cock (already wet and slippery) and pressed it between my buttocks. I was no novice, needing to be broken in gently—but even I was unprepared for the roughness of the assault. He was inside me before I knew it, and there was no holding back; he pushed right ahead, heedless of my grunts of pain.

"Jesus, fuck, that hurts."

"Want me to stop?"

"No."

And that was all we said. He started slowly, all the way in, all the way out, picking up speed until he was pistoning into me. I guessed that Bill hadn't got laid since the last time he was in this room, and he needed the relief as badly as I did.

The pain receded, and all that was left was pleasure, the overwhelming, mind-numbing pleasure that comes from being properly fucked. My conscious mind collapsed, short-circuited by lust. Bill's thrusting got harder, and I braced myself on my forearms, tensing my thighs, pushing backward to meet him, his pelvis slamming against mine. My cock was drooling; if I touched it now, I'd come. But I didn't want this to be over.

I don't know how he managed it, but Bill kept on fucking me, never slowing, for what seemed like hours. Most of us have to take a break, catch our breath and retreat for a while from the brink of orgasm, but not Bill. With superhuman self-control he just kept on fucking and fucking, his breath harsh, sweat dripping off his forehead and onto my back. All I had to do was endure.

I heard a voice, distant at first, then getting louder and louder, shouting a stream of obscenities, and it was with the start of a man waking from a dream that I realized the voice was mine. I had a sudden moment of clarity and then, without the touch of a hand, I started coming, my insides churning around Bill's rigid dick, jizz shooting out over the bedclothes. He picked up his pace, punishing me harder and harder until I could bear it no longer, and then he pulled out, flipped me over, straddled my chest and shot the whole lot in my face. I closed my eyes, opened my mouth and took all that he had to give me.

It was a great deal.

Bill collapsed on top of me, hairy stomach wet with sweat, shirt clinging to him in great dark patches, the spunk on my face smearing onto his as we kissed. We were both wet and sticky, our clothes pulled up and pulled down, creased and stained, chests heaving, hearts pounding.

Even after such an ecstatic fuck as this, the pleasure of lying awkwardly soon turns to discomfort and pain. Bill rolled off me, gave me a kiss and said "I need to piss."

"Me too."

"Come on then. Get your kit off."

We hobbled into the bathroom, shedding garments as we went. Bill's dick was still half hard, and from the look in his dark, hooded eyes, I suspected that he wasn't finished with me yet.

"Get in the bath."

I was right. He stood watching me, two fingers idly flopping his cock from side to side. I climbed into the tub and lay back.

"Want this?"

I didn't have to ask what he was talking about. I lay back and waited. It didn't take long. Bill positioned himself at the side of the bath, pointed his big dick at me and started pissing a great thick stream that hit me so hard on the stomach, chest and legs it actually hurt. It mixed with the sticky film of jizz and washed it away. I rubbed it over me, making the hair go this way and that, scooped some up in my hand and poured it over my cock and balls. I too was getting hard again.

Bill seemed to have a bottomless bladder, and the stream stayed steady for a whole minute. But finally it ended, he shook off the drops and continued to shake until he was fully erect. He climbed into the bath and straddled me—it was awkward, there wasn't enough room—and somehow managed to press our cocks together.

"Your turn."

It's not easy pissing through a hard dick, but with a little concentration I managed. Bill used my cock like a joystick, steering the stream up in the air, over his chest, over my chest, into my face, laughing all the time like a kid playing with a hosepipe. We were both soaked and dripping, and we smelled of piss and sweat, and once I'd finished Bill carried on mashing our slippery cocks together. He spat into his hand, rubbed it into his ass and then, with a bit of shifting that jammed my knees painfully against the sides of the tub, got my dick inside him. He rode it up and down, swearing and grunting, his balls bouncing on my wet stomach, and to my astonishment, went into a second orgasm, spewing out another big load that added to the mess on my chest and face. And suddenly, I was coming too, filling his ass with my sperm. It was the quickest, and without a doubt the dirtiest, fuck I have ever had.

Washed and dried and carefully dressed, our minds clear (for now), we sat in the hotel lounge and planned our course of action. Bill was delighted, to say the least, to be given this extraordinary mission; at Frank Southern's request, he had been ordered to render "all necessary assistance" to Dr. Mitchell for as long as he needed it, pending review in seventy-two hours. That gave us two days in which to solve the case, and another day to fuck each other's brains out, before Bill returned to normal duties. It was a pleasing prospect, combining my two greatest passions (detection and dick), and for the first time in months I felt on the whole cheerful and optimistic about the future. That this feeling arose from the deaths of two young men, and the probable existence of a malicious criminal network preying on homosexuals, says something about me that I will leave to the experts to decipher.

Bill would be the man of action in this investigation while I would do the brain work. A soldier in uniform would pass unnoticed on the island and, more importantly, would be above suspicion, whereas a tourist like me was easy to mark. And unless I was much mistaken, Bill was not in cahoots with the army top brass. It was possible that they'd sent him over to distract me and cover up their role in the deaths, but that was stretching it even for a mystery fan like me. I've met liars and cheats before, some of them even more plausible than Bill, but it seemed from our acquaintance so far that he was honest and eager to help.

And so we decided that I would impose myself on the Jessops at lunchtime, keeping them occupied and asking questions while Bill searched their rooms. If we could rule out their involvement in blackmail and robbery, my investigation would become a whole lot easier. Henry Jessop may have been one of the best fucks in the Mediterranean, but he was also the only person who had been in my room when the money disappeared from my wallet. I caught him—Claire Sutherland didn't. It was possible that his parents knew about his thieving ways, or even controlled them. It was possible that they were using him as bait and messenger in a blackmail operation. A thorough search of their rooms would surely turn up something.

True, if they were guilty it didn't explain the attack on me in Valetta, but that might just be a red herring, the price I paid for wandering in a dangerous place.

It was so easy to manage. Bill made himself scarce, wandering around the harbor for half an hour, while I bided my time in the lounge. And there, on the dot of one o'clock, were the Jessops, all three of them, the parents as neat and buttoned-up as ever, Henry looking fresh and beautiful, hair wet from bathing. Tilly seated them in the dining room, and I waited while the other tables filled up. And then, assuming my best brash American manner, I strode up to them.

"Say, you folks mind if I join you? It's getting kind of crowded in here, and I'd much rather eat with friends than strangers." The parents looked disgusted, Henry looked terrified, but it was too late—I already had my hand on the back of the chair and was pulling it out. "Beautiful day again," I continued, "but I guess it always is here. Not like London, or even Boston. Rain one day, sunshine the next, snow and ice storms in winter. Perpetual summer on Gozo." By dint of not letting them get a word in edgeways, I sat down and signaled to Martin. "One of your lethal martinis please, Martin. What are you folks having? Join me in a cocktail?"

"We do not drink cocktails, Dr. Mitchell," said Mrs. Jessop, dabbing her dry mouth with a napkin.

"What? You don't know what you're missing. How about you, Henry? You ever tried a *cock*tail?" The emphasis was not lost on him. His blue eyes widened, and I half expected to see tears.

"My son is only twenty years old, Dr. Mitchell," said Mr. Jessop, looking like a stern headmaster. "He is far too young to drink."

"Really? I started when I was fifteen." I caught Henry's eye. "Once you get a taste for it, there's no turning back. Sure you won't try, Henry? No?"

He shook his head, blushing and mumbling, and stared down at his hands, fiddling nervously with the hem of the tablecloth. His parents simply glared, aware that no amount of chilly good manners would deter me.

"Now, I'm glad I got this opportunity to talk to you folks,

because you're kind of experts on the island, aren't you?"

"We have been here several times, if that's what you mean," said Mr. Jessop, still far from friendly but just the tiniest bit flattered.

"What I want to know is, what's it really like? I mean, to live here, not as a tourist. I know you're not permanent residents, but you must have got a pretty good feel for the place over the years. Say, how long have you been coming here?"

"This is our seventh visit," said Mrs. Jessop, thawing slightly. "Henry was just fourteen when we first came, and we've returned every summer since. Of course, it's quite a journey from England, but we think it's worth it, don't we Maurice?"

"Oh yes. We are fortunate in that we live near Portsmouth, which is where we embark from."

"I know it well," I lied, wondering if the garrison in Valetta had copies of English telephone directories. If I could verify their address, it might allay my suspicions that they were island-hopping criminals. Perhaps they were just what they appeared to be, and at worst Henry was an opportunistic sneak-thief. He wouldn't be the first good boy who's gone bad from being too strictly brought up. Mr. Jessop's icy glare, and his wife's embarrassment, might arise from some scandal involving Henry's larcenous ways—maybe he'd appeared in the Portsmouth courts and newspapers, a nine-days' wonder which they were in no hurry to share.

"And Dr. Mitchell," said Mr. Jessop, suddenly all charm, "have you travelled extensively in Europe? I know what you Americans are like, always going here, there and everywhere."

"Not at all. I grew up in Boston, Massachusetts, went to Cambridge University in England, and completed my training in Edinburgh, Scotland. The rest of the time, apart from a trip to Paris, has been spent in London.'"

"And I suppose one day," said Mrs. Jessop, with a soft, fond look in her eye, "you will go home and marry your sweetheart."

"I missed my chance there," I said, thinking of Vince.

"Never mind, Dr. Mitchell," said Mr. Jessop, sounding ever more like a headmaster. "There are plenty more fish in the sea."

"Speaking of which, I was rather hoping that Henry might show me some of the good places to swim. How about it, Henry?"

He looked up at his parents but said nothing.

"Not after eating," said his mother. "You, as a doctor, must know how dangerous that can be."

"Oh, I don't think it'll kill us," I said. "And if Henry gets into trouble, I can always give him the kiss of life."

Mr. and Mrs. Jessop took this at face value and laughed politely. Henry blushed to the roots of his hair.

The aged Ralph came to take our orders, so for a while we debated the relative merits of fresh fish or rabbit stew, both of which were pronounced delicious, and I enjoyed my martini. When he'd gone, I switched tack.

"Terrible business about that young man," I said. "Do you know if the police are any nearer to finding out what happened?"

"Oh, suicide, undoubtedly," said Mr. Jessop, not without satisfaction. "I'm afraid he was a very poor sort."

"In what way? He seemed as happy as a lark when I spoke to him."

"A smiling face can conceal great evil," said Mrs. Jessop, as if reading from one of her tracts. "One is given to understand that Joseph Vella was engaged in all sorts of wrongdoing."

"Now now, my dear," interjected Mr. Jessop. "Only God can judge him."

"But surely the police should be finding out what drove him to suicide? If this happened back home, there would be a full-scale investigation."

"Indeed, the police in these islands are not to be compared with those at home," said Mr. Jessop. "Even so, I have no doubt that they know exactly what happened and will see justice done."

"Justice for whom? For Joseph Vella? Will they find the people who drove him to his death?"

"Dr. Mitchell, I hardly think we are in a position to assume—"

"And what about Edward Porter? Has he had justice?"

Mother and son stared into mid-space, while the father rubbed his forehead, as if trying to remember. "Porter? Did we know a Mr. Porter, my dear?"

"Lance Corporal Porter, in fact. Known to his friends as Ned. Fell to his death from the very same cliff a couple of years ago. You would've been here at the time, perhaps, or certainly heard about it."

"It rings a bell. There is a lot of gossip on the island."

"I hardly think talking about an unexplained death could be considered gossip, Mr. Jessop."

"Unexplained? Why, surely the police were satisfied that…" He realized he'd given himself away. "Where is our food? They take a devil of a time in this kitchen."

"What do you think would drive two young men to throw their lives away like that? You're a mother, Mrs. Jessop. Ned and Joseph were only a few years older than Henry here. Can you imagine how desperate they must have felt? What it did to their families?"

"Suicide is a terrible crime," said Mrs. Jessop, but her voice was unsteady.

"If it was suicide."

"Of course it was," snapped Mr. Jessop. "What else could it have possibly been? Now please, Dr. Mitchell, can we change the subject? People are starting to look at us."

"I'll tell you what else. Murder." I kept my voice low, unwilling to alert the whole dining room.

"Please, let us not… Oh dear." Mrs. Jessop used her napkin in earnest this time, dabbing tears from her eyes. "This is most distressing."

"You have upset my wife, sir," said Mr. Jessop, standing. "Ralph! Mrs. Jessop is unwell. You will serve lunch in our room."

They beat a hasty retreat. Henry dawdled, delaying his exit. I hoped that Bill had completed his search; it would do us no good at all to find him on the job, especially after the theft of Claire's earrings.

"I'm sorry about your mother," I said, grabbing Henry's arm and pushing him back down into his seat. "I had no idea she felt so deeply about the deaths."

"My mother is a very sensitive woman," said Henry, but he still couldn't look me in the eye.

"Well, of course she knows much more about them than I do."

He looked up. "What makes you say that?"

"Having been such a frequent visitor to the island, of course. She must have known Joseph, for example, quite well. And perhaps she met Ned. Come to think of it," I said, as if this had just occurred to me, "perhaps you knew them as well. You've been coming here since you were fourteen, isn't that right?"

"Yes."

"Joseph, certainly, was a very attractive man."

"I don't know…"

"And from what I gather, so was Ned Porter. I spoke to his lover, you know."

"I don't…"

"Ned was like you and me. So was Joseph." I waited for a reaction, a denial. "Did you know that?"

"No." Henry was starting to look like a sulky child, his eyebrows contracted, lower lip stuck out.

"If you know something, you'd better tell me."

He shook his head, shrugged.

"Where were you this morning, Henry?"

That shook him. He jumped in his seat. "Nowhere."

"Nowhere? That's quite an achievement, even for you. Everyone has to be somewhere. Where were you?"

"I was out."

"Uh-huh."

"I went for a walk and a swim."

"Which way?"

"Across the bay."

"Did you happen to go anywhere near Captain Hathaway's house?"

"No. Towards the headland."

"Any particular reason?"

"I like it up there."

Cold horror suddenly struck me. Had Henry, too, been contemplating suicide? All my theories collapsed like a house of cards.

"Jesus, Henry, you weren't…"

"What?"

"I mean, you weren't going to...to jump."

At last our eyes met properly and held, and then, after five seconds, maybe more, Henry did the very last thing I expected him to do. He threw his head back and laughed.

"My God," he said, "you don't really think I went up there to... Oh, it's too ridiculous."

Ralph was hovering with plates of food. We were both hungry and started tucking in.

"Sure you won't have a drink, Henry?"

"What the hell. Get me a beer, Ralph. Just don't tell my parents."

"Make it two." The old man shuffled off. A festive mood had descended on us.

"You want to know what I was really doing this morning?"

"Yes."

"All right. You asked for it." He leaned across this plate, and I did likewise. "I was with someone."

"Ah. A man, I presume."

"Jealous?"

"Slightly. I thought I was the first."

"Sorry," said Henry. "I was pretending. I know that men like to think that." Well, I thought, he fooled me, the great expert in sexual matters, the trained observer of human nature. Yes, sweet, innocent Henry Jessop only had to flash his rose-pink hole and look over his shoulder with those baby-blue eyes, giving me that "please be gentle" line, and I was hoodwinked. How many more mistakes had I made?

"Bet you can't guess who it was." He was smiling now, his eyes twinkling.

"You swam across the bay to meet him?"

"Yes. There's a little cave over the other side, with steps leading all the way up to the top of the cliff. I'll have to show you."

"And that's where you go to have sex with people."

"Not *people*. Just one person."

I saw Martin mixing drinks behind the bar. Of course! It all fell into place. Martin's distress, his money worries... A whole new narrative spiraled in my mind, accelerating too fast for reason to keep up with it.

"My God. Martin Dear."

"What? Martin Dear?" Once again Henry laughed. "Oh, Mitch. You're barking up the wrong tree. He's married."

"It's never stopped anyone before."

"No. Guess again."

I racked my brains. Who else was there on the island—a man, young and attractive enough to be of interest to Henry, or perhaps old and wealthy. Someone who could get to a clifftop rendezvous.

It clicked at last. "I see. So you keep away from married men, but you don't mind fucking priests."

"He's not a priest," said Henry, coyly. "At least, not yet."

"Nor is he likely to be, by the sound of it. So—you and Deacon Peter. It was you that he had seen before."

Now it was Henry's turn to look perplexed. "What do you mean?"

"He told me there was someone he knew back home. Someone who presented a danger."

"Is that what he said? Well, that's me. Do you think I'm dangerous?"

"I think some men would be willing to risk everything for you."

"I'm flattered, Mitch."

"And I think you know exactly what you're worth."

"You make me sound calculating."

"And what about your parents? Are they aware of your worth?"

The color drained from Henry's face. Fortunately for him, Ralph brought two glasses of cold beer at that moment. We ate and drank for a while, considering our next move.

Henry was the first to speak. "My parents know nothing about me."

"I don't believe you."

"They may suspect things. But they don't know."

"Is that why they guard you like a prisoner?"

"They are very religious people."

"You mean they appear to be good, but underneath they're the same as the rest of us."

"They're certainly not like you and me, Mitch."

I couldn't come right out and ask him if his parents were, by any chance, using him as bait to blackmail queers all over Europe. I drank my beer and ate my meal.

"Henry, if I ask you a question, will you give me a truthful answer?"

"I'll do my best."

"Did you take money from my room?"

"Of course I didn't."

"Why did you go up there?"

"That's a bloody silly question." He was blushing again, a vein standing out on his forehead.

"You mean you just wanted to fuck?"

"Yes."

"And what about Peter?"

"What about him?"

"Aren't you and he...serious?"

"Yes, we're serious. Very serious, worst luck."

"What does that mean?"

"Would you mind if we get out of here? All this whispering is giving me a headache." He downed his beer, and I watched his throat working, remembering how it had looked when he sucked my cock. I was getting hard again, and I suspected he was too.

"Come on then."

We took a short stroll along the harbor wall, away from eavesdroppers.

"We met a couple of years ago."

"Where? Here?"

"Back in England." He sighed deeply. "I was still at school. It was my last term, and I was supposed to be concentrating on exams. Father wanted me to go to university to study theology. They have this idea that I'm going into the church."

"That doesn't seem very likely."

Henry shrugged. "What else do people like me do?"

"You can do anything, Henry."

"I'm not very clever, that's the trouble. I failed my exams."

"Why?"

164

"I was distracted."

We took a few more paces along the path, then sat. "Go on."

"It wasn't my fault. There was this teacher. Well, not really a teacher. He came in to do extra tuition in divinity. He was a seminarian at the Jesuit college. They were always sending priests in to tell us what to do. Most of them were old and ugly, but this one..."

"Was Peter Allinson?"

"Yes." He sighed. "We both knew it was wrong, but what could we do? Every day I had a lesson with him, just the two of us, and we were allowed to go out into the gardens to sit under the trees by the lake. It was a lovely place, my school. I was quite happy there, away from Mother and Father."

"I thought you said you didn't go to that kind of school."

He shrugged. Another lie, obviously. "With Peter, it was different."

Isn't it always? I thought, but held my peace.

"Usually, with older boys and teachers, I let them do all the running. But Peter was even more scared than I was. He kept telling me that it was wrong for two men to fall in love, to kiss, even to touch each other's hands."

"You believed all that crap?"

"I'd never thought about it before. I mean, all the boys did it, and half the teachers. Nobody thought much about it—we just knew it wasn't something that you talked about afterwards, and you certainly didn't tell your parents. Sometimes there was a bit of trouble, two boys would get a bit too serious, and one of them would suddenly disappear in the school hols and not come back. But most of the time we just got on with it."

"Sounds like a great school. Think they're looking for teachers?"

He shuffled a little closer to me; there was a cool breeze coming off the sea. Our legs touched.

"So when it happened for the first time, it was me that started. He was so frightened, but then, I suppose, nature took over."

"Yeah. It has a habit of doing that. And afterwards?"

"You can imagine. He felt so guilty. He said he would have to ask the college not to send him; he would apply for a transfer or go on a pilgrimage or something. But the next day he was back, and instead of talking about Bible studies he spent the whole lesson telling me that the sins of the flesh would condemn our souls to eternal fire, and so on."

"And then?"

"He fucked me again."

"How was it?"

Henry pressed his leg against mine; one hand was in his crotch. "Wonderful."

"Better than me?" I reached around and grabbed his ass.

"Not the first couple of times. But he learned fast."

"The student became the teacher?"

"I suppose so. And the thing was, well, I don't really know why this happened, what with him being a deacon and feeling so guilty and lecturing me all the time, which was really boring, but...I fell in love with him."

"Forbidden fruit tastes sweeter." I could picture the two of them, Peter with his cassock pulled up, Henry with his school pants pulled down, fucking beneath the trees by the lakes, books and lessons forgotten, just the urgency of cock and ass. I was rock hard, and slipped my hand inside his waistband. He fidgeted around until I could get a finger between his cheeks and find his hole.

"It went on for a few weeks, and every time he said it would be the last. And then, just before the exams, he disappeared, and I never heard from him again. I tried to ask what had happened to him, but nobody would say a thing. Of course, I flunked all my exams. Even divinity. Didn't pass a single one. Bang went all of Mother and Father's dreams of getting me into a good college. Now they're trying to get me in through the back door, pulling in favors to find me a job as a verger or something in a little rural parish where they're absolutely desperate for whatever they can get. In other words, they're ashamed and they want to get rid of me."

"Did they find out?"

"Nothing's ever been said. Father went storming in to see the headmaster, demanding to know why his son had done so badly, but when he came out he was very quiet and wouldn't discuss it. So

I suppose that old bastard told him something. People must have known. It was impossible to keep secrets, and we weren't as careful as we should have been. And now they watch me all the time."

"Your parents? The truth this time, please."

"They think I'm some kind of whore."

I pushed around his hole. "Yeah? Think they might have a reason for that?"

He gasped and bit his lip. "It's not fair. Everyone else is allowed to do whatever they want to. Half the chaps I was at school with are engaged or even married now, and the others are all boasting about how many girls they've had. They don't get consigned to some living death in the country. Oh! You're going to have to fuck me, Mitch."

"All in good time. First of all, I want some answers."

"I've told you everything."

"Why is Peter here? Don't try telling me it's a coincidence."

"It is. It's a horrible, wonderful coincidence. Until I saw him on the ferry I had absolutely no idea he was coming."

"Rubbish. You come here every year. You wrote to him and told him to meet you here."

"How could I possibly do that? I didn't know where he was."

"So you expect me to believe that, of all the places in the world, you both happened to end up on this little rock in the middle of the Mediterranean by chance?"

"I don't care what you believe, quite honestly." He moved his hand to my crotch and started rubbing. "Please just...please...oh—oh God."

I thought for a moment he'd burst into tears, but in fact, he was coming, just from the sensation of my finger up his ass. So much for fucking him. He sat there with his pants full of jizz, breathing heavily. I guess the memory of those Arcadian afternoons with Deacon Pete's dick inside him was just too much.

"I'd better go. Really. I must get back. They'll be looking for me." He stood up, my hand still awkwardly caught inside his pants, and wriggled free.

"Are you telling me the truth?" I shouted after his retreating shadow, but answer came there none.

For the first time in two days the shutters were open at Vella's bar, so I walked slowly in that direction, wondering how much, if any, of Henry's story I could believe. It seemed so farfetched—and yet coincidences do happen, people's paths cross under the strangest circumstances. Perhaps Henry had told Peter that his family came to Gozo every year, and Peter had engineered the whole thing without Henry's knowledge. That's not what Peter told me—he seemed startled, almost terrified, by Henry's presence on the island. One of them was lying. Who? The thief or the deacon?

Peter Allinson wouldn't be the first cleric to lie about sex. Western civilization is built on such lies.

I took a seat, ordered a beer and surveyed the promenade. After ten minutes, I heard footsteps running down from the Continental, pounding across the prom.

"Bill! Over here!"

XI

BILL LOOKED FURIOUS. "MITCH! WHERE THE FUCK HAVE YOU been?"

"Interrogating suspects."

"Yeah, right. While I risk my neck."

"Did anyone see you?"

"I don't think so. I heard the Jessops coming up the stairs so I had to leg it. Climbed over the balcony into the son's room. Just as well I did too."

"Why?"

Bill lifted up his shirt and showed me a loose bundle wrapped in a towel. "Jackpot."

"In Henry's room?"

"Yeah. In a sponge bag hidden in a suitcase under the bed. Looks like our little friend's been busy."

"What have you got?"

He looked around. "Not here. When the Jessops find out someone's been in their room the hotel's going to be in uproar."

"You left tracks?"

"Well excuse me for not tidying up properly, but it was either that or get caught. Next time, do it yourself."

"Okay, okay. Where shall we go?"

"Up to the barracks. You need an operational HQ, mate."

"As long as there's a lock on the door, I don't care where we go."

"Oi, enough of that. Let's get one fucking mess sorted out at a time, eh? Then you can have as much of this as you want." He squeezed his crotch. "I've got some furlough saved up for you, my boy. Wait here. I'll commandeer transport."

He shoved the bundle into my hands and marched up the road. I couldn't resist a peek. Bank notes, letters, and something gleaming in the bottom of the bag.

An engine revved.

"Come on, Mitch. Jump on." Bill sat astride a dusty, rusty motorcycle that he seemed to have conjured out of nowhere. "Don't look so bloody surprised. I know a bloke who owes me a favor. Let's go."

I climbed onto the pillion seat, wrapped my arms around Bill's waist and held on tight as we sped up the bumpy road to Victoria. I could smell his sweat mingling with the pervasive island odors of pine, dust and herbs. It was mid-afternoon now, the sun at its fiercest. Out of the corner of my eye I saw lizards scampering for cover as the bike whizzed past. We made it to the capital in less than ten minutes.

Bill was every inch the regimental sergeant major when we got to the barracks.

"I need a room with a telephone, right now."

"What's your authorization?" said the bored soldier at the front desk.

"Major Fucking Telford, you cunt. And you address me as 'sir,' private. Got that?"

"Yes sir."

"Better." Bill turned to me, a wolfish smile on his face. "These lads need to be reminded who's boss sometimes, Mitch."

The private blushed as he unhooked keys from the pegboard. "Number four, sir."

"What's your name, private?"

"Rhys, sir."

"Right, Rhys. Tell the CO I'm going to need another pair of

hands later on, and he'll need to find someone else to cover the desk. Got it?"

"Sir!"

Bill pocketed the key and led the way upstairs. "He looks useful, doesn't he?"

"Depends what for."

"Oh, you know," said Bill. "Fetching, carrying, fucking."

"Aren't I enough for you?"

"Yeah. But you're not sticking around, are you? I've got to plan ahead."

"Who knows? I might be."

He stopped on the stairs and turned around so suddenly that I bumped into him. "Don't take the piss, Mitch. I like you. I told you that. If you were serious, I'd go anywhere with you. Give up the army if necessary. But you're not. You're here for a holiday and a bit of fun, and somehow we got caught up in all this."

Jesus. A declaration of love was the last thing on my mind, especially from someone like Bill Conrad, especially when my mind was focused on catching a killer—or killers? Was the same person responsible for both deaths? And what about the blackmail? What would I find in the bag?

"Are you even listening to me?"

"Of course I am."

"Could have fucking fooled me. Think I'm in the habit of this kind of—"

Poor Bill. He looked so sad. So I stood on tiptoes, put my arm around the back of his neck and pulled him in for a kiss. "Bill, if there was any way on God's earth that you and I could be together, I'd make it work."

"But?"

"One thing at a time. Let's clean up this mess first."

"And then?"

"We'll see."

"Yeah. Right." He turned, walked ahead. "This should do you. Room four. A desk, a telephone, a bed, and there's a toilet down the hall if you need a piss. Let me know if you need anything. I'll be downstairs talking to Rhys."

"Oh for Christ's sake, Bill, come here." I pulled him into the room and kissed him again. "What do you want to hear? You're probably the best fuck I've had in my life. You're everything I could ever want in a man. But we've known each other for three days. I've got history, Bill. I've made mistakes that I need to sort out before I start something new."

"Right."

"When this is finished, take some time off. Come stay with me. See if you can persuade me there's a future for us."

"You know there is. You feel it as much as I do." He grabbed my hand and moved it down to his cock, which was rock hard inside his pants. "Nobody else does this to me. Nobody. Ever."

"Not even your wife?"

"Fuck off. I'm serious."

"So am I." I was hard too, and made him feel it.

We stood there in the bare, stuffy room, hands rubbing each other's stiff cocks, lips joining in a kiss, both contemplating a future that could never be...could it? Why couldn't it be? Possibilities flashed and tumbled like colors in a kaleidoscope.

"Come on, then," Bill said at last. "Let's get the job done." He was Sergeant Major Conrad again, albeit with a damp patch the size of a dime on the front of his pants. "What are my orders?"

I could think of several things unconnected to the deaths of Ned Porter and Joseph Vella, but with a huge and totally uncharacteristic effort I cleared my mind of sex and concentrated on something else.

"First we're going to see what's in this bag." I put Henry's loot on the desk. "Then, I'm going to have to make some calls and send some telegrams. I need a few key pieces of information. Do they have phone directories at the front desk?"

"Of course."

"Right. Let's do it."

The time had come to arrive at a hypothesis—and to act on it. By now, Hercule Poirot or Miss Marple would have had that moment when they say, "Of course! I have been so stupid! It was staring me in the face all along!" much to the bafflement of their readers. They would then summon all the main characters in the lounge before a long and entertaining denouement in which the chief suspect would say, "you haven't got a shred of evidence for this fantastic story." And then—aha! Evidence would be produced, the guilty would be led off cursing and we would turn off the lights and retire to bed.

I, however, was still in the dark—a somewhat lust-fuddled dark at that—but I had my suspicions and was prepared to act on them.

I emptied the bag.

A pair of heavy diamond and sapphire earrings tumbled out with a crash.

"Bingo," said Bill. "That solves that mystery."

"But why? Why would he steal them?"

"I dunno. Perhaps he's a drag queen."

"Local currency. English currency—phew! Quite a nice little haul. About a hundred pounds. And—here we are. Forty U.S. dollars. Just the amount that went missing from my wallet."

"Fucking tea leaf. Want me to call the cops?"

"Definitely not. We can deal with Henry Jessop."

"Oh yeah?" Bill looked a little too interested.

"Not like that. At least, not yet. Now, what's this?"

A bundle of letters on pink notepaper, tied with a ribbon. Six in all, no envelopes. Addressed to "Fancy" in a loose, flowing hand, blue ink. Signed, "your ever-loving Claire"; "yours forever, Claire"; "adoringly, Claire"; "heartbroken, Claire"; "in anger, Claire" and, finally, just "Claire." It was easy to read in these letters the brief and predictable arc of an affair, passion leading to infatuation, disappointment, fury and resignation. She made assignations that were broken. She chided, she coaxed, she blamed. There was nothing compromising other than the shame of a woman putting herself at the mercy of a man. But where had the letters come from? To whom were they addressed? And why did Henry Jessop steal them?

All that was left was another letter, this one in a plain envelope bearing an English stamp. It was addressed to Miss Patricia Porter, at her home address in England, and the postmark was eighteen months ago. It had been neatly opened with a paperknife.

Patricia Porter—Ned's sister. Now, who on earth would have a letter addressed to Patricia Porter? And why had it been stolen?

Surely the only people on the islands who might have written to Pat were her brother, Ned, and his grieving lover, Alf. I looked at the date again: it was after Ned's death. It must have been from Alf. He'd told me he'd written to her after Ned's death, trying to find out if she knew anything. How had the letter come all the way back here? Had it, perhaps, been returned to sender, and then stolen from Alf's barracks? Why? The answer must be here. My "click" moment was coming. My hypothesis was forming.

With sweating fingers, I pulled the letter out.

Two sheets of paper, covered in neat handwriting. An educated hand—a feminine hand, I guessed at first sight, and a glance at the signature confirmed it.

"Yours sincerely, Alice Butterworth."

Alice Butterworth? Who the hell was Alice Butterworth, and why was she entering the stage so late in the drama? What had she written to Pat Porter, and how in God's name had the letter come back here to Gozo? Had Pat herself returned?

8a Chicheley Street
London SW

Dear Miss Porter,

This is the fourth time I have written to you since your poor father died, on the advice of his solicitors, Messrs Abelforth. As I have not yet received a reply, I will now be placing the matter in their hands, and you will be hearing from them shortly. They have given me to understand that if you do not send me the money that is owed me, I will be within my rights to employ bailiffs to destrain goods to the value of that sum, with all costs borne by your father's estate.

As I have mentioned before, I have a letter from your father in which he promised me a modest bequest in recognition of the services I rendered him in the last five years of his life—services that perhaps would have been more properly rendered by a dutiful daughter, but I need scarcely remind you that you were unable or unwilling to perform them. The sum can mean so little to you, particularly now as I understand you have inherited the entire estate after the tragic death of your poor brother, so shortly after you had visited him in Malta. But it would mean a great deal to me.

Your father gave me to understand that the terms of the bequest were made explicit in his will, but as no will has come to light, I am entirely dependent on you, as next of kin and now sole heir, to honour his wishes. I hesitate to press the claims of friendship, as they clearly mean nothing to you, but I would remind you that I did all I could to help you and your young man during your father's ill health, and to shield you from the worst of his disapproval and anger. He was terribly distressed that the two of you ran off as you did just at the time when he needed you most. You were present at the death, but that's about all you managed. It was I, you will remember, who took care of him, who organised the funeral. I did not think it right to remind you on that sad day of your financial obligations towards me, trusting—wrongly, as it turned out—in your good nature.

Messrs Abelforth will be in contact soon, and if you are no longer receiving letters at this address, they assure me that they will be able to find you.

Yours sincerely,
Alice Butterworth.

A letter that posed more questions than it answered. My little house of cards toppled under the weight of supposition. But there was one more item in Henry Jessop's swag bag. A rectangle of card, ripped along one edge.

I turned it over. A photograph. A naked man, the head missing, but the body gloriously, fully intact.

My head was spinning. I felt drunk. Bill watched me with concern. "You all right, Mitch? Look like you've seen a ghost."

"A ghost. Yes. I think that's exactly what I have seen."

"What are you on about?"

"Every single person on this island has been lying to me," I said. "With one exception."

"Yeah. Me."

"Exactly. Now I need those phone books, and I need to send some telegrams. Can you make that happen?"

"That's what I'm here for, sir," said Bill. He kissed me on the back of the neck, his stubbly chin connecting directly with some nerve center in my brain that controlled my dick, then bounded downstairs.

I had my hypothesis. Now I needed to test it.

A couple hours later I was in the lobby of the Continental Hotel playing the bluff American holidaymaker for all I was worth.

"Hey! Jessops! How are you doing?"

They tried to get past me, but I was not so easily put off.

"Please join me for cocktails this evening. I've decided to go home tomorrow—urgent business back in London, you understand, lives to save—and I really can't leave without saying a proper good-bye to all my new friends."

"I'm afraid we will not be—"

"Of course, of course, you don't drink. I'll make sure there's something suitable. Did you try the lemonade? It's sensational. And of course you must bring Henry. What a nice kid, you should be really proud of him. Say, where is Henry? I haven't seen him for a while. You okay, Ma'am? You look a little pale. You should sit down. Hey! Ralph! Glass of water for Mrs. Jessop! You'll be here at eight, won't you folks? Don't want to have to send out a search party!"

That was enough to warn them. "Thank you," said Mr. Jessop, through bloodless lips. His wife looked quite blue. I moved on.

"Ah, Tilly! Glad I caught you. Could you prepare my bill? I'm checking out in the morning."

"What? Oh, Mitch, no! Why ever are you leaving us? I do hope it's not because of what I said the other day. I thought we'd straightened all that out."

"Not at all. If it was up to me I'd stay here all summer. But I'm afraid duty calls."

"Really? What's so important that it can tear you away from us?"

"A case I'm involved in is about to reach an unexpected crisis."

"I see. Well, of course, if it's a matter of life and death..."

"It is. Very much so."

"I do hope you'll be back, though."

"Definitely. I love it here, and I've made some great friends. I'll come back to the Continental as long as you're here to welcome me."

"In that case," she said, with her loveliest movie-star smile, "I look forward to many more happy summers together, Mitch. You're one of the family now."

"Cocktails at eight, yes? For everyone. Make sure Martin comes. Add it to my bill. Oh, excuse me, Tilly. There's Claire. You know how busy she gets in the evenings. I wouldn't want to miss her."

We exchanged an amused glance, both of us well aware of the nature of La Sutherland's social engagements, and I moved on.

"Claire! Claire! A word!"

"Why, Mitch. How lovely to see you." She looked over my shoulder at a young, handsome man who was waiting at the door. "Have a lovely evening. Toodle-oo!"

I lowered my voice. "Want your earrings back?"

"What?"

"And your letters?"

"Letters? I don't know what you're talking about."

"Then why are you whispering?"

"Well, really."

"Cocktails, here, eight o'clock. Bring your handsome young friend if you wish, although you might not want him to hear what I'm going to say."

She strutted off, arms extended, bracelets clattering, "Marco, darling!" But she looked over her shoulder on the way out and gave me a businesslike nod.

All I had to do now was wait. I had already invited the Captain by telephone, and Bill had his instructions: he was to meet me at the Continental, with whatever information he had been able to collect from the Victoria barracks, at 7:45 p.m. And there was one more important delivery he would make, if the relevant permissions and transportation were forthcoming.

Alf Lutterall.

I took a seat in the lounge with a good view of the lobby, ordered tea and read a book. There was activity all around me—boats speeding across the straits from Valetta, motorbikes and cars plying the island streets, people coming to my party or perhaps getting as far away as possible—and in the air, through the wires, phone calls and cables spanning the continents.

Captain Hathaway arrived first, dressed in his smartest blue blazer and white linen pants, his cap firmly on his head.

"Here I am, reporting for duty."

"Do you have what I asked for?"

"I hope so."

"Good. Take a seat at the table. Drinks will be served when the others arrive. Forgive me for not being more sociable. I have to keep an eye on things."

"Understood, old boy." The Captain did as he was told, fiddling nervously with his buttons. He knew all too well that the crimes he had committed could land him in a prison cell for the rest of his days. He was taking a big risk.

Between paragraphs of Christie I surveyed the lobby. Nothing untoward happened. Tilly was behind the desk, ordering paperwork, speaking to the staff. Stella the housekeeper came in, had a word with Tilly then returned to the kitchen. A couple of other guests drifted through, asking about dinner.

Time passed slowly.

Bill appeared at the door, saluted me and left. That told me what I needed to know. All that was left was to wait for the other guests at my cocktail party.

Claire sashayed into the lobby, high heels ringing out on the stone floor. She'd certainly dressed the part—an elegant, bright-blue cocktail frock, liberally sequined; jewels at her ears, throat and wrists; hair and makeup the full theatrical mask. She was first and always an actress—good at dissembling. If there were revelations or accusations, she would take them without blinking, sure of her lines.

"Mitch, darling." She bent down and kissed the air around my face. "Are there drinks? I was promised drinks."

"Coming right up. Tilly? Tilly!"

I called across the lobby, but Tilly was not there. Instead, Martin came bustling out from the kitchen. "Yes, yes, everything's ready. Ralph? Set up over there, please, on the big table in the lounge. That's it. I've made big jugs of Tom Collins. That'll do, won't it? Nice and cold on a warm evening. Phew!" He mopped his brow which was wet with sweat, his blond hair sticking darkly to the skin. "I'm boiling! And there's lemonade for the non-drinkers. Come on, Ralph! Get pouring! Miss Sutherland." He bowed elegantly. "May I offer you a cocktail?"

"You may," said Claire, extending an encrusted hand, which Martin kissed. He too was playing a part, in his open-necked white shirt, spiffy ascot and canvas shoes. Only the sweat gave the game away.

"Where is Mrs. Dear?" I asked. "I specifically wanted to thank her for her hospitality during my stay."

"She's just coming, Mitch," said Martin. "Finishing off a few things in the kitchen with Stella. Just some canapés, you know. Fiddly little things, but she likes 'em."

"Ah," I said, "here come the Jessops. The full set! I'm so pleased." I walked towards father, mother and son with arms extended in greeting. They froze, as if all three of them might bolt for the door. "Come and have a drink. Three lemonades, I suppose? Sure I can't tempt you to something harder?"

Henry was ashen, his eyes bloodshot as if he had been crying. If ever a man needed a drink it was him, but he meekly accepted lemonade and took a seat. His parents posted themselves on either side, like guards.

"Very good. Once Tilly joins us, we're all here. All my lovely Gozo friends," I said, my voice dripping sincerity. "At least, all those who are able to join us." I paused; nobody would meet my eye. "Those who haven't, you know, died."

The silence was broken by Claire's carrying theatrical voice. "Does anyone have a light? I appear to have left mine in my other purse."

Martin was quick to oblige with matches. His hands were shaking, and the flame flickered as it danced around the end of Claire's cigarette.

She took a long drag. "That's better. Lovely drinks, by the way. So sorry we're losing you, Mitch, just as we were all getting so cozy together."

"I know, I know. But duty calls. Lives to save, you know."

"Now, does everyone have what they need?" asked Martin, bustling around, handing drinks, straightening cushions. "Because if you don't mind, I really need to get on with arrangements for dinner."

"Sit down, Martin. I'm sure Ralph and Stella can manage between them."

"Oh, but I'd better go and check in the kitchen..."

"Tilly is taking care of all that, isn't she? Hope she hurries up with those canapés. I'm starving. I can't wait to see what she's come up with."

"Shall I go and see?" Martin started for the door.

"No." I blocked his path. "Please, Martin. For once, you don't have to be the genial host. You can just be one of us for half an hour." He frowned. "As a special favor to me. I would be really most obliged."

He perched on a stool, but looked ready to bolt at any moment. He wouldn't get far. Guards were posted.

"Now that we're all here," I said, standing with my hands behind my back, "I wanted to tell you about something very strange that happened to me while I was here. I didn't mention it at the time because I didn't want to upset anyone, but now I'm leaving..."

"Aren't we waiting for Mrs. Dear?" said Mr. Jessop, in his most schoolmasterish voice. "I thought she was joining us."

"I have a feeling Mrs. Dear is otherwise occupied just now," I said. "Let's not wait. If I need her, I'm sure someone can go and fetch her. No, Martin. Not you. Please sit down. Refill your glass. Come on, you like a drink, don't you?"

"Oh well, if you insist." Martin gulped down a second Tom Collins. That seemed to calm him.

I paced around the room, keeping an eye on all of my scattered audience. Everyone was engaged in some sort of activity—fiddling with buttons, biting nails, tapping the ash off a cigarette—that allowed them not to look at me.

"It happened in Valetta, of all places. I suppose I should have been more careful—it's a port, after all, and ports are always dangerous places. All sorts of riffraff coming and going. Anyway, to cut a long story short, someone whacked me over the head, knocked me out."

"Oh, Mitch, how frightful for you," said Claire. "A blow to the head is terribly dangerous. But of course you're a doctor, you'd know that…" She ran out of steam and took a drink.

"Are you quite well now, Dr. Mitchell?" This from Mrs. Jessop, sitting with her knees clamped together, handbag in her lap.

"Absolutely fine, thank you ma'am."

"I suppose you were robbed."

"Funnily enough, no. Not there, at least."

"You mean…oh."

"Oh indeed. As we all know, don't we, someone has been helping themselves rather too freely to the contents of other people's rooms. I must say, I was shocked that this sort of thing went on at the Continental, Martin. Burglary."

"Awfully sorry," said Martin. "Got the local coppers onto it, but you know what they're like. Pretty useless bunch."

"Aren't they just."

"I say," he went on, "did you tell them about that biff to the head? Can't have that. Bad for business. Gives the whole country a bad reputation."

"I didn't go to the police, no," I said. "As you say, Martin, they're not much use."

"Bad show. No harm done, though."

"In the event, you see, I didn't need the police. I worked this one out for myself."

Silence in the lounge. A few other guests passed through the lobby, looked in and moved on. Stella came up with a plate of olives and cheese—that stinky local stuff that Bill had such a taste for.

"Is Mrs. Dear joining us, Stella?" I asked.

"I thought she was up here with you, sir."

Martin's knuckles were white as he gripped his drink; any more pressure and the glass would shatter.

"Never mind. Mmm, that looks delicious. Now, does everyone have drinks? Cigarettes?"

"Oh, what the hell," said Henry, reaching out for a cocktail.

"Henry!" said his parents in unison.

"Give the kid a break," I said. "He's not a child any more, is he? He's a man. Come on, Henry. Fill your boots."

He took the glass and stood by the windows at the back of the lounge; they looked out to a tiny paved courtyard behind which the cliffs continued their rise above the town. No escape that way, just in case anyone thought of making a run for it.

"Anyway, where was I? Let me see…" I counted things off on my fingers. "The attack in Valetta, the burglaries in the hotel, what else was there? I'm sure there was something…" I was playing for time, half hoping that Bill would deliver telegrams that his little protégé Private Rhys was under strict instructions to bring down from Victoria the minute they arrived. Without them I was improvising, however certain my hypothesis. But delivery came there none. "Oh yes, of course. How could I forget? A dead body."

The silence was punctuated by the clink of ice as Martin poured himself a third glass of Tom Collins.

"Quite an eventful few days, wouldn't you say? Not exactly the restful holiday I was hoping for." I laughed. "It'll be a relief to get back to work, to be honest."

Six pairs of eyes stared at the carpet, the plants, the windows—anything but me, or each other.

"It's like being in a detective novel, isn't it? All those unexplained crimes, and a lot of people with secrets from each other. Anyone else here read Agatha Christie?"

"I have appeared in some of her works for the stage," said Claire, rather grandly.

"How 'bout you, Jessops?"

"We read serious literature," said Mr. Jessop.

"Well then, allow me to tell you a story. Is everyone ready?"

"What is all this about, Mitch?" Claire was getting restless. "I have an appointment. I thought you said... Well, never mind."

"I'll come to that," I said, aware that she was eager to get her letters back. "For the time being, indulge me. I will try to keep things brief. But where to begin?" I rubbed my forehead, as if thinking hard, still glancing at the door for a delivery that never came. "I have it. My story begins here at the Continental Hotel, two years ago."

"I thought you said this was your first visit," said Martin, his speech starting to slur. "Never set foot on the island before."

"Quite right," I said. "But others were here before me, and others will remain when I leave, I have no doubt. Only two years ago— such a short time, but so much has changed. The Continental was under different management, to begin with."

"The dear Andersons," said Claire. "How we miss them." She looked around the lounge. "Where *is* Tilly? Shouldn't she be here?"

"She should, Claire, but I have a feeling she's suddenly rather busy. As you mentioned the Andersons, let's begin with them. A nice couple, everyone tells me. You all knew them, didn't you?"

"Not me," said Martin.

"What? I thought they were great friends of your wife's."

"Yes, yes, of course." He looked flustered. "I mean, I saw them a couple of times back in England, you know, but I never really knew them."

"And yet here you are, two years later, running their hotel."

All eyes turned to Martin, who stared gloomily into his glass. "Running it into the ground would be more accurate.'"

"Everyone was so surprised when they decided to sell, weren't they, Captain Hathaway?"

"Rather. Told me they'd be here for keeps. Absolutely no desire to return to England, and I for one can't blame them. Horrible cold place. Cold people."

"And yet, without warning, they packed up and left a thriving business and all the friends they'd made over the years, without explanation. Did they ever tell your wife why they were selling, Martin?"

"You'd have to ask her."

"I'd love to. But as she's not here, perhaps you can enlighten us."

"All I can say was that Tilly was absolutely thrilled when they offered it to her. She'd come into a pot of money, you see, and we'd always talked about running a little hotel. Sort of a pipe dream I suppose you'd call it, but suddenly there it was being handed to us on a plate, and we had the wherewithal, you see. Too good to be true."

"How very fortunate for you—and for us, who have enjoyed your hospitality."

"Hospitality?" barked Claire. "I've been burgled. You yourself, Mitch, have been insulted—I was there, I heard it for myself. Added to all those other troubles... Well, I shan't be returning. That's that. I've decided."

"Now, Claire," I said, "let's not make any rash decisions. I'm sure *you'll* be here next summer, at least."

"Don't talk in riddles, Mitch. Get on with the story. Your audience is restless."

"You're right. Two years ago. The Andersons' last summer. The year that Ned Porter died. I'm sure everyone remembers that, or at least heard about it. Tilly was telling me just the other day how upset she got thinking about it, and she wasn't even here. A tragedy. A young man just starting out in life. What made him so desperate that he would throw himself off a cliff? Suicide, that's what everyone said, wasn't it? The police had the note that Ned had written to his commanding officer. But that struck me as strange. If you're going to kill yourself, who do you write to? Your boss or your loved ones?"

"What is the point of this ridiculous story?" said Mr. Jessop. "You're upsetting my wife."

"Mrs. Jessop is such a nervous creature," I said. "Maybe I should prescribe her a tonic. In the meantime, a drink would do just as well. And the point of this story is that everything leads back to the death of Ned Porter. He wrote to his CO—a man whom he disliked and feared. Not to his best friend, not even to his sister, who had only just visited from England. That seems strange, and very much out of character. But then, suicide was out of character too. Ned Porter was a happy, popular young man with everything to live for. Wasn't he, Captain Hathaway?"

"Oh yes, he always seemed a cheerful sort. Nothing morbid about him."

"And he was in love."

"An unhappy love, perhaps," said Henry. It was the first time he had spoken.

"No. He was very happy. He loved a man who loved him in return." *A man*—it was out at last. Throats were cleared, feet shuffled. "Alf Lutterall, a private at the garrison in Valetta. They made plans for a future together—to leave the army, to travel…they didn't much care what or where. They had each other. And then Ned was taken away. Alf, who loved him with all his heart, had his future stolen from him."

"Suicide is such a selfish crime," said Claire, "however desperately sorry for these poor chaps one must feel."

"But murder," I said, "is even more so. Murder is the ultimate selfish act—taking another life for your own benefit."

"But who could possibly benefit from Ned's death?" asked the Captain. "That's what I can't understand. These boys have nothing. That's why they're always touching one for a few bob."

"On the contrary, Ned was rather well off—or would have been, if he'd survived. His father wasn't a millionaire, but he was quite comfortable. Ned would have inherited half his estate—but he died too soon, a week or so before his father."

"You mean," said Henry, interested despite himself, "that someone murdered him for his inheritance?"

"Exactly so. And that person is on the island now."

XII

Everyone stared at me, waiting for an explanation.

Captain Hathaway broke the silence. "Dear boy, you're not seriously suggesting that one of us is a murderer, are you? Things like that simply don't happen."

"For goodness' sake, Dr. Mitchell," whimpered Mrs. Jessop, "tell us what you want to tell us and let us go. This is unbearable."

I had no intention of letting them off the hook that easily—besides, it was in the telling of the story that I hoped to ascertain for certain the identity of the guilty party. In the absence of any hard evidence—nothing had been delivered from the barracks at Victoria—I was putting my hypothesis under considerable stress. I just hoped that someone would crack and confess, or otherwise give themselves away. A desperate action, perhaps. A gun waved around the Continental lounge, a bolt for the door.

"Everyone all right for drinks?"

"Oh for Christ's sake, Mitch," It was Martin, already half drunk. "Can I go, at least? I have other guests to take care of."

"Let's not break up the party yet, please. The fun is only just beginning. Now, where was I? Oh, yes. Two years ago, just before Ned Porter died, he had a visit from his sister Patricia. Nobody here met her, did they?"

There was a general shrugging and nodding of heads.

"From what I understand she was not the sort of person who would make a big impression. Quiet, thin, mousy—nobody would give her a second look. She was the one who stayed at home while her brother Ned travelled around the world with the army. Their parents were in poor health—Patricia had to nurse her mother in her final illness, and when she died the poor girl had the sole care of her father. Imagine it—a young woman just starting out in life, trapped into being a nurse and a drudge for a difficult old man, while her brother was free. She loved her brother, but she resented him as well, particularly as he would inherit half her parents' estate when the father died. Why should he have all that money, when he hadn't been there to earn it? She'd worked her fingers to the bone, sacrificed herself for her parents' care, and she deserved to be rewarded. As time went by, the old man started to get sick, and Patricia became obsessed by the idea of the inheritance. She was determined to keep every last penny—and to that end, she hatched a plan to rob her brother of his share. But how could she disinherit him? He was the apple of his father's eye. There were only two ways of doing it. Firstly, she could discredit him in some way, so that Mr. Porter cut him off without a penny. Secondly, she could kill him. And so, as her father entered his final illness, she left him in the care of a paid nurse and travelled out to Malta to see Ned one last time."

A lot of this was improvisation; I had no evidence, and my reading of human nature is, as we all know, far too influenced by detective fiction. However, the audience seemed to be lapping it up, so I continued with the narrative I had concocted.

"She traveled all the way to Malta and spent a couple days playing the loving sister. Ned brought her over to Gozo, showed her the sights and took her into his confidence. He was in love, he told her, and planning to leave the army to start a new life some-where. Oh, she was so delighted, so pleased for him. Who was the lucky girl, she asked? She couldn't wait to meet her new sister-in-law! And then Ned told her the truth, because he was an honest person, and he believed that his sister loved him enough to under-stand. He wasn't in love with a girl—he was in love with a man, a soldier in the same regiment, Alf Lutterall. This was just what Patricia had been waiting for—an opportunity to discredit her brother, to blacken his name. She was so careful—she pretended she was happy for him, but she kept saying how awful it would be if father found out, how he'd cut him off without a penny. But Ned didn't give a damn. He laughed in her face, told her he didn't care what the old man thought, he and Alf just wanted to be free and together.

"This was a setback for Patricia. She thought she could manipulate Ned into giving up his share of the estate, but he didn't care about the money. I suppose she could have gone straight home and told her father everything, but it was too great a risk. What if Mr. Porter was so disgusted with her tale-bearing that he left all the money to someone else? The kind nurse, for instance, Alice Butterworth. Or the stray dogs' home. She could easily lose the lot. Mr. Porter was a stubborn old man with little love for his children; he hadn't even made a will, he cared so little for them. They would inherit as next of kin, but he made it quite clear he didn't give a damn. Without a will to work on, Patricia Porter was entirely at the mercy of the bank, or whoever ended up administrating her father's estate. They wouldn't be interested in any tittle-tattle about her brother's love life. She would surely lose the money she believed was rightly hers.

"And so, by his honesty, courage and optimism, Ned Porter sealed his fate. Patricia had only one option left to her: murder."

Martin interrupted again. "Are we supposed to believe that this mousy little girl murdered her own brother? Seems bloody unlikely from all you've told us. Why didn't he just tick her off and get rid of her?"

"I don't imagine he suspected a thing."

"What, she took him by surprise? That's ridiculous. He was a soldier. She was just a…just a…"

"Women," said Claire Sutherland, with all the dignity she could muster, "are quite capable of murder, thank you very much."

All eyes in the room were on her. Was this the confession I'd been waiting for? Was my hypothesis about to be proven?

"I don't know why you're all looking at me like that. I didn't kill him. I never even met him or his wretched sister."

"Ah, but you did, Claire. You told me yourself that you had seen a mousy young woman at the Continental. A bluestocking, you called her. The summer before last, you said."

"That could be anyone. Anyway, what of it? People come and go through here all the time."

"But that particular year, at that particular time, just before the death of Ned Porter, and there was someone in this very room answering to her description. Do you remember what you told me?"

"I really couldn't say." Claire was getting nervous and fidgety, no longer sure of her lines.

"You said that the most unlikely people brought guests to the Continental. You even saw this skinny, plain young woman carrying on with a priest! A man of the cloth! Do you recall?"

"Something of the sort, but it could have been someone entirely different."

"I think not. What did the priest look like, Claire? Cast your mind back."

"Oh, you know. Priestlike. Tall. Dark. Handsome."

"What color was his hair?"

"You can't expect me to remember details like that after such a long time."

"You're an actress, Claire. You pick up on these details. Come on. Think."

"Dark hair, then. Not jet black like the local men, but very dark brown."

"There you are. A handsome young clergyman with dark hair. Does that sound familiar?"

Henry was squirming in his seat as if he was desperate to go to the bathroom. I left him to stew for now.

"Well I'm bloody confused," said the Captain. "What's this priest got to do with anything? Island's crawling with them, like black beetles—always turning up where they're not wanted. Admittedly they don't venture in here much, at least they didn't in the old days. But still, I don't see what you're driving at."

"Patricia Porter didn't come to Malta alone," I said.

"You mean she travelled with a priest?" said the Captain. "Was she devout?"

"Far from it. The clerical garb was a disguise, and a very effective one. As you say, the island's crawling with priests. Nobody's going to notice one more."

"Is anyone in this story who they appear to be?" said Mr. Jessop.

"Yes. One person: Ned Porter. He knew exactly who and what he was, and he never tried to hide it from anyone. And that, in a roundabout way, is why he died. If he'd been willing to lie and to hide, he might still be living today. But Ned was happy and in love with another man."

"Disgusting," said Mr. Jessop, which, considering that at least three of us in the room were man-lovers like Ned, was met with a frosty silence.

"Live and let live, Mr. Jessop," said Claire. "Surely you have learned that from your regular trips to the Continental. I have often wondered why you come here, considering your somewhat Victorian views. Unless, of course, you and your wife have a secret as well."

"How dare you?" said Mr. Jessop, but then the wind went out of his sails. He must have guessed that I knew about Henry.

"May I continue?"

"I wish you bloody would," said Martin.

"Patricia had an accomplice on Malta, someone who traveled with her and was just as prepared as she was to do whatever it took to secure the inheritance. He kept out of the way, and only went around in disguise, but when Patricia realized that she had to act quickly, he came over to Gozo and they hatched a plan. He would gain Ned's confidence, get him alone and then murder him. So this false priest befriended Ned, seduced him perhaps, and then smashed his head in with a rock. After that it was a simple matter to push the body from one of the highest cliffs on the island, forge a suicide note which was posted to Ned's CO, plant some evidence of blackmail and leave the rest to supposition. Patricia made a point of leaving Malta a day or two before Ned's death, so that she was above suspicion. Her accomplice stayed around to report on the investigation, and when he was satisfied that the police and the military authorities had swallowed the suicide story, he either rejoined her in England or waited for her here. Patricia had business to attend to at home—her father was near death, and she had to be present at the end and play the grieving daughter. But all the time she was making her plans and waiting for the money to come through.

"She didn't have to wait long. The old man was intestate, which now worked to her advantage. Patricia would inherit the lot. Her father promised gifts to one or two people, including the nurse, Alice Butterworth, but none of it was legally enforceable. Probate was granted in a few months, and Patricia was suddenly a rich young woman. And she knew exactly what she was going to spend the money on. She'd been laying her plans very carefully, getting all the pieces in position. This wasn't the first crime that Patricia Porter had committed. Everyone thought she was just what she appeared to be, a quiet spinster who would never amount to anything. It was good camouflage. For some years, Patricia Porter had been an active and accomplished blackmailer. She knew exactly how to sniff out weakness and secrecy, and she exploited it brilliantly. And now, when she had pulled off the biggest crime of her career, she was ready to move onto greener pastures. While she was in Malta, she'd stumbled upon the most lucrative nest of blackmail victims imaginable—a whole hotel full of people with secrets. She couldn't believe her luck. She wanted it—and in order to exploit it, she had to control it. And so she got to work on the only people who stood between her and this revolting life of crime—the owners of the Continental."

I paused a while to let the words sink in. Who would get there first? Captain Hathaway? The Jessops, father, mother or son? Claire? Martin?

"What the hell are you suggesting?" Martin, of course, as I knew it would be. The outraged husband. "Do you seriously believe that... no, it's too ridiculous."

"Believe what, Martin?"

"That *Tilly* is somehow involved in this?"

"Is that what I'm suggesting?"

"It bloody better not be. Nobody insults my wife like that. And anyway, how on earth could she be this Porter person? She's nothing like her. You're barking up the wrong tree, old chap." He poured himself a long drink and sighed. "Just a load of nonsense from beginning to end."

"Perhaps Tilly herself would like to comment on that?"

"Yes, Martin," said Claire, in vindictive tones, "where exactly is Tilly?"

"She's busy running the hotel if that's quite all right with you. Which is what I should be doing, instead of sitting here listening to Mitch's ridiculous fantasies."

Martin got up, but I moved to block the door. "Not quite yet, Martin, if that's all right. There's just one more thing that I wanted to mention. While Patricia's partner was lying low in Malta, he made one crucial mistake. He left a track."

"What sort of track?" He tried to make it sound trivial, silly. "A footprint?"

"Better than that. A photograph."

"Let's see it, then."

"Very well." I produced the tattered photograph from my pocket. A headless man, the body naked, the cock visible and erect. I placed it on the table. Mrs. Jessop screamed. Her husband shielded her. Claire and Henry both leaned forward to have a better look. The Captain smiled.

"Anyone recognize him?"

Heads were shaken around the room. Henry began to say "It's not..." but then stopped and blushed.

"No, Henry. It's not Peter Allinson, the other clergyman in the story. Nor, indeed, is it our mysterious murdering priest. It's someone that he met while he was on the island, after Pat had left, after the murder was committed, when he was lonely and remorseful, wondering if he'd done the right thing. He went to a bar one night and got drunk. One of the waiters made friends with him, and one thing led to another. They went off to a secret place together and made love." I refrained from saying "fuck" only for the sake of Mrs. Jessop. "After it was over, the young waiter gave his new friend a keepsake—a photograph of himself. And the false priest, the murderer, the blackmailer's accomplice, could never quite bring himself to throw it away. He had one scrap of decent feeling in him—and he couldn't help wondering if life could have turned out better if he hadn't come under the thumb of Patricia Porter. But she had him exactly where she wanted him."

"She was blackmailing him too?" asked Claire.

"Precisely. He feared her, but he loved her as well, in the way that the very weak will always fear and love the very strong. Just for a moment, when Patricia had gone home and the killer was left alone, he thought about escaping her—running off with that waiter and starting again. But of course he didn't. He was in too deep. But he kept the photograph to remind himself that he could be free if he chose."

"And who is it?" asked Henry.

"The killer tried to conceal the identity of his lover by tearing off the top part of the picture—the face. He knew he was making himself vulnerable, but even then he couldn't bear to throw the past away. Now, is there anyone here who can tell us who is in the photograph?"

The Captain sat back in his chair and folded his arms. "I can. That photograph is my handiwork."

"Go on."

"It's Joseph Vella."

"Joseph Vella," I said. "Whose body was found at the foot of the very same cliffs, the temple smashed by repeated blows from a rock."

"I don't see what you're getting at," said Martin. "I know I'm not much in the brains department—I leave that to my wife—but I am completely baffled."

"There's one more piece of information that I think will help," I said. "I need the answer to a very simple question."

"Fire away," said Martin. "I've got nothing to hide."

"It's not for you," I said. "It's for Henry."

"What has my son got to do with—" blustered Mr. Jessop, but I interrupted.

"Henry—where did you find that photograph?"

All eyes turned to Henry, who blushed deeply, just as he had when I was fucking him. How much did his parents know about his activities on the island—with me, with Deacon Peter, and in the rooms of his fellow guests at the Continental? Were they all in it together, or was he a free agent? That didn't matter right now. What mattered was that Henry held the one piece of information on which my entire hypothesis hung. If he'd stolen the photo from Captain Hathaway's house, or found it among Claire Sutherland's jewelry, I was in the shit.

It took everyone a while to realize that I had just identified the Continental Burglar. Henry knew that he was cornered, and had better make a clean breast of it.

"It was in Mr. Dear's office."

"What?" said Martin. "Absolute bloody rubbish. Anyway, what were you doing in the office? You had no right to go in there, you little thief."

"Mr. Dear!" shouted Henry's father. "How dare you!"

I held up a hand. "Quiet, please. Henry. Go on."

"Must I?"

"You must. I think someone out there would be proud of you if you confessed."

He nodded, swallowed and said "I was looking for money, or anything that I could sell. The desk drawer was unlocked. There was no cash, but I found that photo."

"Go on."

"It was in an envelope, underneath a load of paperwork and stuff."

"I don't know what you're trying to do, Mitchell," said Martin, "but the boy is lying. I've never seen that photograph before in my life. What on earth would I be doing with a picture like that? I'm a married man."

"Are you?"

"Of course I am. You all know my wife."

"We know someone who has been introduced to us as Mrs. Dear. That's not quite the same thing."

"Does anyone else follow what he's on about?"

"I think I get the gist," said the Captain. "Go on, Mitch."

"For the last few days, Henry has been helping himself to other people's belongings." I produced the sponge bag, to general astonishment. "Claire, your earrings. Forty U.S. dollars—they belong to me. You had only to ask, Henry, I'd have gladly given you the money. Some love letters—yours too, Claire. Be more careful with your private possessions in future."

"You ghastly little sneak," said Claire, glowering at Henry. "How dare you?"

"The rest is odds and ends of cash, and another letter. You really weren't cut out to be a criminal, Henry. You wouldn't have got very far on this lot."

"But why, Henry?" This from Mrs. Jessop, who looked truly stricken. "Why?"

"I can't tell you," said the boy. "It's not my secret."

"There are altogether too many secrets on this island," I said, "and two of them have led to death. It's time for honesty. Henry was planning his escape."

"Escape?" said his mother. "I don't understand. From what?"

"From you, mother!" Henry burst out. "From all of this! From being treated like a child, like a prisoner, watched all the time."

"It is for your own good," said Mr. Jessop. "If we hadn't removed you from England... Well, it's too awful to contemplate."

"But your plans didn't work, Mr. Jessop," I said. "Danger followed Henry to Gozo—by chance, I believe, but some would call it fate. The one person you most wanted to protect him from is also on the island. Henry saw him on the crossing. You didn't recognize him, of course—you'd never met him, just heard about him from your son's headmaster. A young seminarian who had been disciplined and dismissed. But Henry knew him, because he loved him. And as soon as he could get away, they met. Where was it, Henry? Across the bay, in the caves?"

"Yes."

"And together they arranged their getaway. I don't suppose it was easy to convince him, was it Henry? But you can be very persuasive when you try. You told him that you'd take care of everything. You'd raise the money for your passage off the island, and then—well, you'd both have to work. I wonder where you thought you'd go? Even if you sold Miss Sutherland's jewelry and made her pay for the letters, you'd only get as far as Sicily, perhaps mainland Italy, if you could find a boat that would take you."

"And if you think," said Claire, mustering what dignity she could, "That I would stoop to paying you for those letters, you are very much mistaken. Why, the very idea of blackmail disgusts me. Do your worst! I regret nothing!"

"And yet," I said, unwilling to let Claire claim all the moral high ground, "I presume you had paid for their return in the first place. Why else would you have a packet of compromising letters you yourself had written? Don't worry. I'm not going to ask you who 'Fancy' is. That's none of our business."

Claire blushed, and for once seemed genuinely embarrassed.

"So, Henry, what was the plan? Where are you going?"

"Sicily to start with. We thought we might get work bringing in the grape harvest or something."

"Oh Henry," sobbed Mrs. Jessop. "Oh, my little boy." Her husband put an arm around her. Any idea I may have entertained about the Jessops being international criminals, pimps or black-mailers evaporated. They were just holidaymakers, returning year after year to the same hotel, not because they particularly liked it, but because they could afford it.

"I'm sorry, Mama. I should have told you. But every time I tried to talk about it, you looked so upset, and Papa was so cross. But this is the truth." He took a deep breath. "I love Peter, and Peter loves me. We want to be together."

"But he's a priest, son," said Mr. Jessop, "and you're a child."

"He's a deacon, actually," said Henry, "but not for much longer. He decided yesterday that he's leaving the church. And I am not a child. I'm a man. I must be allowed to make my own decisions."

"I cannot stand by and let you condemn yourself."

"You must, Papa. I know what's right for me. I don't want to end up like Ned Porter. I want the future that he never had."

"And you shall have it, Henry. I imagine Peter is waiting for you right now, isn't he?"

Henry looked at his watch. "I'm very late. He must think I've got cold feet or something."

"Don't worry. We'll send someone up to the ferry port to reassure him. Is that where you were meeting?"

"How did you know?"

I tapped my temple. "Call it a lucky guess. But you'll have to find some other way to pay for your tickets."

Henry smiled for the first time all evening.

"This is all very well, Mitch," said Claire, "and of course I'm pleased to have my possessions back. But what has this got to do with the photograph...or the death of Ned Porter?"

"We know that Henry stole the photo from Martin's office."

"I absolutely refute that," said Martin.

"And the photograph is of Joseph Vella."

"Bloody rubbish," said Martin. "It's actually me, when I was, you know, doing a spot of bodybuilding."

"No," I said. "It's Joseph all right. I was familiar with his body."

"Prove it."

"Captain?"

The Captain produced a buff envelope from his blazer pocket. "This is the negative from which that print is taken," he said. "The face is quite clearly visible. Joseph Vella modelled for me on many occasions. He was rather proud of that particular photograph." He sighed. "I did several prints for him."

"Useful in his line of work," I said. "A business card, perhaps. Or, in this case, a reminder."

"Reminder of what?" said Martin.

"That he would expose you if you didn't pay up. That's where the money's been going, isn't it? You're no more of a gambler than I am. You've been paying Joseph Vella to keep his mouth shut about what happened one summer's day two years ago, when you were drunk and remorseful and you let him take you up to his little hut on the top of the cliffs. You looked different then, of course. Dark hair. Your natural color, I wonder, or did you dye it? Was it a wig?

And I suppose you wore glasses, or a false nose or something. You looked the part—a dark-haired young priest. The islands are full of them. Nobody else recognized you when you came back as Martin Dear, the blond hotelier. Different hair, different face. But Joseph remembered your body, and one day he spotted you out swimming across the bay, and he saw his opportunity."

"Good God, Mitchell, you have a sick imagination."

"Thank you, Martin. I shall take that as a compliment. Did Joseph send you the photograph straightaway? Did he get money out of you first, then use it to get more? Was he threatening to tell Tilly? How long did it go on? It must have been horrible—no wonder you've been drinking so much. And finally, you couldn't stand it any more. There was no money left, and Joseph just wouldn't give up. You couldn't go to the police of course, so you took matters into your own hands. You'd done it before. When you've killed once, it's so much easier to kill again."

"You aren't seriously suggesting that I... That it was me who..."

Whatever Martin was about to deny we would never find out. There was a crash as the hotel doors burst open, followed by a banshee wail and there, standing in the middle of the lobby's marble floor was the Black Crow, her eyes wild, hair disheveled, a stream of hysterical Maltese screeching from her lips, and her hands covered in blood.

XIII

"WHAT IS SHE SAYING? FOR GOD'S SAKE, WHAT IS SHE SAYING?" hissed Claire. "One of you must understand Maltese."

The Jessops, Martin Dear and I looked at each other and shrugged, but the Captain held up his hand. "Just a moment," he said. "I'm far from fluent, but I've picked up a few words here and there." He listened again. "There. Hear it? 'May yet. May yet.' She keeps saying it. 'May yet.'"

"May yet what, for heaven's sake?" said Claire.

"No, *mejjet*." He spelled it out for us. "It means dead."

"Who is dead?"

"Wait," said the Captain. "I'm trying to figure it out. *Alla, alla,* that means God, God. And there's *mejjet* again. The rest of it I can't quite catch. Who is dead, dear?" He spoke loud and slowly, as one would speak to a child or an idiot. "Can you tell us?"

The old woman pointed one red, reeking hand towards Martin, shrieked a few further imprecations in Maltese and rushed from the room as suddenly as she had come. We all followed her, scrambling to get out of the door and down the steps to the harbor.

The skinny body wasn't quite dead. Her head was bleeding from a massive gash that ran from above the left temple down to the corner of the eye and into the cheek: a blow from a large, blunt blade, I guessed, or a very hard piece of wood. She lay, drenched and almost drowned, her feet still in the water, her nails digging into the sand at the edge of the bay. Her neck was turned at an awkward angle, and seaweed clung to her mouth, obstructing her breathing. Her hair was plastered flat against her skull, and the black shirt and pants she was wearing were torn in places, clinging to her skinny body.

"My God," said Claire, standing in a stage attitude of shock, "who is it?"

"Stand back everyone." I knelt by the body, cleared the airways and used my handkerchief to staunch the wound. "Someone call an ambulance. She's alive. We may yet save her."

"But who is it?" repeated Claire, becoming increasingly hysterical. "Who?"

"Here's someone who can tell us."

Bill came running down from the hotel, where he had been waiting for my signal, with Alf Lutterall in tow. I had been keeping them in reserve for what I hoped would be a dramatic identification scene in the Continental lounge, but Tilly had taken matters into her own hands. "Alf, step forward, please. Do you recognize this woman?"

It was getting dark now, but the lights along the promenade lit the white, blood-smeared face quite enough for identification.

"Yes," said Alf, frowning. "It's Pat. Patricia Porter. Ned's sister."

"My God," said the Captain, "she was here all along?"

I stood. "Does nobody else recognize her?"

A tense silence, just the waters lapping, the seabirds calling eerily above the cliffs.

"Martin?"

Martin swayed and staggered on his feet, and just when it seemed that he would surely collapse, he bolted. Bill was on him in a flash, launching himself through the air to grab Martin by the legs. They fell together with a thump and a gasp onto the promenade.

"My God," said Captain Hathaway, as the scales fell from his eyes at last. "It's Tilly."

"But...but..." Claire Sutherland was struggling to comprehend. "Her hair... Her face... And where are her breasts?"

"You of all people should understand the power of theatrical illusion," I said. "The hair was bleached and set; now that it's wet she looks more like herself. The makeup has washed off her face. As for her body—well, that's why Tilly Dear never went near the water. She couldn't appear in public without her disguise—a bit of padding here and there turned skinny spinster Pat Porter into blonde bombshell Tilly Dear. Tilly hated the sea and the sun; Patricia was an excellent swimmer and climber and runner. Remember this morning at your house, Captain? When I tried to chase the person who delivered the blackmail note?"

"Her? Tilly? Well I never."

"But I don't understand," said Henry. "Who did this to her?" He glanced down at Martin who was on his knees, his arm twisted behind his back in Bill's iron grip. "Nobody had the opportunity. We were all in the hotel."

That worried me for a moment. Was it the same person who had tried to kill me, perhaps—hired and paid by Martin Dear, no doubt? Was there still some mysterious unknown? No. Of course not. The truth dawned at last.

"What you're looking at, my friends," I said, pointing down at Tilly's—Patricia's—battered, bleeding but still breathing body, "is the only real suicide on the island."

"Typical!" snapped Claire, turning on her heel and heading back to the hotel. "She even managed to mess that up."

Alf looked as if he might faint at any moment.

"Captain, could you get him up to your house, please? I'll join you as soon as the ambulance arrives."

I was trying to staunch the flow of blood from Tilly's head while checking that her airways were clear and that she was still breathing. Whatever she'd done, I still had to try to save her life—even if it was only to hand her over to the police for trial and inevitable execution. Bill, meanwhile, was sitting on top of Martin's prostrate body, pinning him with his knees and holding one arm backward in a painful twist. If Martin struggled, Bill would break his arm.

We heard the bell first, jangling as the police car hurtled down the hill from Victoria. The Captain flinched then hurried up the steps to the Continental with Alf leaning heavily on his arm. Tires scrunched on the sandy promenade, and three uniformed officers got out of the car.

"These," I said, "are the killers of Ned Porter and Joseph Vella. And, incidentally, the perpetrators of a major blackmail operation."

An ambulance joined the police car on the promenade. Tilly was loaded into one, Martin into the other.

"We will need a statement, sir," said the senior cop, who was about seven feet tall and looked as if he needed to shave three times a day. "But first, you'd better get cleaned up."

I looked down at my clothes—the smart suit and fresh shirt I'd put on for my little cocktail party—and they were covered in blood.

Bill and I washed and changed quickly, barely taking time to kiss. My responsibility now was to Alf Lutterall, and for once I was able to put my appetites second to my duty. Obviously I groped Bill to full erection before we went back downstairs, and he slipped a thick finger into my ass, but by the time we reached the lobby we were decent. Frank Southern was waiting for us. Baffled guests, some of whom had witnessed the waterfront drama, were pressing around the front desk where Claire Sutherland dispensed information and advice as to the manner born, ordering Ralph and Stella around like her own vassals.

"Now all of you listen!" she commanded, quelling the hubbub with a sparkling hand. "Dinner may be a bit late, but it will be served in the very near future. We all have to muck in together during this crisis. All for one and one for all! And if you would like to make your way to the lounge, I'm sure Ralph will find a bottle of something drinkable…"

We left her in charge and made our way down the steps, along the harbor wall, past Vella's bar (closed again) and up the steep, rubbish-strewn steps to the clifftop. Some holiday this had turned out to be—a murder, an attempt on my life, a suicide bid that may yet prove successful, three lovers in four days… Yes, I reflected, it was pretty much perfect.

Captain Hathaway had made Alf comfortable on a couch with

rugs and brandy. His eyes were closed, his face still pale, ghostly. But he looked up on our arrival, and even managed a weak smile.

"Mitch...Doc...Bill..." He tried to stand.

"You stay right there," said Frank, moving in beside him to check his pulse and feel his brow for any sign of fever. Bill, standing at my side, nudged me in the ribs. I could read his mind, and I agreed with him: Frank and Alf would make a lovely couple. Something to sort out before I left, perhaps. I had to stick around for the police investigation. What was one miracle more or less?

"What happened to them?" asked Alf, once Frank had pronounced him fit to talk and the Captain had furnished us all with drinks. The seaward windows were open, admitting the eerie sound of the shearwaters flying back to their roosts as the last light of the sun went down into the sea.

"They're gone," I said. "She'll be in the hospital for a while, then she'll join Martin in custody while the police prepare their case."

"I suppose I'll have to give evidence."

"We all will," I said. "Between us, we know everything."

"Do we?" Alf rubbed his forehead. "I feel like I don't understand anything anymore. That woman... Was that really her? Ned's sister? Was it a dream?"

"No dream," I said, sipping a whiskey. "She's been here all along, right under our noses, hiding her identity under bleached hair and makeup and padding. She was already a hardened criminal back in England; we've had a telegram from Scotland Yard that confirms they were investigating her for a string of blackmails. She was biding her time, waiting for her father to be near death before she made her decisive move."

"You mean she planned to kill Ned all along? Her own brother?"

"I think first of all she intended to force his hand by threatening to reveal his secret to their father, in the hope that Ned would renounce his share of the inheritance. That didn't work, because Ned wasn't ashamed. He wanted the world to know."

"That's what he always said," said Alf. "It was me who thought we had to hide."

"And when she realized that she couldn't blackmail him, she

resorted to the only means she had left to secure the money. She ordered Martin to kill him."

"Why in God's name would he do that?" said Frank. "He didn't seem like such a bad sort. Stupid, but fundamentally decent."

"Don't you believe it," I said. "Martin was putting on just as much of an act as his wife. He's just as greedy and immoral as she is. He spun me a lot of lies about how they were being blackmailed, how his wife was dragging them down, and at the time I believed it all. She may have been the brains in that partnership, but he was a very willing accomplice. He killed Ned by bashing his head in with a rock, then dumping him over the cliff. Patricia wrote the suicide note to Captain Haymon and planted the blackmail note in Ned's room when she was visiting. She made sure that she was out of the way when the murder took place; no suspicion must be attracted to her, the sister who inherited her father's entire estate due to a horrible coincidence."

"And I thought that the army had done it," sighed Alf. "I thought they wanted us out of the way."

"No. They are no more guilty of Ned's death than you are. Their culpability lies elsewhere."

"What do you mean?" said Frank, looking angry.

"They failed to investigate the death properly. They took everything at face value, just as Patricia hoped they would. By trying to avoid a scandal, they abetted a murderer. There will have to be an enquiry. I'll make sure of it."

"Don't stir up trouble," said Frank.

"Why not? How will things ever change if we don't?"

"I admire your ideals, Mitch, but I think you should leave the decision to Alf," said Frank. "He's the one who'll be in the spotlight. As things are, they'll probably make it up to him somehow. An honorable discharge with a generous pension—"

"You mean hush money."

Frank ignored me; he was addressing himself to Alf. "Or a good chance of promotion if he decides to stay." They looked into each other's eyes for a long time. The rest of us held our breaths. Perhaps my suspicions about Frank Southern were not entirely groundless, despite his protestations. Either that, or he was taking the good doctor act to ridiculous extremes.

"I'll do whatever Lieutenant Colonel Southern advises me to do," said Alf. "If it wasn't for him, none of this would have been sorted out. I'd have been sent back home to the loony bin. It was only because he believed me..." He swallowed hard, his eyes wet.

Frank cleared his throat. "Well, I didn't make a very good job of it, did I? Too scared of asking the right questions. Had to get expert help." He sounded gruff and embarrassed. Alf sighed, leaned into Frank until his head was resting on his chest, and closed his eyes.

"Well, you know the system better than I," I said at last. "If it was up to me, every officer who was complicit in the cover-up would be thrown out..."

"But it's not up to you, thankfully," said Frank. "The army will deal with this. And I will make sure that it is handled properly."

"I bet he will," Bill murmured in my ear.

"So there was never any blackmail," said Alf. "I knew it. He would have told me."

"Nobody was blackmailing Ned," I said. "That rumor was very efficiently started by Patricia. But pretty much everyone else was involved in blackmail, either as perpetrator or victim. Patricia blackmailed the Andersons into selling up in the first place. She's been collecting from Captain Hathaway, after stealing certain incriminating photographs from his studio."

"I must review my security arrangements," mumbled the Captain, blushing even redder than usual.

"Martin Dear was being blackmailed—not by the Black Crow on account of his wife's promiscuity, as he tried to make out, but by the man he'd been foolish enough to have sex with after he murdered Ned. Exhilarated or remorseful, but almost certainly drunk, he allowed himself to be picked up by Joseph Vella, the experienced gigolo, and put into a highly compromising position. When Martin and Patricia returned to the island with their new identities, nobody recognized them: different hair, different clothes, different shape. But then Joseph saw Martin out swimming, and he remembered the body he had made love to. He saw an opportunity to earn some extra money by threatening to tell Martin's wife what had happened. Martin kept his secret—at the cost of Joseph's life. Same crime, different motive. He bashed Joseph's head in and placed the body at the foot of the cliffs. Another suicide, it seemed, and this time our friend the Captain nearly swung for it."

"I suppose I'm off the hook now," said the Captain, looking more cheerful than he had in days.

"I might have been next," I continued. "Tilly, I mean Patricia, tried me out as a blackmail victim the morning after I'd been entertaining a certain Sergeant Major in my room at the Continental." I put an arm round Bill's shoulders and squeezed. "Tried to tell me that the guests had been complaining."

"And basically," said Bill, looking rather proud, "Mitch told her to fuck off."

"Which nearly cost me my life. She sent Martin chasing after me in Valetta."

"We even gave the bastard a lift," said Bill.

"He followed me around the docks and bashed me over the head. I'm pretty sure he had a knife. I'd have been found with my throat cut in an alleyway if someone hadn't stopped him. I don't suppose I'll ever find out who that was," I said, thinking of the blond, bearded sailor. "And that's when it started to unravel for Tilly and Martin Dear. The façade was crumbling. Martin was drinking too much, cracking under the pressure of what Tilly was forcing him to do. She was planning to leave him—he was too much of a liability. But when she figured out that I was onto her, she panicked. Perhaps she was trying to run away over the cliffs, and she slipped. But I think she realized there was only one way out of the trap."

"Suicide," said Alf.

"With proper medical care, she'll recover," said Frank. "She won't escape justice that easily."

"But I say," said the Captain, pacing up and down with his hands behind his back, "there's one thing I don't understand. That young chap at the hotel, the Jessop boy. What on earth possessed him to go sticking his fingers in other people's possessions?"

"He was desperate to escape from his parents. And who wouldn't be? Year after year, coming back to this beautiful island, and he had no more freedom than a child. He's in love, he wants to live his life. Who knows if it'll last? But he deserves a chance, the same as all of us. So he stole whatever he could lay his hands on. Money, jewelry, letters, photographs. Unwittingly, he provided the clue that I needed to solve the mystery—the headless photograph of Joseph Vella, sent as a warning to Martin Dear, who, fool that he was, could not quite bring himself to throw it away. Perhaps it represented the last moment of freedom he knew before he became bound to Patricia by guilt."

"And why on earth did they keep coming back here?" asked the Captain. "I shouldn't have thought this was their kind of place at all. They always looked so disapproving."

"I wondered if they were in on the blackmail act themselves at first," I said, "but now I believe they just enjoyed being onlookers year after year, observing all the sin and depravity around them. Little did they know, it was going on right in the bosom of their family."

"Serves them right," said Bill. "Good for Henry. I bet he's a great fuck."

I'd fill Bill in on the facts of the case later, if at all. "Even Claire Sutherland was being blackmailed, I suspect, by one of her island boyfriends. We may never know the true identity of 'Fancy,' the man to whom she wrote those passionate letters, and paid for their return. There are plenty of men on these islands willing to take advantage of the generosity and recklessness of visitors. Claire Sutherland is easy prey."

"She and I will have to watch our step," said the Captain, "if we're going into business together."

"What?"

"Why not? She's been due to retire for donkey's years, although it's not very chivalrous of me to mention it. She can sell up in London, I can sell up here, and damn me if I don't think we could make a bloody good go of the Continental between us. And there won't be any more blackmail or murder or any of that nonsense. Just good food, good drinks and a discreet, sympathetic landlord.

We've discussed it before, as a kind of pipe dream. We could both carry on our...private interests. But it might be rather fun."

"She's already taken over, by the look of it," said Bill. "Bossing people around. She's in her element."

"Perhaps for starters," I said, "you could offer a room to Henry Jessop and Peter Allinson. I imagine the parents are clearing out pretty soon."

"They're welcome as my guests, either here or at the hotel."

"That's the spirit. Happy endings all around." I looked at Bill, who winked at me.

"What about that awful old woman who's always pestering me?" said the Captain. "The one you call the Black Crow."

"She's crazy, but she's not stupid. She sees everything that goes on—including your liaisons with Joseph Vella and...others," I said, unwilling to reveal that Ned had been another of the Captain's models. "And I suspect she recognized Tilly and Martin as the skinny young woman and the dark-haired priest that Claire spotted in the Continental bar a couple of summers ago. The summer that Ned died and this whole story began."

"Well I'll be blowed," said the Captain.

"And now I think we had better return to the hotel," I said. "I shall leave my patient in your hands, Frank. Come on, Captain Hathaway. I'm sure Claire could do with some help."

"Yes, right. Right you are. Of course. Absolutely," blustered the old boy, barely able to tear his eyes away from the two men on the sofa.

Alf was asleep now, cradled in Frank's arms. Frank—the robustly normal Frank, hero of the rugby pitch, adored by the island women—did not move. He blushed, and his beautiful blue eyes were wider and shinier than ever, but he stayed there holding the sleeping soldier, and he looked content.

Dinner at the Continental that evening had a carnival atmosphere, as the news spread among the guests that their picture-perfect hosts, Tilly and Martin Dear, were languishing respectively in a hospital bed and a cell, both in police custody, under arrest for a range of crimes, including murder. Every so often Claire Sutherland's voice rang above the hubbub—"of course one never trusted them for a moment; one sees through such falsehood; I knew there was something wrong the moment I set eyes on them," and so on, her back reading of events fast establishing itself as truth in her mind. At last she had found the role she was born to play. I hoped that she and the Captain would make a go of the Continental. Perhaps an investment of some of Aunt Dinah's money might help. That way I'd always have a place to stay on the island—if I returned.

Bill and I were quiet as we ate, both knowing that our time was coming to an end. He had some leave to use up, and we could spend the whole time fucking each other's brains out, but the shadow of parting was already falling. What had it meant, this last few days of danger and excitement? Was it just a distraction from the muddle and misery of my real life, the life to which I'd have to return in a few days, weeks or months? Yes, for four days I had hardly given it a thought—the guilt and sadness of losing Vince; the frustration and anger I still felt towards Morgan; the anger I felt towards myself for turning everything I touched to shit... And here it was, happening again right in front of me, as Bill mechanically ate his food, jaw working, brows contracted, barely glancing up at me. He wanted me to stay, or to give him some sign that we had a future—whether here or in London or America; it didn't much matter to him as long as we were together. And why not? I would never find a better lover, or one with his feet planted as firmly on the ground. Bill would bring out the best in me, and he wouldn't stand for anything less. Cheating, dishonesty, lies—all that would have to end. With Morgan, half the attraction had always been the thrill of the chase—the knowledge that he could never be mine. I could win him over for a while with my cock, but he'd always go back to his wife. He was the one that got away, the eternal "what if?". But look what happened when I found someone who wanted me as much as I wanted him? I betrayed Vince with every breath I took. If a man loves me, I run away. Was that why I was already thinking of how soon I could leave Malta? What was I in such a hurry to get back to? My freedom? Freedom to be alone, to grow old unloved and disappointed, regretting every chance I missed?

Even Captain Hathaway had more of a future than I did. Frank and Alf, Henry and Deacon Peter, all of them starting off on something new, full of hope. I was the only one who was looking for a way out. I'd been given everything—money, opportunity, good health and the wherewithal to enjoy it, a big dick that men wanted— and I was throwing it away.

"Is everything all right, Mitch?"

Claire Sutherland was towering over me. She made me jump.

"Sorry, Claire. Miles away."

"You've hardly touched your food. I know it's not exactly cordon bleu, but under the circumstances I think Stella did rather a marvelous job. Now come on. Eat up, or she'll be offended."

"Thanks." I toyed with a fork.

"Oh for heaven's sake!" she said, rolling her eyes, "Why are you so glum? You should be crowned with laurels and carried through the streets! Come on, Sergeant Major, try to cheer him up. We don't want any long faces at the Continental, dear me no! Ralph, find a bottle of something nice for Dr. Mitchell." She clapped her hands and went onto another table, a word for everyone. At least she'd broken the ice. Bill put his hand on mine.

"Want me to go? It's all right if you do. I understand." He smiled, deep lines forming at the corner of his eyes. "We had fun. You're a great bloke, Mitch. I'm glad I—"

I didn't wait to hear any more. "Come on. We're going to bed." I stood up. "Ralph? A bottle of champagne to my room as soon as possible."

"On the house!" said Claire. "Three cheers for Dr. Mitchell!"

Bill embraced me as the diners cheered, their voices echoing as we climbed the twisting stone steps to my room.

It was dark, the sun long since set into the sea. Bill opened the windows and stared out over the harbor, up to the cliffs and down to the rocks where our story had begun. His ass—the first thing I ever noticed about him when I saw him on the ferry—was stretching the cotton of his pants. He lit a cigarette, the smoke blowing back into the room on the cool night air.

I put my arms around his waist, rested my head on his shoulder blade, feeling the warmth and strength and solidity.

"What are we going to do, Bill?"

"Don't know."

"I'm so tired."

He turned around to face me, and held me tight. "I know. It's all right. We've got a couple of days. Let's make them good." He was getting hard already, pressing his groin into mine. Of course I wanted to fuck him, for him to fuck me, but I wanted more. Something to fill the void at home, to protect me from age and loneliness and disappointment. Could it be this man, this soldier in my arms, his cock against mine? Was happiness so easily found?

"I'm not a very nice person," I began. "I lie and I cheat and I can't keep it in my pants."

"Why are you telling me this?"

"Because I want you to know."

"I don't care. I like you, Mitch. That should be enough." He grabbed my ass. "And I want to fuck you."

"And if I want more than that?"

"Greedy bastard," he said, giving my ass a hard slap. "I've got mates back at the barracks who could come over and join us if you want."

"That's not what I mean."

"Then what."

"I want you."

"You've got me already."

"Really?"

"Yeah. For what it's worth."

He kissed me on the mouth, the tobacco strong on his tongue.

"I could stick around for a while. I've nothing to rush back to."

"And then? Next month? Next year?"

"That's kind of up to you."

We kissed again, deeper and longer this time. I could feel Bill's cock throbbing against mine. It's hard to make decisions about your future when you have a hard dick and a man's hands kneading and spreading your buttocks.

"Mitch," he said, coming up for air, "I need to fuck you. Now."
There was a knock at the door. "Your champagne, sir."

Ralph, of course. Bill let him in, took the bottle and glasses and shooed the goggle-eyed old man out of the room as fast as he could.

"Take your clothes off, Mitch. Right now."

The champagne would have to wait. I stripped, my cock harder than ever.

"Kneel." He pointed to the window. "Right there."

I did as I was told. Perhaps if someone on the cliffs had binoculars they might see us. I didn't much care. Bill was behind me, slicking himself up with lubricant. He eased himself in, then grabbed my hips and drew me back on to him. God, he was big. My ass stretched as wide as it could, but it wasn't enough. He seemed to be growing, stiffening with every thrust.

And gradually the swirling mess of anxiety and pain and fear in my mind was calmed, and my breathing fell into the rhythm of Bill's dick pounding in and out of my hole, and there was only one thought left. Barely a thought. Just a word. Yes. Yes.

I was saying it aloud, I realized with a little surprise, as my body arched upwards. My hands reached around to pull him in, and I shot my load without touching my own cock, sperm flying out onto the balcony and into the night, to the sea, the sky and the stars.

Bill pushed me down, and that's when the serious fucking began.

www.ingramcontent.com/pod-product-compliance
Lightning Source LLC
Chambersburg PA
CBHW020513120726
47904CB00003B/818